LA
LIGHT

ALSO BY HELEN PHIFER

HELEN PHIFER

LAST LIGHT

bookouture

Published by Bookouture in 2018

An imprint of StoryFire Ltd.

Carmelite House
50 Victoria Embankment
London EC4Y 0DZ

www.bookouture.com

ISBN: 978-1-78681-509-5
eBook ISBN: 978-1-78681-508-8

For my amazing Mam, I love you forever and always xx

CHAPTER ONE

18 February 2016

Detective Inspector Lucy Harwin parked in the small car park on the opposite side of the road to the crime scene and got out of her car. She surveyed the area; there were no houses which faced directly onto what was left of the derelict St Cuthbert's Church. A row of terraced houses that backed onto the fringe of the car park had upstairs windows which gave a view of the side of the church. But each house was in darkness; there wasn't going to be much scope for any witnesses. They were too far away and the wrong angle. Her only hope was if they had external CCTV but judging by the peeling paint and graffiti on the walls it was unlikely.

An ambulance was parked further down the street. She crossed towards the two officers standing by the entrance of the church; the older of the two had been in the job longer than she had, while his student, judging by their collar number, was fresh out of training. As she got closer she knew by the look on the student officer's face it was going to be bad. The crime scene log was clutched in his shaking hands, and she felt sorry for him. Dead bodies were hard to cope with no matter how long you'd been in the job. The loud roar of her friend and colleague Detective Sergeant Mathew Jackson's pick-up as it turned into the deserted street made her pause: she might as well wait for him before she started. He parked and jogged across the road to where she was standing. Much to her annoyance he never looked as if he'd been woken up in the middle of the night. His suits were always immaculate, his shirts never creased.

'Lucy.'

'Mattie.'

She turned back to the officer and held out her hand to shake his. She'd never met him before and wanted to show him a little respect.

'DI Harwin and DS Jackson, would you mind talking us through what happened?'

He shook his head. 'Some teenagers decided to do a spot of ghost hunting and found a way in to the church. They got a lot more than they bargained for. I mean I got a lot more than I bargained for; I thought they were pissing around when they called it in.'

'Ghost hunting in a church? In this church? It's falling to bits and a deathtrap.'

'I suppose it's as good a place as any. One of the kids is in the back of the ambulance under sedation. He wouldn't stop screaming. His parents are on their way to collect him.'

'Where are the rest of them?'

'In the back of the van.'

'Are they suspects?'

'No, at least I don't think so. They're twelve and thirteen years old. She looks like she's been here awhile.'

'So, we're treating them as witnesses?'

'Yes, ma'am. Well sort of, I don't think we can actually assume they saw anything apart from discovering the body. They were in the wrong place at the wrong time.'

'You can say that again. Thanks, I suppose we better get suited and booted.'

She turned to walk back to her car where she kept a supply of protective clothing. Mattie followed. He was quiet for a change and Lucy wondered if he'd been busy. He didn't look like he'd been rudely dragged out of bed. She opened the boot and passed him some packets. Ripping them open they dressed themselves in paper overalls, shoe and leg covers. Pulling on rubber gloves last; as they crossed the road Mattie whispered, 'You can go in first, Lucy.'

'Thanks.'

There was a small gap in the metal fencing which had been erected around the building to keep the kids and teenagers out. The church had been boarded-up for a couple of years, set on fire more times than she could count. Squeezing through the gap, she walked towards a small doorway with a wooden board that was hanging on by a thread and just big enough to get through. She noted the faded, dark red, upside-down cross that had been spray-painted onto it. Turning on her torch she stepped into the blackness and shone it onto an overgrown mess of weeds, litter, rubble and empty beer cans. The woodwork, or what was left of it, was a charcoal mess. She didn't need an expert to tell her it was also unsafe. She waited for Mattie before she moved further in. He clambered through the gap.

'Bloody hell, this place *is* a deathtrap. I bet we're not supposed to be in here. It looks like it might collapse at any moment.'

Lucy inhaled. The faint smell of decomposition filled her nostrils. They were lucky it was February and freezing cold, otherwise it would smell a whole lot worse. She moved forward, trying to keep to one side as best as she could, until finally the horror was clear to see. The dead body, hanging upside down on a crudely fashioned crucifix made from mismatched pieces of blackened timber, was bad, but it was nothing that she couldn't cope with as she shivered and stamped her feet to keep the circulation flowing. She moved closer – it was the smell of the thick, congealed, sweet-smelling blood that had run down the body in rivulets, staining the white nightdress and turning it into a crimson, bloody, wet mess that made her gag.

'What happened for you to end up this way?' she whispered to the body. She knew that sometimes humans were not as innocent as they appeared; the dark secrets they kept locked away could sometimes be the reason for their murders.

Mattie stood behind her and whispered, 'What the fuck?'

Lucy nodded in agreement. What else was there to say about it? This image was now ingrained in her memory. It would never be erased. She might well be able to store it away, but it would always be there, threatening to appear when she was doing her best to live a normal, happy life. Doing things that normal, happy, people did. She tried to remember exactly when the last time was she'd done anything remotely normal, but couldn't, having devoted the last ten years of her life to serving her queen and country with every inch of her heart and soul.

For some reason she'd lost her voice; it didn't want to come out. It was caught in the back of her throat.

CHAPTER TWO

'I think we need to get the scene examined and the doctor here. There's nothing we can do for her except find whoever did this.'

Mattie nodded, and Lucy turned and walked out the way she'd come in. Outside in the car park there was not only an assortment of police vans, but also two fire engines. The whole circus was here. Detective Chief Inspector Tom Crowe had arrived and was talking to the fire officers. He waved her over, and she headed in his direction.

'Lucy, you're not to go back inside until the fire service has assessed the scene and made it safe.'

'Sir, that could take hours.'

'I know, but we need to put the safety of the officers and civilians working the scene first. There's nothing we can do about it if you're in there and the building collapses – it's going to be a nightmare.'

He pulled out his phone, and she wandered back to Mattie.

'What's happening?'

'We have to wait for the all-clear to go back in.'

He shook his head. 'Christ, we're going to be stuck here all night.'

She shrugged. 'Did you have something better to do?'

'Well, yes. Sort of and it's bloody freezing.'

'Come on, we'll go and talk to our expert eye witnesses. At least it's warm in the van.'

*

Two hours later the fire service had agreed the safest point of entry, which, surprisingly enough, was the same one that Lucy and Mattie had already used. Tom was shouting into his phone, and Lucy got the gist as she heard the words: 'Crime Scene Manager, patrols to secure a cordon and the area locking down'. He was a bit slow tonight. She'd requested everything on arrival, and the crime scene investigators had gone in to document the scene.

'So, how did we find her?'

'Well, sir, some kids scaled the fencing to come into the church and do a spot of ghost hunting. She looks like she's been here at least twenty-four hours, but the doc will tell you more than I can on that score.'

'Where are the kids?'

'I've spoken to them and got first accounts, and they've all been taken home. I'll send officers to get statements tomorrow. I think they've had enough excitement for one night.'

'You can say that again. I bet it's quite some time before they decide to go ghost hunting again. Do we have any ID on the vic?'

Lucy shook her head. 'We have nothing, although the body hasn't been searched yet. It's highly unlikely, because she's wearing a nightgown, but you never know. Do you want to take a look?'

She could tell by the pained expression on his face that he most definitely didn't want to take a look, but it was his job. He had to.

'Should I lead the way, or do you want to go in alone?'

'I'll follow you.'

She led him to the metal plates that had been put down by the on-duty CSI, Amanda. Walking single file, he looked at the upside-down cross on the board which was now propped against the side of the church. She smelt the Home Office pathologist before she saw her, swathed in a mist of Chanel. Catherine Maxwell caught all of the bad jobs she did – they were an unlikely pair of crusaders in the fight against evil.

Lucy turned to her and smiled. 'Catherine, thanks for coming.'

'There's nothing I'd rather be doing, except maybe sleeping. At my age I need my beauty sleep you know.'

Lucy smiled at her; Catherine Maxwell was the most attractive, glamorous woman she'd ever laid eyes on. She most definitely didn't look her age, which Lucy guessed to be somewhere in her late forties.

Tom paused, lifting his arm for the doctor to go first. 'We'll let you take a look and be in shortly.'

'That's very kind of you.' She walked in, carrying her heavy case.

Lucy whispered in Tom's ear, 'Anyone would think you didn't want to go in, boss.'

He whispered back, 'I don't. My stomach feels a bit off to be honest and I have the headache from hell. The last thing I need is to stand in close proximity to a decomposing body.'

'Bless you, if it's any consolation she doesn't smell that bad. At least if you don't get too close she doesn't.'

'Thanks.' He inhaled deeply then stepped inside, walking as near to the corpse as he dared yet not getting too close.

Catherine was taking samples from the body. She nodded at them both.

'Do you know how long she's been here, Catherine?'

'Hard to be exact, Tom, but you know that. Judging by the fact that she's in full rigor I'd say at least twelve hours. Her body temp is the same as the ambient surroundings, so she's been dead awhile.'

He stared at the deep wound on the victim's throat. 'Cause of death is pretty obvious even to me.'

'It might look obvious, but you never can be one hundred per cent sure until the post-mortem. For all we know she could have died several ways. It doesn't look as if there's enough arterial spray for blood loss to have been the cause. I'm tempted to say her throat was cut after death, but that would be speculation and we all know what that can lead to.'

Tom took a step closer, crouching down. He looked up at the body that was tied to the roughly fashioned cross, studying the open, blood-crusted wound on her neck. 'Did you notice the inverted cross on the board outside? It looks to me like someone decided to take up devil worship. Have we got any devil worshippers on our books, Lucy?'

'Sir, are you being serious? Devil worship? In Brooklyn Bay? I've never heard of it, and as far as I'm aware no, we haven't got anyone who is a self-confessed devil worshipper on the system. Apart from the body and a faded piece of graffiti outside there's nothing to suggest it. I'd have expected candles, pentagrams, some kind of altar.' Just to be sure she slowly moved her torch beam over the darkest corners of the building.

'Yeah, well neither have I but what else have we got to go on? It's a definite line of investigation and I want it looked into. We can't rule anything out, just because it seems ridiculous.'

Catherine arched an eyebrow at Lucy. 'I think I'd prefer to go off the hard evidence and work it out. We can't go around saying there's a bunch of satanists in town.'

'I didn't say we could, it's just a suggestion.'

He stood up and walked back outside.

Catherine whispered, 'I think he watches too much television.'

'You and me both.'

'This is going to be an interesting case, Lucy, aren't you glad you were on-call for your first official murder investigation?'

She shook her head. 'For once, I wish I wasn't. My stomach almost fell out when I took the call; it's not a straightforward sudden death, is it? There's a lot to be said for rest days and working upstairs in the Intel unit.'

Catherine placed her samples in the heavy, metal case. Taking out brown paper bags, she secured them around both hands of the corpse to preserve any evidence.

'You can let the undertakers move her when you're ready. I've taken my preliminary samples. I'll see you tomorrow.'

Lucy watched the doctor leave then turned to look at her nameless victim.

'I don't know who you are or why you were killed, but I promise I will find out, and catch whoever did this to you.'

Taking one last look, she left; there was so much that needed to be done. She glanced down at her watch – it was almost two. She was going to the station for a large mug of strong coffee and to get the investigation going. Her bed wouldn't be getting slept in tonight.

CHAPTER THREE

Lucy came out of the daily morning meeting, which had been held at nine thirty prompt with the heads of each department and the chief superintendent, with glazed eyes. She went back downstairs to the first floor where the CID office was situated. The members of her team that were on shift today were waiting for the list of jobs she would have been tasked with, though they looked as enthusiastic as she felt.

'Well that's thirty minutes of my life I'll never get back. Nothing of note: a couple of attempted shed breaks overnight that I said we'll pick up, and a domestic that Public Protection Unit have picked up. The Super wants to know why we haven't got an ID on the victim and a half-decent suspect for the crucifix killing. I've told him that we're working on it as a matter of urgency.'

She walked over to the whiteboard, where she'd stuck a photograph of the victim's face to it and a couple of the crime scene photos. 'Gather round you lot. I need an ID on her like now.'

Detective Constable Colin Davey, Lucy's go-to guy for Anything computer related, shuddered.

'That's a terrible way to die, having your throat cut and bleeding to death upside down. I can't even begin to imagine the horror of what was going through her mind, and why here, why would anyone choose Brooklyn Bay? It's not a big city or even that busy for a town.'

'Col, please can you check the intelligence system for me? I've sent a global email with a photo of her face asking if anyone can ID her.'

Col, who was now staring back at his computer monitor, held up his hand. 'We have an ID; one of the PCSOs has just emailed to say that she looks like a woman called Sandy Kilburn who lives on Bridlington Court. Give me a minute.' He began tapping on the keyboard. Lucy wanted to kiss Col – having an ID made her life so much easier.

'Here you are, boss, it's her.' Crossing the room she looked at the enlarged mugshot on the screen; it was a few years old, but it was definitely their victim.

'God I love it when things go right for a change. Brilliant, so Col, you do the background checks.' She looked at Mattie, and Rachel who was another of her detectives. 'Can you two grab CSI and go to her flat? I want it locked down and searched for any evidence.'

They both nodded. Lucy began to write 'Sandy Kilburn' above her photograph in red marker. The overwhelming tiredness she'd felt sitting in the morning meeting had been pushed to one side. Forgotten; now they had viable information and an ID, they were closer to finding whoever was responsible. Somebody had to know something. As Mattie and Rachel stood up she turned to face them.

'Oh, and the DCI's mum's decapitated cat needs looking at.'

There was a loud groan and several head-shakes.

'Seeing as how Detective Sergeant Browning is late, he can have the dead cat.'

Browning walked in just as she'd finished speaking, and Lucy waved him over.

'That was good timing. We have a murder enquiry on the go, and there's a dead cat waiting for you to look at.'

'What's a dead cat got to do with me? Give it to some nice, keen student on section or a PCSO – they love that kind of stuff.'

'I would if it wasn't the boss's mum's beloved cat. Its head's been hacked off and left on her front doorstep; she's very upset.'

Browning grimaced. '*I'm* very upset; I don't like cats.'

'The boss has it in his head that the victim found last night in the burnt-out church was killed by a devil worshipper. I don't want anyone saying we didn't check the dead cat to make sure it wasn't another sacrifice to Satan.'

'You're kidding me, right?'

'I'm afraid not. I'm being serious. If there are any satanic symbols or candles then call CSI out to photograph the scene. I need someone with a bit more experience to assess the situation and that's you.'

'Bloody hell, what's happened? I feel as if I've stepped into an episode of *The Twilight Zone*.'

'Look, I don't really believe it either. Hopefully there won't be anything to suggest it's anything more than a neighbour with a grudge.'

He shook his head in disbelief, turning to walk back down the stairs. Lucy wondered what had put him in such a bad mood so early in the day: she hadn't meant he had to go right now.

She went into her office and closed the door, needing five minutes to clear her head. Her mobile began to ring; glancing at the number, she wondered if she should answer. No doubt it would be some drama. It didn't stop, so she picked it up.

'Morning, Ellie.'

'Did you tell Dad I couldn't go to Maisie's party tonight?'

Her daughter's voice echoed down the phone and she knew she should have ignored the call.

'Yes.'

'Why?'

'You know why! You didn't go to school all week and spent most of it in that shithole of a cellar at the youth club. Not to mention you broke into the bloody cellar in the first place. There are laws against that kind of behaviour, Ellie.'

'I hate you.'

The line went dead, and Lucy sighed. 'Yes, I know you do.' She'd had no idea being the parent of a teenage girl would be quite this traumatic. She'd been ready for the mood swings and attitude, something which had marred her own teenage years. She hadn't been ready for the lies and borderline criminal behaviour, not to mention the drinking and manipulation. Ellie was spending a couple of nights at her dad's. Lucy was well aware that Ellie was trying to push her luck with the both of them. She'd only recently split up with George, and already their daughter had figured out that it might not be a bad thing, realising that she could play them off against each other to her advantage, which she supposed any teenager in the same situation would do. As frustrating as her attitude was, Lucy loved her more than life itself.

There was a knock on her door and she waved Col in. He handed her a sheaf of papers still warm from the printer.

'Sandy Kilburn has quite a dossier; she has previous for drunk and disorderly, assault, sex in a public place, shoplifting. It's all there for you to read.'

'Thanks, Col, at least it gives us something to work with.'

He nodded. 'Yep, you can say that again.'

Closing the door, Lucy wondered if this was some kind of revenge killing. Revenge for what though? What could Sandy have done to have made another person so angry with her that they wanted to leave her in the burnt-out shell of a church, bleeding to death on a makeshift crucifix?

CHAPTER FOUR

Browning parked the unmarked Ford Focus outside the tired-looking semi. He'd imagined the boss's mother living in one of those new retirement flats on the seafront. Not sure what he was going to do with a decapitated cat, he sighed. Getting out of the car he pushed open the rickety gate and walked up the uneven brick path. The weeds were winning the battle for this garden, which was a shame. A selection of rose bushes sported some beautiful blooms despite being strangled by copious amounts of bindweed running through them. He didn't care much for the organic stuff; he much preferred a short blast of chemicals to do the job. As he approached the front step his eyes fixated on the bloodied corpse of the headless cat. She could have at least covered it with a bin bag or something. It was lying there in all its stiff, dead glory for the world to see. He looked around for its head and was taken aback to see it sitting in a plant pot as if it was a prize flower that had been nurtured and grown for display. He felt his stomach lurch. The poor bastard was staring right at him, its green eyes now covered with a milky film. Browning shuddered. Normally it was the cat who was the hunter – who had decided to turn the table and hunt the cat? There were no satanic symbols or anything else to suggest devil worship.

'He was such a good boy, who would do such a thing?'

Browning tore his gaze away from the cat and looked up to see the old woman dabbing her eyes with the corner of a tissue.

'I'm sorry, I don't know. It's horrible. I'm Detective Sergeant Peter Browning, Tom asked me to come. Should we go inside for a chat?'

She turned and he followed her inside, relieved to not have to stare at the abomination any longer, although someone was going to have to scoop its sorry arse into a bin bag to get rid of it. She led him into a living room which was an explosion of eighties floral and striped paper, the bright yellow faded enough he was thankful he didn't have to shield his eyes from the glare. It was messy, nothing like he'd expected, and in the corner on the floor was a place mat containing bowls of dry cat biscuits and water. He tried not to draw attention to them. The woman was still wiping her eyes with a tissue. She pointed to the gap on the sofa next to a pile of *People's Friend* magazines, and a stack of newspapers which were yellow and turned up at the corners. He never imagined the boss would let his mother live like this. It wasn't dirty, just cluttered and full of junk. He squeezed his bulk into the space and waited for her to sit down in the chair opposite him.

'I really thought that Tom would have come himself. I suppose he's too busy. He's always at some kind of meeting; if they held a meeting about the sky turning grey when it rained he'd probably be there.'

She began to chat away about the weather and the price of milk.

He smiled at her. 'Mrs Crowe, can we talk about the cat?'

'Please, call me Margaret. The cat? Oh yes, you mean Mr Biscuit. Who would do such a thing to him? He's a friendly little thing, so trusting he would let anyone stroke him.'

'I don't know, it's very cruel, whoever it is. Have you fallen out with any neighbours recently?'

'No, I have not. I'm too old to be falling out with my neighbours. I talk to everyone, even the ones I don't like. That couple next door but one is always arguing in the street and having noisy parties, but I still speak to them. I don't hold grudges.'

'Are there any kids, teenagers you might have shouted at because they've been a nuisance lately? You know the annoying ones who always play football outside your house when you're trying to watch the television?'

She shook her head. 'I love kids, I even love teenagers. We were all that age once. They get a tough time. I don't shout at them. They have to play somewhere, and the kids in this street are pretty good to be honest. I pretty much keep myself to myself, it's the best way.'

'Well, I'll look into it for you. I'll make some enquiries. What are you going to do about Mr Biscuit?' Browning felt himself cringe, his fingers crossed behind his back.

'I don't know. I asked Thomas to come and sort him out for me. I didn't expect him to send someone else. That's just typical of him – he will find any excuse not to come here and visit his mum.'

'Erm, would you like me to take him with me? The CSIs might want to take a look at him?'

He knew fine well what the response from Jack or Amanda would be if he walked in with a dead, decapitated cat and it would more than likely end in *off*.

'Could you do that? I don't really want to have to dig a hole and bury him, my knees won't stand for it. They ache so much.'

'Have you got a bin bag?'

'You can't put Mr Biscuit in a bin bag, he won't like that. Haven't you got one of those paper sacks they use on *CSI*?'

Browning felt his jaw drop; Lucy owed him big time for this. Not only did he have to deal with Loopy Lou, she expected him to bag up the dead cat and take it with him.

'I'll just go and see if there's one in the car.' He stood up, his cheeks burning. That pack of wankers would all be tucking into their breakfasts and he was here trying to find something to scoop up a dead cat with. He had a good mind to dump it on the boss's desk so she could sort it out.

He opened the boot of the car and found a plastic evidence bag. Tugging on two pairs of latex gloves, he grabbed another bag. Storming back towards the dead cat, grimacing, he bent down, picking the cat up by its tail. He shoved it into the plastic bag, then, grabbing its head by its ear, put that in the bag too.

Sealing the bag, he stripped off the gloves and threw them into the overflowing wheelie bin. Then he threw the bag into the boot of the car, slamming it shut.

He went back into the house where the old woman was now frying bacon.

'Margaret, I have to go now. I've got your cat. I'll let the CSIs take a look at him.'

She waved the spatula in the air. 'Thank you, what a nice man you are. I'll tell Tom you've been very helpful. Try and find the brute who hurt Mr Biscuit, won't you? Would you like a bacon sandwich before you leave?'

He shook his head. Hungry as he was, after handling that manky cat he didn't think he could face eating anything just yet, and for all he knew she might have been touching it with her bare hands. He shuddered at the thought.

'No, thank you. I'll be in touch if I find anything of any value.'

He turned, leaving her to it, wondering how often Tom visited her. If you asked his opinion Margaret should be in a retirement home, being looked after. That's where his mum would be if she was still alive – being looked after and not having to worry about some nutter killing her pet.

He drove back to the station, to the tune of his phone ringing all the way. As he parked up in the back yard he answered it to his flustered wife, who began shouting at him. Hauling himself out of the car, he began walking to the station, the dead cat all but forgotten about as he began shouting back at her as she continued their earlier argument.

CHAPTER FIVE

December 1987

The wet sound of skin slapping against skin was so loud it broke him from the daze he was in. He was lost in the world of 'The Bash Street Kids', tucked under his bedcovers, reading with his torch because it was late. He heard the noise from his bedroom, which was at the opposite end of the hall to his parents. He had cried so much when his mother had made him move from the nursery next to their room and into this one, not realising at the time she was doing it for his benefit. He'd cried like a baby despite being eight years old, not wanting to be so far away from her, and she'd begged him to be a big boy. Promising to buy him new comics every week, the ones his father wouldn't let him read because he didn't agree with them. She wasn't allowed to go out of the house unless it was to go shopping or for his father's daily paper. Some of the other kids at school had mums who worked at the shoe factory. He'd heard her pleading with him last week to let her get a job there to help pay the bills, but of course that had led to another beating. Now, when he heard the all-too-familiar muffled cry as his mother tried to hold the pain inside so he couldn't hear her, it made him flinch. Every single time it happened she tried to hide it from him, the cuts and bruises. The broken jewellery, the clumps of missing hair, and heavy eye make-up she'd take up wearing after a beating. He knew she was trying to protect him from the horrors she suffered, but he knew exactly what went on behind their bedroom door. He heard the sound carry along the draughty hallway. Whenever it happened his father's angry voice filled the air. Not quite a shout, but too loud to be considered a whisper.

"'If we confess our sins, he is faithful and just and will forgive us our sins and purify us from all unrighteousness.'"

The silence filled the air more than the noise. He knew he would be there, standing over his mum with his hands together as if in prayer. Taking the same stance as Father Vincent did every Sunday in church. Only Father Vincent wasn't scary like his dad, who would demand she repeat the words after him. He knew this verse, and many others, off by heart because his father wouldn't let him read about naughty school kids having adventures with their friends. Instead he made him read and memorise the different passages of the Bible. This in his opinion was far worse than Dennis the Menace could ever be. It was all bloodthirsty fights and scary stories of burning bushes and the sea parting. This particular favourite of his father's was from 1 John 1: 9. The sound of another slap filled the air, and he buried his head under his pillow. Squeezing his eyes tight shut, trying to force himself to go to sleep because there was nothing he could do to help.

'I said: "If we confess our sins, he is faithful and just and will forgive us our sins and purify us from all unrighteousness". What are you waiting for woman? You can still speak, can't you? I saw the way you smiled at that man who delivered the post today. I know what you were thinking. This is your last chance to come clean and make it known in front of God and me that you didn't have any impure thoughts.'

Her sob filled the air. 'I smiled at him because it's polite. I wasn't thinking anything except thank you for bringing the letters.'

'Then say the words and we can move on, woman. You need to absolve your sins and admit your sinful behaviour.'

She whispered the words, and he silently mouthed them in unison with her, begging her not to get it wrong or to say anything else, because he knew the bastard would keep on hitting her until she got it right. When she finished the sentence, he let out the breath he was holding. If he came in here and found him awake, he would beat him as well. He'd done it so many times before he couldn't keep count. He wanted more than anything to run in there and protect her, but the last time he tried it hadn't gone to plan. Instead of him stopping at the shame of being caught, his father had turned his anger on him. Beating him black and blue – the bruises had taken for ever to fade to yellow and his body had ached for days after. His mother had cried for hours over his cuts and bruises then had made him promise never to interfere in whatever happened behind their bedroom door again, and he'd promised. Unable to leave the house, he had been kept off school until the marks disappeared. Missing his first speaking part in the end of term assembly, his mother had cried more about him being hurt and not being able to take part in that than for the beating she'd taken.

He knew what was coming next and he hated this part even more. He'd rather listen to the endless Bible verses than this. A sob so loud he imagined it shook his bed carried along the hallway; it was always like this and he hated him. The anger, the beating, the preaching, the crying and then the begging for forgiveness. His mother, who was terrified of his father, would soothe him as if he was the one who was hurting – it was all so wrong. His small, chubby hands curled into tight fists. One day he would be big enough to punch him back. He would hit him again and again. Nothing would feel better than watching him curl up on the floor in a ball and cry, like he made his mother. Then he'd be sorry, because he was pretty sure God wouldn't help him. He wondered what verse he could shout as he buried his fists into his nose and face. He wouldn't hit him where the bruises wouldn't show. He'd hit him everywhere they would; he wanted people to know what a bastard his father really was. If the Father could see him now he wouldn't welcome him with open arms into the church or laugh and joke with him. He wouldn't want anything to do with him, and who would blame him.

CHAPTER SIX

Natalia Costella pulled the sleeve of her daughter Isabella's coat, dragging her into the church hall despite the fact that the kid was digging her heels down and grumbling.

'Bella, stop it. I promised that we'd help set up the stalls for the winter fair tomorrow.'

'I want to go with Daddy, I don't want to stay here.'

'Daddy is busy, he has to go to the restaurant and talk to the staff. You'll be in the way; you can help to set up the toy stall. You'll like that. You might find something to spend your pocket money on.'

'Good afternoon, Natalia, how lovely to see you both. I can't thank you enough for giving up your spare time to help.'

'Oh, it's nothing, Father David. I like being here and helping out, it's such a beautiful church.'

Isabella rolled her eyes; the grip on her sleeve released as she spied Ellie hovering around by the kitchen door and she raced towards her.

He laughed. 'I think your daughter has a slightly different opinion of the church if I'm not mistaken.'

Natalia's face began to turn crimson. 'I'm not going to lie, she's a daddy's girl. She wanted to go with him.'

The vicar nodded. 'Well there's nothing wrong with that. If my father owned the best pizzeria this side of Brooklyn Bay I'd want to spend my time there as well.' He patted his round stomach. 'Although, I don't think my trousers would be too happy. Can I ask a personal question, are you and your husband Italian?'

Natalia shook her head. 'I'm part Italian, my mother was from Sorrento, my father is English. Tony is definitely English. He just loves Italian food. When we first met, we spent hours in the kitchen while I taught him to cook. It turns out he's a far better cook than I'll ever be. I'd better go and find Margaret, I'm sure she'll have a clipboard with everyone's assignments ready to be ticked off.'

She wandered off, and Father David watched her; she had one of those perfect, hourglass figures, complemented by a head of lustrous, black curls and the most seductive lips he'd ever laid eyes on. She had the look of a young Sophia Loren.

The slight touch of a cold hand on his broke his trance and he turned to face Jan, his much plainer, rounder wife of fifteen years. She was glaring at him, and he smiled. 'Yes, dear.'

'What are we going to do about Street Saviours on Saturday night? Is it still going to happen or are we going to cancel it?'

'Why on earth would we cancel it?'

'You can't expect people to volunteer at the fair and then come back later on, David. That's taking their loyalty a little too far.'

'They won't mind.'

'How do you know that? It's taking the piss if you ask me.'

He winced. 'You have such a way with words. I'll ask them and see what they say. I'm sure they'll all agree it's far too important to not bother. We're just getting it off the ground. If we want to be taken seriously then we can't pick and choose when to go out. We have to be out there, making it a regular thing so the patrons of the pubs and clubs know that we're here, ready to help them in their hours of need. We're providing a valuable service and if it stops one drunk from getting into a fight or passing out on the street corner and choking on their own vomit, then it's all worth it.'

He walked away, and she stared at him, her eyes narrowed and the distaste radiating from her in waves.

Oblivious to the withering look from his wife he began to make his way towards the hall where Natalia was talking to the sullen teenager who had been volunteering with the soup kitchen and organising the winter fair as part of her coursework. But he was intercepted by Margaret.

'Father, I need to talk to you about the running order of events tomorrow. We need a clear itinerary.'

He tried his best not to roll his eyes, mustering up the warmest smile he could.

'It's a winter fair, I don't think it needs to be precision timed, down to the last minute, Margaret. We open the doors at one and let the rabble do their worst. When we've had enough, and the tea and cakes have run out, we'll draw the raffle and let them all go home.'

'We can't do that, we need to be organised. It won't do to have a free-for-all, things need to be done properly, otherwise it will turn into a disaster. If we don't get the raffle tickets sold before the end, who knows what could happen.'

'Margaret, why don't you tell everyone what you think is best? Have a chat with Jan, she'll be happy to help you get everyone organised if that's what you think it needs.'

'Thank you, David, that's better. It will be chaos if we don't keep to a schedule.'

He blinked several times, and then forced his mouth muscles to work and smile.

'Well, you know best. I'll leave it in your capable hands; just give me my orders tomorrow and I'll do my best to follow them.'

His hand reached out, squeezing her frail shoulder. She was so tiny, he doubted Margaret had ever had a curvaceous, lustful figure. In fact he didn't even know if she'd ever been married; if she had, the poor sod deserved a medal. If he thought his wife was sent to try him, she was almost a saint compared to Margaret.

CHAPTER SEVEN

Natalia had been given a raffle ticket book, and a roll of Sellotape to stick all the tickets with a zero or a five on to the selection of donated prizes. She reached the table and looked at the assortment of tat; surely people wouldn't pay a pound to win a bar of yellowed lavender soap that had been hidden away in someone's drawer for the last six years, or a bottle of sherry that had years of dust stuck to it? She wasn't a snob but she enjoyed the feeling of helping others who were far less fortunate than herself. Her favourite was working in the soup kitchen, and she'd helped out with the Street Saviours the last couple of times. Much to Tony's annoyance: he didn't like her spending her spare time here. He thought that church and religion were a waste of time and delighted in telling her she should spend her time helping out in the restaurant. She did when she had to, but he paid staff to work there. She hated his attitude at work, he was always so bossy. The hustle and bustle of it all was too much for her, and he didn't need her. They nearly always ended up arguing whenever they worked together, so it was better if she kept away. She wasn't too keen on helping the drunken people that the Street Saviours targeted, but despite her reservations about it, she loved helping others. Father David had a way of making you feel bad for saying no and that was how she'd got roped into it. She looked around to see where Bella was and smiled to see her chattering away to Ellie, the surly teenager who was pulling stuffed toys out of boxes. Ellie's face broke into a smile and soon the pair of them were giggling at something, which made Natalia smile.

She was blessed to have a loyal husband, a beautiful daughter and a thriving restaurant. Life was good to her and if she could repay the favour by giving a couple of hours of her spare time to help others less fortunate then so be it. At least she could say her prayers and go to sleep each night knowing that she was being a good person, which was all that mattered.

'Mamma, Ellie said I could help her tomorrow. Can I?'

Natalia turned around to look at her daughter, who was a miniature version of herself. 'Help her where, Bella?'

'Here, on the toy stall. Please, Mamma, I want to.'

She looked at Ellie. 'She's certainly had a change of mind; earlier she was crying to go with her dad. If you don't mind listening to Bella's never-ending chatter, then of course she can help you.'

Ellie laughed. 'No, she's cute and funny. She also passes the time on.'

'Why are you here on your own? Shouldn't you be out with your friends shopping and hanging around Costa on a half term Friday afternoon?'

'Yes, but I have to get good grades in my citizenship. It's my last chance to impress my dad; he's kind of mad at me. I've messed up everything else, and I wanted to prove to him I'm not a waste of space.'

Natalia studied the girl. 'That's very noble of you. What about your mum?'

'She hates me, I hate her and besides she spends more time at work than she ever does at home. My dad says she's married to her job in the police more than she was ever married to him.'

'I'm sure she doesn't hate you. It's tough being a teenager though, I remember it all too well. The arguments with my parents were terrible.'

Ellie rolled her eyes. 'Tell me about it.'

Bella, who was bored of their conversation, nudged Natalia. 'Can I?'

'If Ellie says yes, then yes.'

Bella smiled; turning to Ellie she whispered, 'I told you so.' She grabbed the teenager's hand. 'Come on, I'll show you where they keep the sweets.'

Natalia turned back to her dismal tombola prizes before she got another order from Margaret. Tony might hate her spending her spare time helping here with the church, but it was the right thing for her to do. It gave her peace of mind and a feeling of satisfaction – which was worth far more than the odd grumbling from her husband.

CHAPTER EIGHT

Lucy yawned. Her eyes were feeling heavy. She had to get out of this office – it was too stuffy – if she didn't, she might fall asleep with her head on the desk. She also needed to go back to the church. The body had been moved to the hospital mortuary a couple of hours ago. She needed to have another look at the scene now it was daylight. The office was empty. Everyone was out on follow-up enquiries, which suited her just fine: she would go on her own. She needed to get a feel for the place, to try and recreate what had happened in her mind. Why had the killer chosen this particular building? It must have some meaning to him – was it symbolic? Maybe Tom had something: even though CSI hadn't found anything else to substantiate devil worship it didn't mean that he was wrong. Staring at the checklist she'd written down, there wasn't anything missing. The worry of being responsible for catching whoever was responsible for Sandy's death was weighing heavy on her shoulders. This was her first, solo major case and she wanted to make sure she did everything she needed to without being told. No one had bothered to warn her that with the promotion came the relentless worrying about not fucking up.

The church grounds, which were more like an overgrown tip, were still cordoned off. They'd had to open the street an hour ago after task force had been in and done a fingertip search. It was one of the main roads into the town centre and a logistical nightmare to keep it closed for too long. The search had found nothing of evidential value; drains, refuse bins, flower beds along the edge of the car park had all been painstakingly searched and photographed. No weapon had been found, which was what Lucy had been hoping for. She parked in the car park once more: the street was busy. Brooklyn Bay residents enjoyed the thrill of a good murder; the Facebook rumours were spreading like wildfire. Thankfully no one knew the extent of the horror which had happened inside the church. It was a good job it wasn't summer because Lucy was pretty sure some of them would have brought their kids and picnics along to watch all the police activity. There was an unmarked car parked to block the entrance, and Lucy waved at Sam, one of the PCSOs.

Sam got out of the car with the scene guard book.

'Morning, Sam, is there anyone left inside?'

'No, ma'am, task force left about an hour ago. It's been quiet, well, apart from the crowds of onlookers.'

Lucy smiled. 'Just the usual then. Do you need anything or want to go and get a drink while I'm here? I need to go back in and look at the scene.'

'No thanks, I'm good. Phil is going to bring me a coffee in half an hour then take over. To be honest I don't mind sitting here all day. It's warmer in the car than being out on foot, and at least I can listen to the radio or read a book.'

Lucy took the scene log off her and signed herself in; there was no need for protective clothing this time. As far as she was aware the scene was clear, but they were keeping it secured in case the post-mortem brought up anything later. She walked around the back of the car, snapping on a pair of gloves. The car door slammed shut making her jump, then she walked towards the doorway.

All around the edges of the board were now covered in black fingerprint dust. She stepped through it into the vast space, where wintery light filtered through the missing tiles in the roof and the cracks between the walls and boards. It was different to last night, still dark around the outer edges, and she turned the torch on. Shining it into each of the corners, walking forwards she didn't see the charred chunk of wood that had been moved in the search earlier. A screech escaped her lips as she tumbled over it, landing on her hands and knees, and an ear-splitting shrill, rattling whistle filled the church as the air above her turned black with startled pigeons that had been nesting in the eaves. Lucy screamed even louder: she hated birds and the furious flapping and squawking terrified her. She cowered, covering her head to protect it. They took off out of the gaps in the roof, and she heard Sam shout: 'Lucy, is everything okay in there?'

Standing up before she got caught curled up in a ball on a pile of rubble, she shouted back: 'Yes, thanks. I think I gave the pigeons a bigger fright than they gave me.'

Her knees stinging, she could feel her cheeks burning, it was lucky for her there was no one around to see her make a tit of herself. They'd have a right old chuckle about it at the station and she'd never live it down.

'Okay, if you need me shout.'

She waited until she heard the muffled sound of the car door shutting and exhaled; a white cloud of her breath filled the air in front of her. The torch had rolled some distance, and this time she kept her eyes on the ground while she went to retrieve it. The church was eerily calm now the birds had left. Lucy shivered. She made her way to where the cross had been positioned, staring down at the dark stained rubble it had been wedged into. Closing her eyes, she pictured the scene exactly as it had been in the early hours when she'd first set her sight on it. Sandy Kilburn must have been terrified. Of all the godforsaken places to die, this wreck of a church must be one of the worst. She tried to imagine how the killer had lured her inside: he must have removed the board from the door beforehand and had the cross made and waiting. It wasn't the sort of thing you could carry down a busy town centre street – even at night the area had plenty of passing foot traffic. And how did he get her to go in with him, had he promised her alcohol, sex, money? All possible reasons for her to follow him, or had she known and trusted him? There were so many lines of enquiry to follow; what they needed was to start interviewing the list of associates on Sandy's intelligence profile. She studied each wall to see if there were any satanic symbols, not that she was really aware of any. A pentagram or an upside-down cross was about the limit of her knowledge on matters concerning devil worship, and even these had come from re-runs of old Hammer horror movies on the TV.

When she went home she knew that was how she would spend her evening before falling into a coma. She would search the internet until she had a grasp of the knowledge she needed to know about these sorts of crimes. She yawned, she was exhausted and still had the post-mortem to attend, which would take hours. It crossed her mind that she could send Browning and Mattie on her behalf while she went home for a couple of hours' sleep. Then she ruled it out. How would it look if the new DI couldn't hack the first twenty-four hours of a murder investigation? There was no way she would let anyone scrutinise or criticise her. She needed strong coffee, some food and she'd be good to go for another few hours. It didn't matter how tired she was, all that mattered now was catching this killer, and she was going to do everything in her power to bring him in to custody to answer for this heinous crime.

CHAPTER NINE

Margaret was the last to leave the church hall. She had assured David she was more than capable of locking a door behind her. She wanted to check everything was in order one more time and she couldn't do it while there were people milling around. The sound of their chattering voices filled her mind and gave her a headache, which made it hard to concentrate on anything longer than twenty seconds. They also made her forget what she was doing, which was why she needed the damn clipboard. Old age wasn't what it was cracked up to be; her memory was playing up. Some days she could remember what she'd done from the moment she opened her eyes until she closed them at bedtime. Others she couldn't remember what her cat was called or how long she'd owned it. She paused as a sob escaped her lips; her cat was dead, murdered. She kept forgetting that as well. Some evil person had taken away the poor innocent thing for no reason at all. Her well-meaning son had suggested she made an appointment with her GP about her forgetfulness, but she hadn't. Her mother had started with dementia at an early age and she was terrified it might run in the family. She didn't want to end up in an old person's home like her own mother had. Visiting her mother had been heart-wrenching to say the least. Her vacant eyes staring into space and never at her, wandering around asking for scrambled egg all day despite being fed less than ten minutes ago. No other conscious thoughts or memories left inside, her mind an empty shell – the thought made her shiver. She'd always been such an efficient person. There was no crueller fate than to make someone who feared losing their mind actually lose it.

She walked around the trestle tables, nodding with pleasure at how good they looked. The tombola was set out beautifully; Natalia had done a splendid job. She reached the toy stall and sighed. It was a shame she couldn't say the same for this hotchpotch mess. The books weren't stacked in a very good order and the stuffed toys were all over the place – this would never do. Shaking her head she began to rearrange everything, not noticing how dark it was getting outside. Margaret didn't go out at night on her own: she didn't mind helping out with the Street Saviours because there was a large group of them and they weren't truly alone at any one point.

A loud bang from inside the entrance to the hall startled her, and she looked up and saw the large hall, which was normally filled with light, was now filling with dark shadows. She shuddered and the skin on her arms broke out in goosebumps.

'Hello, who's there?'

There was no answer. Her first thought was those pesky kids off the council estate who loved to spend their spare time terrorising all the nice people who came to church. Straightening up she heard the bones in her back creak. She hadn't realised she'd been stooped over for so long. Leaving her clipboard on the toy stall she walked towards the entrance, opening the heavy wooden vestibule door. Releasing the breath she'd been holding she smiled, shaking her head. *You silly old fool.*

Throwing open the front door she looked around the car park – it was deserted. She couldn't even see any kids out on the street. It was time to call it a day. Her stomach let out a loud groan; she was going home for a nice pot of tea and a couple of crumpets. Going back inside the hall she grabbed her coat off the rack and the keys from the stage. Taking one last look around she nodded, it would have to do. After the crowds had been let in tomorrow it would look like a jumble sale in five minutes anyway.

Despite the fact that it was almost completely dark outside and there was a biting nip in the air she decided to walk the short distance home, as it was quicker than waiting for a bus. There was no way she was phoning a taxi, which was a frivolous waste of her pension when it was such a lovely evening. As she hurried along, the feeling of being watched settled over her and she turned to see if anyone was following her. There was no one, she was being silly. Who would want to follow her anyway? It's not as if she had a purse full of money they could steal. She didn't have a mobile phone or expensive jewellery – if anyone decided to mug her they'd be pretty disappointed. Having scared herself she turned the corner and came face-to-face with the now-abandoned care home that was her mother's last address. The council had built a new, super home and closed all the ones in need of updating. Basterfield House loomed larger than life as she walked towards it, with its boarded-up windows and door. The front of the building had a wall of graffiti covering it; foul words and the crude outlines of a man's private parts took pride of place across the double doors. She shook her head, it was disgusting – another of the town's landmark buildings that had been left to go to rack and ruin. It was a sin the way the council had let the pier go the same way. When she'd been a girl Brooklyn Bay had been such a fun place to live. A bustling seaside town with a fairground, ice rink, theatre and the beautiful Victorian pier, which now looked as if it was about to collapse into the sea at any moment. She'd noticed it had been fenced off and no trespassing signs warning of its danger put up around it. Not that it stopped the teenagers and drug addicts from using it. That pier was a disaster waiting to happen; it could collapse into the sea and take the old bingo hall and amusement arcade with it, along with whoever happened to be dossing down in it. She'd met her husband on that pier: they'd both been sixteen and in the queue for the big wheel. It had been love at first sight. She let out a sigh; she missed him dearly even though he'd been dead for ten years.

A loud moan piercing the air stopped her in her tracks. Looking around she couldn't see anyone, considering it was a cold but dry evening. People would be out walking their dogs, but it was typical there was never anyone around when you needed them. Just like the bloody police, she thought. Tom had been an officer, or whatever rank it was now, for eighteen years and he was never around when she needed him. She paused as she heard another groan, wondering where it could have come from. Then she heard a faint, 'Help me.' Wondering if she should knock on someone's door and ask the occupiers to ring the police, she didn't, worried in case it was her mind playing tricks on her and she would look like a silly old fool. Instead she followed in the direction from where she'd thought the sound had emanated. It was probably the wind whistling through the old, draughty building in front of her. Or it could be distant memories of that place and the pained voices of residents she used to hear calling out whenever she visited her mum. She'd spent her entire life trying to be a good person: she could no more ignore a plea for help than she could a kitten stuck up a tree.

As she walked around to the rear of the building she paused for a moment. It was cloaked in dark shadows, a single security bulb above a fire exit gave off a little light. Enough to see that the door was ajar. Another moan filtered through it, and she scurried towards it. She was stubborn enough to go inside and see who was in distress despite her reservations about her own safety. As she stepped into the building the memories came flooding back making her pause, remembering the number of times she'd sat holding her mum's hand, desperate for those flickers of recognition which had been few and far between. Inhaling, her nostrils filled with the scent of damp and mildew. There was another groan. It was so dark inside it was difficult to see and she wished she had a torch or even a cigarette lighter to hold up.

'Hello, is there anybody there? Are you hurt, do you need help?'

There was movement on the floor in the distance, and she felt her heart begin to thud against her ribcage as she realised it was a person huddled on the floor. Margaret hurried towards them.

'Oh my goodness, are you hurt? What happened to you?'

There was an even louder groan. Whoever it was they had a dirty grey blanket covering them and the hood from their sweatshirt pulled tight over their face. Margaret's first thought was that it was a homeless person. Stepping closer she leant down, reaching out a hand to shake them, but then she screeched as a thick, much stronger arm than hers shot out from underneath the cover. She pulled as hard as she could to get away, but the fingers dug deep into her wrist.

'Let go of me, you're hurting.'

She felt herself falling towards the ground as she was being dragged down. She kicked out at the hand as she fell, and it released its grip. She crawled on her hands and knees as fast as she could to put some space between her and whoever it was that had tried to hurt her. The cover was thrown off and terror filled her veins when a dark shadow loomed over her. Margaret pushed and pulled as hard as she could to get away, but she was no match for the stranger who was now standing over her brandishing the biggest knife she'd ever seen.

Opening her mouth to scream she felt the knife cut through the air in front of her, heard it as it whooshed towards her throat, silencing her for ever.

CHAPTER TEN

May 1989

He hated school: he didn't like maths, he couldn't do maths and the teachers always liked to pick on him because of this. The more he tried to hide at the back of the classroom and keep quiet, the more they would bombard him with questions. They seemed to take great enjoyment in making him look and feel stupid in front of the rest of the class, so his mother had let him stay off. As long as he didn't let his father know he was home because then he would be furious with the both of them. He was old enough to understand the consequences of his father's fury. He was to stay hidden in his bedroom and not make a sound – it was their secret. They had a few secrets that they didn't share with his father; he wouldn't approve of his love of comics and sherbet fountains.

His mum had left early to go to an appointment at the hospital. He'd asked her what was wrong. She'd smiled, held him close and told him nothing. It was just a check-up, all women had to have one when they reached a certain age. He didn't know what she meant; ruffling his hair she'd bent down and kissed his forehead. This time he hadn't wiped her kiss away. There was no mistaking the tears threatening to fall from her eyes. She blinked and they were gone; an expert at hiding her feelings, he wondered briefly if there was something wrong. Too afraid to ask her, he did what any other ten-year-old boy would do and built a makeshift tent to hide in. If his father came in he wouldn't see him in there, he'd be safe.

Watching his mum from his bedroom window as she got into a taxi he felt his heart tug inside his chest. He was hungry; he'd eaten his sandwich ages ago. He wondered if he dared go down and get some biscuits, or was he too scared? He didn't know where his father was: he should be at work, but he might be anywhere, although he didn't usually stay quiet when he was home. If he wasn't shouting or talking like Father Vincent, he was hitting them or crying. He wondered if this was what all families were like. Somehow, he didn't think that it was. Why would anyone behave like that? He listened at the door, he couldn't hear the television. That didn't mean he wasn't in. He might be asleep on the settee. He often fell asleep if he'd been drinking or after eating. Thinking about food, his stomach let out a loud groan. He couldn't wait hours to get something to eat. He didn't think there was anyone here – he should be safe.

Tugging his bedroom door open he put one bare foot onto the hall carpet and listened. Before he knew it he was in the hallway; his parents' bedroom door was shut. Creeping down the stairs he made it to the kitchen before he heard the front door slam, and a woman's voice he didn't recognise began to chatter. He did recognise the loud grunt which came from his father. Panic making his heart race, he whipped his head from side to side, realising he couldn't get back upstairs without being caught. He ran over to the back door and let himself outside into the garden – he could hide behind the huge bush in the corner where his den was. It wasn't the warmest of days, there was a breeze in the air and the grass was damp from the rain shower earlier. His feet were cold without any shoes but he couldn't go back inside. He ran across and dived inside his den, in case he came out and saw him. From there he could watch the house and see if he was coming. He was angry with himself now, wishing he'd done what his mum had said. Stayed in his room and kept out of sight like he was supposed to. The thin cotton pyjama top he was wearing was too short; it didn't cover his bellybutton and the cuffs on the pants were halfway up his calves. A dark shadow appeared at the living room window, and he caught his breath, holding it in, wondering if all that praying to God had given his father X-ray vision so that he could see through leaves and branches. Then the curtains were pulled shut, and he frowned. Why had he done that, it was the middle of the day? He sat huddled on an overturned plant pot wondering what he was going to do about the mess he'd got himself into. If his dad was in the living room with the curtains closed, he wouldn't see him sneaking across the garden. A huge drop of rain fell onto the bridge of his nose, and he looked up to the sky. It had gone that murky grey colour, signalling it was about to hammer it down. Another splash fell onto the back of his hand, and he made up his mind. He stood up and sprinted across the grass.

Curiosity getting the better of him, he made his way to the window and crouched down. Counting to three to build up the courage, he peered through the crack in the curtains to see if his father was in there. He was in there all right, so was a strange woman with white hair and huge red earrings that looked like the buttons on his mum's best coat. She was standing behind him, running her hands up and down his father's shirt, undoing the buttons. The boy stared wondering who she was and what she was doing in his house. Then she moved in front of his dad, and her fingers began to unzip his trousers. He didn't want to look, but he couldn't tear himself away. He watched as the woman pushed his dad onto the settee and buried her head in his lap. He knew this was wrong – they were doing something bad. Who was she? He wanted to run in there and pull her hair, rip those huge earrings out of her ears and scream at her to get out of their house. But he couldn't because the beating would probably kill him and then he'd beat him some more. What about his mother? He'd probably beat her as well and none of it was any of her fault because she wasn't even here. He took one last look at the scene in front of him – his father had his eyes shut and was groaning so loud he could hear him through the cracked pane of glass. Her head was bobbing up and down, and he felt his stomach lurch.

He ran to the back door and slipped inside, making his way back up to his bedroom, the hunger pains had been replaced with a spreading feeling of sickness. He went into his room and crawled inside his makeshift tent where he lay on a pillow, pulling a blanket over himself to try and stop the shivering. He didn't know what to do, so he closed his eyes and waited for sleep to come. Maybe he was having a bad dream and when he woke up his mother would be home from the hospital and that strange woman wouldn't be in his house doing dirty stuff with his dad.

CHAPTER ELEVEN

Lucy tried to ignore the annoying ringtone of her mobile phone. She was lying in a bath filled with Lush-scented bubbles, a hair mask on, trying to soak away the horrors of today along with the stench of the post-mortem, where the only trace evidence Catherine had found was a few stray hairs on the nightdress. She wasn't on call, so whoever it was could bugger off and leave her alone. She was beyond tired, in fact she didn't know if she'd ever felt so exhausted before. Not even the hours in labour with Ellie had seemed as long as the last twenty-four hours, and they'd been horrific. It stopped, and she punched the air, slipping under the water to rinse off the conditioner that her bleached-blonde hair had desperately needed. When she resurfaced the house phone was ringing. Now she was pissed off because that was just plain rude. Who the hell needed to speak to her so urgently? Ellie was at her dad's, so it wouldn't be her, and anyway she never rang the house phone. Getting out of the bath, she wrapped a bath sheet around herself and dripped her way into her bedroom, where both of the offending phones were. She looked at the display on her mobile: three missed calls from a private number. The groan she let out was loud, almost as loud as one of Ellie's when she was asked to hoover or wash the pots. As she stared at the phone in her hand, the house phone began to ring, making her jump. Snatching it from its holder she snapped, 'Hello.'

'Ma'am, it's the control room. We have a major incident that we need you to attend.'

'I'm not on call, you should have a list. DS Browning is the duty sergeant tonight, and the duty inspector is out west.'

'We know you aren't and I'm sorry about this. DS Browning requested we phone you. A body has been found at the back of Basterfield House.'

Lucy felt her heart sink; it must be bad if Browning had asked for her to be called out instead of the on-call DI. 'Right, okay. Tell him I'm on my way.'

She began frantically towel-drying her hair, her stomach churning. Whatever level of relaxation she'd achieved had been wiped out in a thirty-second phone call.

She parked her tiny Fiat behind a police van, its flashing blue and white lights blinding her. The first thing she was going to do was find the idiot who thought it was necessary to have a full-on eighties disco lightshow going in the middle of a quiet, residential street at midnight. There was no need for it, the police tape blocking the road was enough to let the few people who were still out and about at this time of night know the area was cordoned off. Before she could say anything to the two officers who were standing there, she heard Browning mutter: 'Will one of you turn the bloody blues off, you're blinding me.' She smiled, he was a grumpy old bugger, but at least they were on the same wavelength. She glanced at the officers, neither of them looked that much older than Ellie. She supposed she would have been the same once upon a time. Having a teenage daughter and working on almost every grisly murder in Brooklyn Bay had given her more than a few wrinkles and aged her beyond her years.

Browning came striding towards her.

'Boss, I'm really sorry to have called you out. I didn't know what to do and kind of panicked.'

'It's okay, I realise this must be quite something for you to do that.'

He nodded, running his hand through what hair he had left. 'It's really bad – and what makes it even worse is I know who she is; I can identify her. I was only speaking with her yesterday about her dead cat.'

Alarm bells began ringing in Lucy's mind and she looked at him, her eyes wide in horror as she put two and two together. 'Please tell me it's not?'

Browning shrugged. 'I wish I could.'

Turning, Lucy ran to the back of her car where she tugged out the packets of protective clothing she was going to need. Deftly pulling on the white paper overalls, boot covers, and gloves she slammed the boot down. Ducking under the tape, one of the officers rushed over, and Browning glared at him.

'Sign DI Harwin into the scene, there's a good lad.'

'Yes, sir. Sorry, ma'am, I didn't realise.'

She couldn't speak, her tongue felt as if it was three times its normal size as it stuck to the roof of her mouth. She needed to see for herself how bad this was before all hell broke loose. Browning led the way and she followed, the thudding of her heart filling her mind. She turned the corner, which was pitch-black, and lifted the Magnum torch that Browning passed to her. Unable to stop herself, the gasp which left her lips was loud.

'Holy Mother of God.'

'Something like that.'

Lucy stepped towards the frail woman who was hanging upside down from the rear fire escape of the abandoned care home. Lucy's hands lifted to her mouth as she began to shake her head from side to side. The woman had been left there, on show for the world to see, like some gaudy scarecrow, her head almost hanging off because the cut severing her throat was so deep. Her arms were spread wide apart, tied to the railings.

'I didn't bother with the paramedics, even I could see she's sustained an injury which is incompatible with life. I mean her fucking head is hanging on by a thread. Who does this to an old woman?'

Lucy nodded, inhaling through her nose and out through her mouth. 'You said you were speaking to her about her cat. It's Tom's mum, isn't it?'

Browning nodded. 'Who is going to tell him?'

They heard the brisk footsteps coming towards them that signalled the DCI's arrival. Browning turned, moving as fast as he could to block him from getting any closer. Lucy followed.

'Sir, you need to go back. Leave this one to us.'

'Lucy, while I appreciate the offer I've already been dragged away from my warm bed. I know you're both very capable, but I'm here now. Can't hurt to take a gander at whatever poor bugger has come to a sticky end this time. You know it's a shame people don't get murdered in more sociable hours, it's always a bloody awkward time or place. Two nights on the trot, it's unheard of. Is it a full moon or something?'

Lucy was shaking her head, wishing she could find the words to stop him before he said anything else. Browning's eyes were so wide she thought they might actually pop out from their sockets. She didn't know who to look at or what to say.

'Move out of the way then, Lucy, come on. It's too late to be messing around. The quicker we get this over with the quicker we can get back to bed.' He went to sidestep her, and she slammed the palm of her hand into his chest.

'You need to stop right there. I'm so sorry, Tom. We think it might be your mum.'

He began to laugh.

'Nice one, that's the most ridiculous thing I've ever heard. She'll be tucked up in bed fast asleep. Why the hell would you think it's her? She wouldn't be out at this time of night. Stop messing around and let me past, Lucy.' He went to walk around her, and Browning grabbed his arm.

'Tom, I'm really sorry. You can't go back there. It's bad.'

Tom pulled his arm away from Browning's grasp and made a run for it. Lucy dashed after him, muttering *Oh fuck*. They stopped behind him as he was shining his torch at the grotesque sight in front of him, the light wavering in his trembling hands. Lucy put her hand on his arm and squeezed gently.

'Is it your mum?'

His head moved up and down slowly. He turned to look at her, his eyes full of tears.

'Why, I don't understand? She's an old woman, for Christ's sake; she lives at the fucking church, she volunteers there so much. Who would want to do this? I only spoke to her this afternoon when she rang me, she was fine. Why would someone want to kill her?'

Lucy was processing all the information he was telling her for later, because at some point, she would have to question him about his movements today. She needed to rule him out as a suspect. She looked at Browning, who turned and walked away, speaking into his radio. They needed him out of here now; he was in the scene and, as ridiculous as she knew it was, they couldn't rule out his involvement. She didn't think that he was involved in any way, shape or form. But she had a job to do and sometimes it called for harsh decisions to get to the right solution. She could not have this scene jeopardised further regardless of who the victim was, and Tom would understand this, eventually.

'Sir, I need you to leave the scene now. You have to let me do my job and I can't while you're here, I'll keep you updated. You know that I will.'

He glared at Lucy, and she took a step back, the animosity in his eyes taking her by surprise. She understood, though – because if it was her mum, she'd want to punch the nearest person to her for telling her to leave.

'Yes, I do know that you will because I'm not about to be pushed out in the cold with no information. I need to be kept in the loop, you realise that don't you, Lucy.'

He turned and began walking away, his pace slow, his shoulders stooped. She didn't know this man, he wasn't the one from a few moments ago, and she had to ignore the churning in her stomach. This was one big headache. She pulled out her phone and rang Mattie.

'I need you to take a statement for me.'

'Lucy, I'm not on call and neither are you. Is this some kind of joke? Let that lazy arse Browning sort out whatever it is.'

'No, I wish to Christ it was. Can you go to the station and update yourself with this log? I'm at the scene for a body behind Basterfield House? Tom's mum has been found murdered. I need his first account of where he's been tonight since he left work and then he'll need taking home. I don't want someone who doesn't know him questioning him. He needs a familiar face.'

'I'm on my way.'

CHAPTER TWELVE

He stripped his clothes off in the rear yard – they were beyond messy. She'd bled a hell of a lot more than he'd expected. Stuffing them into a cardboard box to take to the council refuse site tomorrow, he planned how he'd throw the box into one of the huge skips where it would be crushed with all the tonnes of other crap. He'd panicked a bit more than he should have, he knew; although the back of the empty home wasn't overlooked by any neighbouring properties it was still all a bit too daring. The possibility of being caught had played on his mind, and made him rush more than he would have liked to. He hadn't had time to make the cross, but it didn't matter. He'd made use of what he had available. The rusted metal fire escape had been almost as good. The rope he'd found dumped behind the skip where he'd parked his car had come in very handy. His car would have to be deep cleaned, although he'd left the plastic cover on the seat from the garage, so it shouldn't be too bad. He slid the key in the lock and opened the door – going inside it was silent. There was no one here now; he liked it when everyone had left and he had the place to himself. He could hear himself think and relive the last twenty-four hours. It had been intense to say the least, but what a ride.

He went into the bathroom to scrub at his hands and arms with the antibacterial handwash. It smelt of Fizzy Cola Laces and transported him back to his childhood. He'd lived off ten pence bags of penny sweets and pickled onion Monster Munch; every time he got pocket money he'd go to the shop to buy them. If he hadn't been good enough to earn his pocket money he would steal it from the loose change that his dad kept in the bowl on the kitchen counter. He'd always been scrupulous and had stooped at nothing over the years to reach his goals.

He pictured the look on the old woman's face, it had been priceless. The fear and shock would keep him smiling on his darkest days. He'd got her good. If she hadn't been such a do-gooder she'd still be alive; any normal person would have carried on walking past the deserted building. He had known she wouldn't be able to resist, just like she rushed to help all the drunks on a Saturday night or the homeless people at the soup kitchen. People really were gullible. She could have scurried past and phoned the police. Where had it got her trying to help a stranger? Dead was where it had got her. Although he'd have been in trouble if they'd turned up instead of her. He would have blagged his way out of it though, he could talk himself out of anything, and he'd had enough experience over the years. His public persona was a lot different to his private one – only those close to him ever got a glimpse of that. He smiled at his reflection; with his dark hair and good looks he could have been an actor – he had the skill that was for sure.

He looked around; this job was almost the same. Being nice to people you wouldn't piss on if they were on fire any other time. Listening to their mindless conversations, the rubbish and lies they told each other. He could pick a liar out from a room full of people; instead he greeted them all as if they were his long-lost friends. Shaking hands, hugging, chatting, giving them the attention they so badly craved. No wonder he liked to go home, kick off his shoes and drink copious amounts of red wine. If he didn't use something to relax he'd lose his mind, end up in the mental health unit at the hospital and he didn't want to end up back there. Switching off had always been a huge problem for him, though not so much when he was younger and could lose himself in a comic. Now he was older he didn't find they did the trick quite as much, not like a quality bottle of full-bodied red.

Splashing the tepid water over his face, he decided he would have a shower when he got home. Drying himself on the rough paper towels he put them into the bin and removed the liner, tying it into a knot. He then slipped on the spare clothes he'd left earlier: a similar outfit to the one he was wearing so his wife wouldn't notice.

Grabbing the bag he let himself back out of the back door, pushed the bin liner into the box and stuffed it into the boot of the car. His first port of call tomorrow would be the tip; it would be shut now. It was time to go home and play the doting husband.

CHAPTER THIRTEEN

Mattie walked into the deserted police station rubbing his eyes, glad he'd stayed in to play his Xbox tonight instead of going to the pub with his mates. He was saving money; he was going on holiday in two days, and he didn't need this. Another major case when he wasn't going to be here to help. He hated leaving Lucy to run it on her own, because she would be thinking she had the world to impress. He'd warned her going for the DI position would bring her more work-related stress than she needed. Especially now that idiot George had upped and left her for another woman; she was going to make herself ill. Although it was Browning who was the on-call DS tonight, technically he should be the one to run it, but Lucy would be overseeing it and as usual she would get too involved. Too hands-on, especially if it was the boss's mum. What a mess. He went to the kitchen where he made two strong mugs of coffee.

As he carried them upstairs to the open-plan CID office, the motion sensor lights flickered on. It was eerily quiet this time of night. They'd only pulled a couple of all-nighters before, but he'd never been here on his own. He sat at his desk and got his notebook out. Then pulled a couple of statement forms out of the filing cabinet from behind him. Although he should be using the hand-held device they'd all been issued with, it was a pain in the arse – he'd stick with good old pen and paper. He heard voices carry up from downstairs, then heavy footsteps as they came up the spiral staircase. The boss, who was flanked by one of the new officers, looked whiter than the sheet of paper he was holding.

Mattie jumped up.

'Sir, I'm sorry. I don't know what to say, there are no words.'

'No *sir* crap, it's Tom.'

He walked to the chair opposite Mattie's and flopped down into it so hard it made a loud cracking noise. Mattie pushed the mug towards him, and he took it from him, wrapping both hands around it. Mattie noted how clean his fingernails were. There were no bloodstains or dirt under them, which was a good sign, and he immediately felt guilty for even checking. His dad, who was Brooklyn Bay's equivalent to Derek Trotter, disliked the fact that his only son had become a police officer and had a saying that he liked to bring up at every opportunity: *Once a cop, always a cop.*

'I'm so cold, I can't stop shivering.'

'It's the shock, sir, I mean Tom. I can't begin to understand how you're feeling. I've got a spare fleece jacket in my locker, should I go and get it for you?'

'No, thank you. I don't know how I'm feeling if I'm honest. My stomach is churning so much I feel as if I might throw up my supper. I can't get that horrific image of her out of my mind. It's not the kind of picture you want to remember your mother by, is it? All these years and all the memories of the happy times we've spent together and that's what I'm left with. It's there in my mind, burning a bloody big hole in the front of my eyeballs. There was so much blood, it was everywhere. And her head. I always imagined her dying peacefully in her sleep, isn't that what old people are supposed to do?' He sucked in gulps of air and lifted the mug to his lips to take a sip; though his hands were trembling that much Mattie was amazed he didn't end up wearing the hot drink.

'No, it's not. I'm so very sorry. If you can give me a first account of where you've been tonight after you left work I can get you home and back to your family.'

He nodded. 'Yes, let me see. I left here at six and went to Sainsbury's to pick up some groceries, and I was home by seven thirty. Alison was watching *Coronation Street* and it had just started. I had a shower, ate my tea and put my boys to bed. Then I argued with Alison over the television; it was a stupid argument. She loves watching soap operas and I don't. I went to bed sulking to watch the television up there. I must have been tired because the next thing I know I got a call from Control asking me to attend the scene.'

Mattie finished writing and looked up at him. 'That must have been a terrible shock? Did they tell you who the victim was before you got there?'

Tom shook his head, taking a huge sip from the mug.

'No, they weren't to know, were they? I think it was Browning who recognised her. When I rang her this afternoon, Mum said he'd been to take her dead cat away. Look, for what it's worth I didn't kill my mother. I know this is standard procedure, but I want to go home to my wife and boys now. So if you don't mind can you give me a lift back; my car's at the scene and I don't want to go back there.'

Mattie nodded. 'Of course, come on.'

Tom put the mug down, and he stood up. 'Some days I fucking hate my job. There have been some very dark days over the years. None as dark as this though.'

Lucy waited for the on-call CSI; they were coming from the opposite end of Brooklyn Bay. So was Doctor Maxwell; she spied Tom's Land Rover parked down the street and walked over to it, peering through the windows. Tugging at the handle she was surprised it opened. The interior light came on, and she saw the keys dangling from the ignition. Pulling them out she pushed them into her pocket – that's all she needed, some idiot stealing the boss's car and, in this town, it was quite possible. Shining the torch around she checked the interior; the feeling she was betraying him was overwhelming and she felt like a complete bitch. But it had to be done. She couldn't see any signs of blood splatter or anything of evidential value. She checked the back seat which was a sea of coats, school bags, football boots and empty crisp packets. She paused at the boot before opening it, afraid that she would find a wet, bloody patch betraying him. Lifting it up she breathed out a sigh of relief to see a couple of cardboard boxes, a Sainsbury's shopping bag, and a black, heavy-duty kit bag with various pieces of uniform hanging out of it. There was a football, two tennis rackets, and a pair of gym trainers. She slammed the boot down and locked the car.

Browning was watching her, a look of disgust on his face. It didn't matter what he thought of her, she knew he was still pissed off that she got the promotion over him. Tom might be their boss, but she wouldn't be doing her job properly if she didn't check him out. And she owed it to Margaret Crowe to find who had killed her and left her dangling like a life-sized marionette, bleeding to death all over the overgrown car park of a boarded-up retirement home. Was this some kind of statement? An old woman at the back of an old people's home? Lucy sighed to herself. At this stage nothing could be discounted. She hoped Mattie wouldn't be too pissed with her for calling him in to deal with Tom. If it had been the other way around she couldn't say that she'd have been ecstatic about it. This was definitely up there on the list of shittiest jobs she'd ever asked him to do and there had been a few; but at least Mattie would be out of it in two days. The lucky sod was flying to Greece. What she'd give to be going with him. Her phone began to ring and she answered it without looking at the display.

'Well if that wasn't the most awkward thing I've ever done I don't know what was?'

'Yeah, I realise that, thank you. Where is he?'

'I've dropped him off at home. Boss he looks like shit. You know it wasn't him, right?'

She counted to five. Whether she knew it or not she couldn't let her loyalty to Tom get in the way of the investigation.

'Yes, I'd like to think that was the case. However, you and I both know that the pool of suspects for the murder of a seventy-year-old woman isn't going to be huge. Regardless of who he is, we have to follow protocol and do this the right way. The quicker we establish his whereabouts the quicker we can focus on catching the killer.'

He didn't answer, so she continued. 'It might not seem that way now, but the boss wouldn't want it any other way. Once he's come to terms with what's happened he's going to want to see whoever did this in custody. If it means ruling him out first, then so be it. He might not thank us for it now, he will later though. I want this bastard caught.'

'Do you want me there?'

'No, there's nothing you can do. Browning is here. I'm waiting for the doctor and CSI; you can go home. Thank you.'

'Bye, Lucy.'

''Night.'

She hung up; there wasn't anything he could do. One of them might as well get some beauty sleep because it sure as hell wasn't going to be her.

CHAPTER FOURTEEN

October 1989

He sat staring at his mum; she was asleep. He wanted to shake her and wake her up, but the medicine wouldn't let her open her eyes. It sucked her down into a world of blackness that he couldn't penetrate. Instead he stroked her pale face, wiping away the droplet of water that had appeared on her cheek. He hadn't even realised he was crying until another fell immediately, replacing the first. She'd been in hospital for three days: three long days, and she hadn't looked at him once. The searing pain which ripped through his heart was almost too much to bear; he wanted to sob until he had no voice left and then he wanted to punch everything in sight. Was this why his dad cried all those times after he'd hit her again and again? Was she in here because of him hitting her? He needed to know, because if she was, then he would kill his dad. He didn't care if he went to prison for the rest of his life. If that Bible-quoting freak was the reason why his mum couldn't open her eyes, then God help him – because once he started to hit him he wouldn't be able to stop. He might only be ten years old, but he didn't care. He would take the biggest knife from the kitchen drawer and slice his throat open with it when he was asleep.

He heard raised voices from the corridor and turned to look. His dad was arguing with the doctor. He heard the words 'cancer' and 'too late to treat successfully'. He knew what cancer was, Robbie's grandad had it last year. It made his skin turn yellow and his long, straggly, white, nicotine-stained hair fall out. Robbie had said his grandad changed into the skeleton dude off *Tales from the Crypt*. He'd laughed at him, and Robbie had punched him in the gut, knocking the wind out of his belly. Then Robbie had cried, saying it wasn't funny, he was too scared to go and sit with him because he looked so bad. This couldn't happen to his mum; she was beautiful. He didn't want her long, black, wavy hair to fall out and her skin to turn yellow. She couldn't be this poorly. She'd always wanted to go on holiday to Rome and he wanted to take her there when he was old enough. He bent down and kissed her cheek; her eyelids fluttered and she opened them. Staring at him it took her a moment to realise who he was, then she smiled, and he felt all the blackness that was churning inside his stomach melt away.

'When are you coming home, I miss you?'

Her voice a whisper, she beckoned him nearer. 'Soon baby, soon.'

'Good, I don't like reading the Bible and going to bed early every night.' He had to stop himself from saying it was because his dad was sneaking out of the house and leaving him on his own. He knew it would upset her. If he was honest he'd rather be alone than have to suffer his mood swings and violent outbursts. He came back late, smelling of whisky and horrible, flowery perfume. Not the soft, delicate scent that his mum always smelt of. He knew he was spending all his time drinking in The Dog and Ball; he'd followed him one night to see where he was sneaking off to. He'd sat on a wall up the street, waiting until he'd been in there for a while before going and peering through the steamed-up windows around the side. The pub had been busy, and he'd searched for the familiar outline of his father, gasping when his eyes found him. He was standing next to that woman with the blonde hair, who this time had huge white buttons in her ears. She had her arm around him and he was rubbing his hand across her back. His mum's voice brought him back to the funny smelling hospital room.

'Is he taking good care of you? Has he hurt you?'

He shook his head, to be fair he hadn't. He hadn't really seen much of him, so he'd taken to feeding himself.

'If he hurts you, and I'm not there, you tell your teacher, I won't have it. Promise me that you'll tell someone.'

He saw her brown eyes fill with watery tears and he felt his own do the same.

'I'm okay, I can look after myself. If he hits me, I'll tell. You get better, don't worry about me. I just want you to come home.'

'You're such a good boy, I know you can. I'll be home soon.'

He reached down to hug her, squeezing her gently. Then he felt himself being dragged upwards and pushed to one side.

'Don't touch her like that, you'll hurt her.'

He glared at his dad, the black fury filling his mind making it hard to speak. He would never hurt her, not like the bullying bastard, standing there with his hands on his hips. His dad stared at him, opened his mouth, then closed it again. Sensing that something had changed within his son, realising there had been some kind of shift in his attitude, he turned away from him and didn't look at him again, which suited him fine.

CHAPTER FIFTEEN

Lucy splashed cold water into her eyes, which were puffy, red and tired. Next to her, two of the PCSOs were chattering about an upcoming night out. She envied them: fresh-faced, no forty-eight hour shifts with no sleep. They were two of the good guys. Always keen to help, always friendly, always nice.

'Erm, boss. Would you like some breakfast and a nice coffee getting from Costa? You look knackered.'

Lucy smiled at Lindsey. 'Yes, I would. That would be the most amazing, life-saving thing in the world that anyone has ever done for me. Thank you.'

Lindsey reached out and patted her arm. 'I hear you've pulled an all-nighter again, you work too hard.'

'Someone has to do it and this time it was me. Can I have a vanilla latte and a bacon roll please?'

Patting her pockets and realising she had no money on her, Lindsey shook her head. 'I'll get it, you can pay me later. Then we'll go and take over scene guard.'

'Thank you.'

'Anytime, just don't let them forget about us.'

Lucy shook her head. 'I won't, anyway you don't need us to sort it out. You can sort it out between yourselves, I'm happy to go with what you do. It will need a couple of you though, and tell the officers there I said you're to keep the vehicles. I'm not having you standing around in the freezing cold for hours.'

'See this is why we love you, Lucy, you trust us to do the right thing. Most of the sergeants and inspectors treat us like we haven't got a clue.'

'That's because most of them are idiots and haven't got a clue.' She winked at them and they laughed. They left her staring at her reflection a few moments longer; closing her eyes she inhaled deeply then let it go. *You can do this Lucy, you know that you can.* She took a couple more deep breaths trying to loosen the knot that had formed inside her stomach and was refusing to shift.

Inside her office she sipped on the hot coffee that Lindsey had delivered. It tasted like liquid gold as it warmed her insides and started to shake the fog which had begun to fill her brain. Browning had gone home to shower and change; the briefing was scheduled for nine. She had twenty minutes before she had to confront her team and tell them the disturbing news about Margaret Crowe. She'd pulled up the file for Sandy Kilburn. There had to be some connection: bodies found with throats cut, hanging upside down, were not a common occurrence in Brooklyn Bay. The only differences between the two murders were that there'd been no dead cat which had belonged to Sandy and no homemade, life-sized wooden crucifix for Margaret. She stared at the photographs from both scenes. They were horrific, bloody, gaudy, shocking – they'd been killed for a specific reason. Lucy's job was to find out what the reason was and hunt down the killer before he struck again. She knew in her heart that he would. Because a killer needed three victims before they were elevated into the higher ranks of serial killer. But what would happen then? Was this what he wanted – to become famous in his own right? Brooklyn Bay had its fair share of murders over the years and double murders weren't uncommon. The first big case Lucy had worked on had been a double murder, a jealous ex had murdered his lover and her new boyfriend. Tom had been the lead detective, and she'd worked under his expert guidance. The killer had been caught hours after the bodies had been discovered, practically leading the police to his door because he'd left behind so much evidence. There had been a huge argument in a nightclub in front of witnesses, then he'd followed them home and killed them before the pair had made it through the front door of her ground floor flat. Neighbours had been woken by the screams, and there had been CCTV footage of the entire thing captured by the camera on the house next door.

This was something else though; these killings weren't acts of revenge or passion that she could see. Tom could be right, if there was a connection to devil worship she needed to work out what it was, and soon. Maybe there wasn't one and the killer was trying to throw them off guard. The more she thought about this angle the more she liked it. He was trying to be clever and send them on a false trail, wasting time looking in the wrong places so he could kill again. Her fingers clenched into tight fists. Well whoever it was hadn't reckoned on having Lucy hunting him down, and she would even if it meant she had to survive with no sleep at all to catch him. It had to be a *him*, there was no way Lucy could envisage a woman having the strength to carry out this kind of killing, or the reasoning. Not that it was impossible, but her instinct was telling her she was looking for a man and that was good enough for her.

The briefing room was full to capacity, which irritated Lucy, as she knew that most of them wouldn't be here if it wasn't for the fact that it was Tom's mother. She walked to the front of the room to the wooden lectern, placing her clipboard on it. Then she looked around the room.

'Morning, while it's lovely to see such a great attendance at one of my briefings, I think most of you are not actually needed. Section staff that are currently at the scene guard should be getting relieved at any moment by PCSOs. So that means any of you off section can leave; I know you're all very busy, so I won't take up any of your time.'

The entire back row, which was filled with uniformed officers, began to stand up, grumbling under their breaths. Lucy waited for them to file out and the last one to close the door. That left her team, Jack and Amanda from CSI.

'That's better, it was a bit too crowded. I don't know how much you've heard through the grapevine, but I'll give you the facts.'

The door opened and in walked an ashen-faced Tom. Lucy felt her heart sink, while doing her best to smile at him despite the shock of his unexpected appearance. 'Sir, I'm just about to brief the team. It might be better if you wait in my office.'

He shook his head and took a seat next to Mattie. For the first time in a very long time Lucy didn't know what to do. She couldn't discuss his murdered mother with him sitting there listening, after all, they didn't know one hundred per cent if he had anything to do with it. The silence in the room was so heavy she could feel the weight of it pressing down on her shoulders. She glared at Mattie who had pulled out his phone and was tapping a message to someone.

'Well, as you know a call came in at 23.35 last night from a man who lives further along the same street as Basterfield House. He said he was out walking his dog like he does every night when the dog started whining and straining at its lead. He followed the dog and it led him around to the rear car park of the abandoned building, where he discovered—'

Mattie gave her a thumb up just as the door opened, and Lucy had never in her life been so happy to see the chief superintendent, who made a beeline for Tom. He bent down and whispered something into his ear, and Tom nodded. Then he stood up, and left the room. The Super turned to look at Lucy, who mouthed 'thank you' to him. Waiting for the door to shut a second time, she ran her fingers through her hair and whispered: 'Thank fuck for that.'

A collective sigh from around the room agreed with her. Taking a deep breath, she continued the briefing.

'Anyway, he discovered the body of Margaret Crowe, aged seventy-one, hanging upside down with her throat severed so brutally her head was only just attached.'

She passed some photographs around the room for them to look at – it was better for them to witness the horror first-hand. Lucy preferred using visuals to make her team become invested in a case. Somehow, listening to the gory details didn't seem as effective as seeing them for yourself.

'So, we have a huge problem. We haven't caught Sandy Kilburn's killer and now we have another victim with similar injuries, found hanging upside down in the car park of a disused care home.'

'Don't forget about the cat, boss.'

'I won't, thank you, Browning. You attended Margaret's house yesterday because her cat had been found decapitated on her front doorstep. Why did he not leave the decapitated cat at the scene last night? Was it some kind of warning to Margaret or even to us?'

Browning stood up. 'Oh shit. He didn't leave the cat there because I bagged it up and took it away?'

'Where is it?'

'In the back of the div car; it's going to stink.' He left the room in a hurry, and Lucy had to stifle her laughter. It wasn't funny in the least, in fact it was highly inappropriate, but on days like today it was the dark humour that got you through the shit.

'While Browning hunts down his dead cat does anyone have any burning suggestions about why he's not only killing the pet but its owner as well?'

Several heads shook.

'No, me either. Right today's plan of action. Mattie and Rachel, can you two coordinate the house to house of the area? Col, can you do the background checks, see if we've had any other incidents reported involving dead cats? I'm going to speak to the family, get some more details and try and find someone to do a forensic search of the cat. I want CCTV checks of all the surrounding properties. I noticed there were cameras on the outside of the building, however they are quite rusty and knackered-looking so I'm not holding my breath. Thank you.'

She walked out, leaving them alone for five minutes to give them a chance to talk, gossip, speculate or whatever it was they needed to do without her listening in. It was human nature to be inquisitive; she wanted her team to get it out in the open with each other. Get whatever might be bothering them off their chests and then it was all hands on deck. She would expect one-hundred-and-ten per cent effort from them, things had escalated already. She wanted to be fully ready to make an arrest as soon as possible. Lucy ignored the nagging feeling of doubt in her head, the voice which was whispering in her ear, asking if she actually thought she was good enough to do the job she'd worked so hard to call her own.

As she ran up the stairs she almost bumped into the Super; he held his hands up so he could grab her if she lost her balance.

'Thank you for coming and getting Tom, sir, I honestly didn't know what to do.'

'You're welcome; that could have been a disaster for all of us. You need to thank Mattie. He texted Anna, who came to tell me I needed to get down there pronto.'

She smiled at him. 'I will. Is Tom okay? Well, as okay as he can be. I suppose he's never going to get over this for the rest of his life. The shock must be horrendous; I don't know what I'd do.'

'No, I don't suppose he will. God forbid anything so awful could happen to any one of us. I've sent him home, Lucy, and given him strict orders he's not allowed back in the station. I've told him he needs to be there for his family; he needs to grieve and to give you the chance to work the case without him breathing down your neck.'

The urge to hug the older man in front of her was too over-whelming; she nodded, thanked him once more and walked away. She went back to her office. Trust Mattie to have the phone number of the Super's admin assistant. This time she was thankful that his serial flirting had come in useful. A deep debt of gratitude calmed the churning in her stomach; that the Super believed she could do this brought a sense of calm over her. She would repay the favour by proving just how bloody ready she was to do this, telling the voice in her head to shut up. She drank the remainder of her now-cold coffee and waited for Mattie and the rest of the team to come back up to the office.

CHAPTER SIXTEEN

Lucy parked the Ford Focus outside the gorgeous detached house that belonged to Tom and his wife. There were only three houses in the cul-de-sac, which was a dead end, and his was the one in the middle; each house had a huge front garden. She couldn't see his car and wondered if it was still at the scene, although she didn't recall seeing it earlier. Mattie waved his hand in front of her face.

'Penny for them.'

'I was just wondering if he'd managed to collect his car from the scene. What a mess this is. I mean it's bad enough that his mother has been murdered, and here we are about to go in and question his family about his whereabouts yesterday evening. It's not right, is it?'

'Yep, I've got to admit it's not been the best twenty-four hours, has it?'

Lucy shook her head. 'It doesn't matter who it is, it could be the queen and we'd still have to question her. Come on, let's get this over with.'

The front door opened and she expected to see Tom standing there, instead she was greeted by Alison, who nodded at her.

'I'm sorry, Alison, it must have been a terrible shock for you all.'

Lucy followed her into the light, airy hallway and down to the open-plan kitchen. Alison pointed at the bar stools, and Lucy perched herself on one, slightly more elegantly than Mattie.

'You can say that again, Tom is in a right state, which isn't the calm and collected man that I know. I don't know what to do or say to him.'

'Is he here?'

'No, he left this morning. Said he had to go to work, that he needed to find out what was happening. I haven't seen him since.'

'Oh, I was hoping to speak to him. I didn't want to do it in work.'

'I don't know why, he bloody lives there. He spends more time at the station than he does here with me.'

'Can I ask where you both were last night?'

'I was here, just like I always am with the boys. He was at work again till seven thirty, but you should know that. Then he got the call to go to the scene. To be honest I thought he was taking the piss when he said there had been another murder, but when he came in and his face was whiter than that marble worktop, I knew he was being serious.'

Lucy looked at Mattie, who was the one taking notes. Tom had left the station at the same time she had last night. It had been just after six; she'd followed him out of the electronic gates. A heavy feeling began to fill her stomach, settling inside it like a chunk of lead. She didn't like this. Why had he lied to Alison and told her he was working until seven thirty? She needed to know where he'd been for those ninety minutes – because ninety minutes was more than enough time to kill someone, clean yourself up and carry on pretending that everything in your life was hunky-dory. This wasn't good news at all.

'Can you ring him and find out where he is, please? Don't tell him I'm looking for him, as he might not want to speak just yet. I just need to make sure he's okay.'

Alison picked the latest iPhone off the counter, which Mattie was staring at wistfully. They waited for him to answer, but it rang out. She ended the call and shrugged.

'I should have said he never answers my calls unless I text him first to say it's an emergency. Is it an emergency?'

Lucy shook her head. 'Gosh no, I'm worried about him. I wanted to make sure he was okay. Don't worry, I'll catch up with him at work. Thank you, we'll leave you to it. If you need anything don't hesitate to phone, anytime.'

*

Once they were inside the car and Alison had closed the front door, Lucy began manoeuvring to turn the car around.

'What the fuck is going on? I don't understand why he's lied to Alison.'

'You really don't know why he's lied to her? Come on, Lucy, either your brain's tired or you're far too trusting.'

'What do you mean? Yes, I am beyond tired if I'm honest, so be kind to me and explain.'

'Well it's simple, isn't it? He's shagging around. It's not as if she's the nicest woman he could be married to. You can tell who wears the trousers in that house and it's certainly not our Tommy lad.'

Lucy, although horrified, began to laugh. 'You're terrible, do you think he is having an affair?'

'Yep, for our sake we better pray that he is, because I'd rather him be a philanderer than someone who's committed matricide.'

Her phone began to ring, and she passed it to Mattie. He mouthed to her, 'It's the doc.' After a brief conversation he ended the call.

'She said can you go to the mortuary in thirty minutes? She's cleared the decks and wants to get started.'

Lucy felt a wave of tiredness wash over her. What she wanted to do was to go home and have a hot shower, something to eat and crash into bed. Looking at the clock on the dashboard she felt her stomach lurch. Jesus Christ she needed to get to the church fair: Ellie was helping out and she'd promised she'd go. Making a sharp left she sped off in the opposite direction of the hospital.

'Where are we going?'

'I have to go to church.'

CHAPTER SEVENTEEN

The heat was getting to David. It was uncomfortable wearing a starched dog collar when the winter sun was beating through the many glass windows of the church hall and someone had left the heating on all night. He handed out tickets and kept smiling at the varied bunch of parishioners flocking through the doors. If there ever was a return of freak shows he was pretty sure that most of this lot would be taken on without a second thought. That was the thing about town centre churches like this one; it didn't have an acre of lush graveyard and gardens to set up their stalls in. All they had was a badly tarmacked car park with potholes big enough to launch a boat in. It was currently hosting the bouncy castle, coconut shy and an inflatable paddling pool filled with rubber ducks. The raffle tickets hadn't been sold, and the kitchen was struggling to keep up with the demand for teas and coffees. He felt a finger poke his back and whipped around to give whoever it was a telling off.

'Where the fuck is Margaret?' hissed his wife.

He smiled at her; taking hold of her elbow he pushed her through the crowd into the kitchen and slammed the door shut.

'How many times must I tell you not to talk to me in public like that, it's not nice.' He shook his head, trying to calm himself down. Lord if anyone pushed his buttons it was Jan, his pain in the arse wife.

'I don't know where she is, this isn't like her. I expected her to be here two hours ago double-checking everything. If I'm honest I'm a bit concerned she might be unwell.'

'Have you tried phoning her, Jan?'

'Yes, and it rings out. You phone, she'll answer to you. You're the one she fawns over like an overprotective Rottweiler that's just had a litter of pups.'

He wanted more than anything to tell her to sod off, only he couldn't because she'd love it and so would the freaks outside; they thrived on drama and stupid television shows like Jeremy Kyle. If the vicar and his wife had a major meltdown in the middle of a winter fair, it would be the talking point for months. He peered over the top of Jan's head and caught a glimpse of Natalia – her head thrown back as she laughed at something that moody teenager had said to her. Christ why couldn't he have found a woman as beautiful as her instead of an angry little woman the size of a house? He looked back at Jan, who had her arms folded across her chest and was now staring at him with eyes the size of pinholes. How did she manage to make them go so small and beady? He was surprised she didn't fire venom from her vulgar foul mouth.

He pulled his phone from his trouser pocket and found Margaret's number. Showing the display to Jan, he pressed the green button and waited for it to ring. It rang and rang until the voicemail kicked in.

'Margaret, it's David. I'm just checking that you're okay, I'm a bit worried about you. Please ring me back as soon as you get this message. Bye.'

'"I'm a bit worried about you", David you're pathetic.'

'What did you want me to say?'

'How about, get the fuck to the church hall to sort out the bloody fair *you* arranged?'

About to answer her, he then saw the woman with the platinum-blonde hair, dressed in a smart suit, come flying into the hall and head straight for the stall the moody teenager was standing behind. His interest piqued, he bent down and pecked Jan's cheek.

'Come on, Jan, you know you can handle this. Please try and keep calm.'

She glared at him, turned around and stormed back to the waiting queue of customers. He grinned when he heard an old guy with no front teeth address her: 'Bloody hell, love, I'm gasping for a cup of tea. I thought you'd gone on strike.'

He left, not wanting to witness her assaulting a customer, and briskly walked over to the toy stall where the blonde was doing her best to chatter to the sulky teenager. This was interesting. Moments ago the kid was laughing and smiling with Natalia. Now she looked angrier than Jan.

'Hello, I'm Father David.' He held out his hand.

The woman took it, grasping it much more firmly than he'd anticipated.

'Lucy Harwin, Ellie's mum.'

'Ah, yes I can see the connection. You both look alike.' He ignored the eye roll the girl behind the trestle table gave to him.

'Yes, I suppose we do.'

He heard his name called, and he shook his head. 'I'm sorry, please excuse me. The whole thing is falling to bits. The lady who arranged it all and has the clipboard with a running order of the itinerary hasn't turned up, which isn't like her.'

Natalia nodded. 'Where is Margaret? It's very unlike her not to be here after all her hard work. I hope she's okay.'

Lucy asked. 'Who's Margaret?'

David looked at her. 'Margaret Crowe, do you know her?'

Lucy shook her head as a cold shiver ran down the full length of her spine, technically, she didn't. All she knew about Margaret was that she was a nice old lady who lived with her cat and volunteered to organise the church fair; that was until someone had decided to murder her and her cat so violently that both of their heads were almost severed. Lucy obviously couldn't tell them anything, it was all confidential.

'Well it was nice to meet you, Lucy, Ellie is doing a grand job running the toy stall. Thanks for coming, we need all the support we can get.'

'My pleasure, David.'

He wandered off back in the direction of the door; he was going to have to sell the bloody raffle tickets as well as take the entrance money.

CHAPTER EIGHTEEN

December 1989

The ground was frozen solid; a coating of snow covered the rows of graves. He shivered. His coat had seen better days; the zip had broken. His mum wouldn't have let him walk to school in this weather with a coat that had a ripped pocket and didn't fasten. The few friends he had were excited for Christmas Eve in ten days. He wasn't, Christmas meant even more time spent at the church listening to the vicar, and his dad preaching about how wonderful God was. If he was that wonderful, he wouldn't be here freezing his arse off trying to find his mum's grave to lay some flowers on it. Instead his mum would be at home baking those awful mince pies no one except her liked, and singing along to the cheesy Christmas songs on the radio. His heart tugged sharply at the pain of the memories, and a tear leaked from the corner of his eye. He missed her, missed her more than he could ever have imagined. You don't really think about a world where you have no mum when you're ten years old; he didn't even think your mum could die and leave you like that. He didn't know anyone else whose mum had died; the vicar had taken to being extra nice to him. He kept patting him on the head and asking him if he was okay. As if he was okay; he was probably never going to be okay again.

He slipped on the frozen ground, falling hard onto his arse.

'Bastard.'

He'd said it a lot louder than he meant to. A dark shadow fell over him, and he looked up. Terror filling his veins. If it was his dad, he'd be for it: swearing and jigging school would not be a good combination.

'Hello, are you okay?'

He squeezed his eyes shut, it was even worse than his dad. It was the bloody vicar. Nodding, he whispered, 'Yes.'

A firm hand grabbed his arm, dragging him off the frozen grass which had been so cold his arse was numb. He looked around for the bunch of flowers that he'd stolen from outside the grocer's on the high street. The vicar handed them to him.

'What a lovely bunch of flowers, I bet they cost you all of your pocket money.'

He nodded, *oh shit, he knows I don't have any pocket money. I bet he knows that I nicked them.*

He waited for the accusation, but it didn't come.

'If you want I can wait for you while you go and put them on your mum's grave, then I can give you a lift home and you can get changed out of those wet trousers.'

He shook his head. 'No, it's okay. I can walk back, thanks.'

'Come on, don't be daft. It's freezing, your trousers are wet and your hands are frozen. Where are your gloves, young man? Your mum wouldn't be too happy with me if I left you here on your own to freeze to death, would she, and I can't be bothered doing any more funerals now right before the big day. I need to get on with my Christmas shopping.'

For the first time in what felt like for ever he laughed. He hadn't realised the vicar could make a joke. The mention of the wet patch on his trousers made him realise just how cold he was; he couldn't feel his fingers anymore and his toes were probably turning black right now and about to snap off with frostbite.

'Do you not mind?'

The vicar laughed. 'Of course not, I'll wait in the car. It's that blue one on the top of the hill. Take your time. Although you don't want to be too long, you might get hyperthermia.'

He had no idea what he was talking about, but he wanted to get out of these wet trousers more than anything. The vicar walked off, and he ran the rest of the way to her grave, which was nothing more than a huge mound of soil and stones. It was horrible, it didn't look like the rest of the graves. There was no headstone to tell anyone who was there, but he knew. He'd never forget who was buried underneath that ugly mound. He tried to pull the bunch of dead brown flowers from the top of it, but the wrapper had frozen to the soil and was stuck solid. He tugged and tugged, but it wouldn't move. He'd have to come back when the ground wasn't frozen to bin them. He laid the fresh bunch on top of them so it hid the withered ugly ones beneath. Patting the soil, he whispered goodbye and turned to run up the hill to the knackered blue car that was blowing out clouds of black smoke. He didn't care as long as it was warm inside, he'd have accepted a lift in a hearse.

He tugged open the door and clambered in the back seat. He sniffed a couple of times, his nose wrinkling. The vicar, who was older than his dad, looked at him through the rear-view mirror.

'Sorry, it's the engine. It overheats if I have it running when the car isn't moving, then it smells like burning rubber. It's okay though, it won't set on fire or anything.'

He shrugged, right now setting on fire wouldn't be so bad he was so cold. His teeth began to chatter as he rubbed his hands together to try and get some feeling back in them. He didn't pay much attention to where they were going, he was tired. He hadn't been sleeping more than a few hours at a time, instead he lay in bed listening to his dad carrying on with the woman with the blonde hair. Which was both terrifying and exciting at the same time. The car juddered to a halt, and he felt his head snap back. He opened his eyes.

'Where are we?'

'I didn't know if you wanted to go home all wet and soggy while school is still open. I thought you might want to come and dry off at the vicarage. Have a hot chocolate, sit by the fire and then I'll take you home when it's school kicking out time. I won't tell your dad where I found you. I have a sneaking suspicion he won't be too pleased about you bunking off school to go to the cemetery. I, however, think that it was a very kind thing to do; you must really miss your mum.'

Faced with the chance of getting caught out by his dad this sounded like a great idea. His dad would kill him, and he was cold and would die for a hot chocolate. The downside was, what if he had to spend the next hour talking about God? He hated God. If there was even such a thing, God wouldn't have let his mum die. God wouldn't have turned Robbie's granddad into the scary, skeleton dude, would he?'

'You can watch the television; I promise I won't make you read the Bible if that's what you're worried about.'

He grinned, wondering if the vicar was a mind reader or if he had some kind of special powers, and then he was out of the car. He followed him into the huge house next to the church, glad to be escaping from his rubbish life for an extra hour.

'Come in the kitchen and you can tell me how you like your hot chocolate; it's warm in here. You can take those soggy trousers off, and I can put them over the radiator to dry.'

He went inside the huge kitchen that was big enough to put the downstairs of his house in. The vicar began to pull a pan down from the rack, then he opened the fridge, taking a bottle of milk out. At least it was warm in here, but he was still cold. He didn't know if he wanted to take his trousers off in a vicar's kitchen; he couldn't sit around in his underpants, it wasn't right.

'Take your trousers off; they won't take long to dry on the radiator.' He pointed to the long heater on the wall.

'Erm, it's okay. I better not.'

The vicar turned to him and smiled. 'Come on now, don't tell me you're shy. We're all men here. I won't look, I promise. You can wrap a towel around your waist if it makes you feel better.'

He reached out, grabbing a towel off an airing rack and hurled it in his direction. Grabbing it he mumbled *thank you* then unzipped his trousers and deftly wrapped it around his waist. He was relieved his shirt wasn't wet as well; there was something not quite right about sitting in front of a vicar with no clothes on. The vicar set the milk to boil then turned to him and held out his hand. He passed him the damp trousers.

'Seeing as how we know each other a little better you can call me Vincent, or Vince if you prefer. What should I call you?'

He froze, he didn't want to call him Vince. It was a little too friendly for him. He shook his head.

A loud knock at the door broke the awkward moment between them. The vicar turned the heat down on the milk and went to answer the door. There was a lot of shouting and a woman began to wail – he didn't know what was happening. But he didn't want to get caught here, bunking off school with no trousers on. He grabbed his pants, threw the towel off and tugged them up. Pushing his feet into the shoes he ran towards the back door, the hairs on the back of his neck standing on edge. He ran across the back garden, pausing to turn around and look up at the windows. Someone was watching him, but he had no idea who and he wasn't waiting around to find out who they were. He was getting out of here; he'd rather try and sneak into his house and risk getting caught than listen to whatever commotion was going on back there. Especially dressed in his underpants. He wondered who would be shouting so loud at a vicar.

CHAPTER NINETEEN

Lucy left the bustling church hall with a handful of raffle tickets and some paper bags. Mattie, who couldn't get parked any nearer, had waited a couple of streets away and she was relieved he was still there. Church had never been her thing; she felt even worse for Margaret because it had clearly been hers. How were they going to take it when they found out about her and what about Ellie, how was she going to question her? It also widened her suspect pool; both murders had some links to religion to them. Sandy Kilburn had been found in a church, and Margaret spent a lot of time helping out at one. Before she'd even climbed into the car Mattie was holding out his hands for the paper bags. She passed them over.

'I hope you've got some decent cakes in these – you bloody took long enough. What did you do, go to confession while you were there? I suppose that would have taken an awful lot longer though, with all your sins.'

'First of all what sins? I'm not a sinner, you cheeky git. And who said you could have a cake? You don't deserve one, especially after that remark.'

She glared at him, and he smiled. 'Sorry, you're not a bad person. In fact you're one of the good guys. Can I have the chocolate-covered flapjack?'

'You can have what you want, I'm not in a cake mood. They were the only things I could buy that were useful. You'll never guess what?'

'What?'

'Margaret was a parishioner there, and a popular one. The vicar was very friendly; though I got an odd vibe off him. I wonder how he'll take the news about her?'

'Well let's go back and arrest him then, haul him in for questioning. A friendly vicar that gave you a bad vibe could be a good suspect; I mean two women found hanging upside down with their throats cut. He might have major mummy issues.'

'Very funny. I can't go and drag him out of the middle of his fair when he's surrounded by his congregation. They might turn on him and lynch him if they suspect him of any wrongdoing. What I can do, though, is get Col to run him through the system and do all the social media checks. There's something about him I don't like. I'm not saying he's involved, but I don't trust him; plus, the first murder was a definite huge fuck you to God. She was killed in an abandoned church and hung upside down on a cross. We need to find out if Sandy Kilburn came to church, see if there's any connection. At least we have something to go on now. We'd come to a bit of a standstill despite our best efforts. This could be the catalyst we need.'

'And if she's never set foot in St Aidan's?'

'Then it's back to square one. Come on we need to get to the mortuary or Catherine is going to be seriously pissed off with me.'

He pushed the rest of the flapjack into his mouth and started the engine.

Catherine was a sight to behold standing there in her bright pink scrubs and matching rubber boots; though the arms folded across her chest wasn't a good sign. Lucy dashed in and took her place next to Mattie. She looked drab compared to the glamorous doctor. Holding up her hands in submission, Lucy whispered, 'I'm sorry. Something came up.'

'Apology accepted, now let's get down to business.'

The tag was cut from the sealed body bag, and Lucy inhaled, not sure if she wanted to meet Margaret Crowe under such tragic circumstances for a second time in less than twenty-four hours. The elderly woman looked out of place lying on the cold, steel mortuary gurney with her head almost severed, crusted black blood around the gaping wound. This wasn't how your mum should die; you expect them to have a stroke, a heart attack or, God forbid, cancer. You don't expect them to end up like this.

Catherine waited for Jack to photograph her inside the body bag before they removed it. Then she began to examine every inch of her clothing, pausing partway down her left leg. Stuck to the polyester trouser leg were three grey hairs. She pulled down her magnifying glasses and looked closer.

'I don't know whether these are human hairs or pet hair until I have a closer look. They don't look humanoid; did she have any pets?'

Lucy nodded. 'She had a cat; it was found with its head cut off two days ago.'

'Well that's interesting, poor cat. Do you think there's a link between the cat being brutally killed and its owner?'

Mattie looked at Lucy. 'There has to be, it's too much of a coincidence.'

Catherine turned her attention back to the body. Removing the hairs to examine and send off for identification.

'Where is the cat now? If these turn out to be pet hair, I'll need to take some sample hairs from it for comparison. I can't see any tears or defects of the outer or inner clothing. Andrew, you may remove the clothes.'

Mattie whispered, 'I'll go phone Browning.'

The mortuary technician, who had been doing his job longer than any of them, began to deftly unbutton and remove Margaret's clothes. He laid each piece on another steel gurney to be examined again. There was a puckered band of smooth skin on her wedding finger. She had still been wearing her gold wedding band and a large diamond solitaire engagement ring when they'd brought the body to the mortuary. Lucy wrote in her notebook – *definitely not a robbery gone wrong.* Catherine began to take fingernail scrapings.

'So, we have a female Caucasian, approximately seventy years of age. Height five feet two inches, weight one hundred and thirty pounds. Grey hair, green eyes, in a good physical shape for her age. Some muscle loss, which is to be expected, no scars or tattoos, all of her teeth have been removed some time ago, she was wearing dentures at the time of death.'

When she had finished her preliminary examination, and Margaret's cold, naked body was laid out, she stood up, stretching her back.

'Andrew, you can wash her down now.'

Lucy couldn't tear her eyes away from the gaping wound that used to be Margaret's neck. She watched as Andrew placed a body block under her back, making her chest protrude forward and her arms and head fall back. Lucy knew this was to make it easier to cut open the chest cavity.

Catherine pulled the clear, protective plastic face shield down and smiled.

'Are we ready to begin?'

Mattie turned away so he wasn't staring straight at the body, and Lucy wanted to do the same, only she couldn't. She owed it to Margaret, and to Tom, to be there by her side, to share the cold horror of the post-mortem with her.

CHAPTER TWENTY

Four hours later and Lucy could feel her eyelids getting too heavy to keep open much longer. Her bones were weary, all she wanted was food and her bed. Apart from the stray hairs on Margaret's trouser leg there had been no other trace evidence. As she stripped off the faded blue scrubs and ran her hands under the scalding hot water she knew that was enough for today. Even though she hadn't touched anything in the mortuary apart from her notepad and pen, she still scrubbed at her skin until it was red, as if somehow washing away the horrors of the past forty-eight hours.

When she was satisfied she was clean enough and germ free, she walked into the corridor where Mattie was typing so fast with his thumbs on his phone she wondered if he'd taken a course on touch texting or something similar. He looked up, his cheeks turning slightly pink, and she felt a twinge of envy. He had a life outside of the job; no doubt he'd been sending a message to his current girl of choice. He certainly never wanted for female company; they seemed to be lining up to go out on dates with him. Which was good for him, but it was crap for Lucy, knowing that the love of her life had upped and buggered off after a brief affair with some girl who was old enough to be his daughter. It had only been two months since George had packed his suitcase and walked out of the door, so it was all too fresh and raw. It was his house she was living in, which he'd already owned before they got together, so Lucy was determined as soon as she could find a place of her own that she'd move out. She didn't want a fucking penny from him; she wanted her life back how it was or nothing.

'You look exhausted, Lucy.'

She stared at him, blinking her eyes and stifling a yawn to hide the fresh tears that were threatening to fall down her cheeks. Christ she was tired, she got soppy and emotional when she needed sleep.

'I am and I was just wondering how we are going to get hold of Tom and find out what the hell he was playing at feeding Alison that bullshit story about not leaving work until seven thirty last night.'

'Boss, I think we should let it be. I don't think it's our business, do you?'

They had been walking down the corridor, side by side, towards the busy front entrance of the hospital. Lucy stopped dead and looked at him. 'You're being serious?'

He nodded. 'Do you really think he killed his mother, hung her upside down and then went home to play happy families, Lucy? He's one of us, one of the good guys, and a decent boss. We've never had reason to doubt him before.'

'Yes, you're right. We haven't, and I agree to a certain extent. But we're not talking about him forgetting to pay for a bottle of wine, are we? We're talking about murder, cold-blooded murder.'

She hadn't realised how loud her voice was until she glanced around and saw several people watching her, their mouths open. She didn't say another thing until they reached the car at the far end of the car park.

'We have to ask him, Mattie, he has to account for his where-abouts and he needs to do it truthfully, because there are two dead women who need us to figure out who killed them and why. It's in his best interest. I want to get him out of this mess as quickly as possible, but he's not helping himself, is he? He could have texted or rung me, and I've had no missed calls.'

He shrugged. 'Your funeral, Lucy.'

She tugged the car door open, then slammed it shut behind her.

Mattie carried on talking. 'I suppose it might be better if you pass it over, you know, hand the cases to the big boys from the city. Tell them there's too much of a conflict of interest, then it's out of all of our hands. I mean, you have a lot of stuff going on at the moment at home, no one would blame you.'

'Are you insinuating that I can't handle it, that because my husband has cheated on me and left me that I won't be able to work the cases in my normal, professional manner? None of that has anything to do with how I'm handling this investigation.'

She glared at him, daring him to answer. The sting of betrayal felt like someone had jabbed a red, hot poker straight through her heart. Mattie always had her back and here he was telling her to pass the case on because it was making him feel uncomfortable.

He shook his head. 'You know that's not what I meant.'

She didn't answer because she couldn't. She wanted to talk to Tom, find out if he had an alibi, then go home and get shit-faced, because what was the worst that could happen? It wasn't as if her shitty life could get any worse.

As he parked the car in the rear yard of the station she broke the silence.

'I'm tired, I need to go home and sleep. If anything urgent comes in, ring me. Oh and find out where the hell Browning put that dead cat.'

She strode off to her mint green Fiat 500. Scanning the parked cars for Tom's, unable to see it, she knew that before she clocked off for the day she had to speak to him. She didn't understand if it was a man thing with Mattie or whether he was just being incredibly naive, but she would not put her investigation in jeopardy by being too scared to interview a potential suspect regardless of his rank. If the tables were turned and it was her mother who had been murdered and she had ninety minutes of time that couldn't be accounted for, she'd be demanding another detective to deal with the case if they hadn't bothered to chase her up. That was the key to being a good detective: no matter how small or painstaking something might seem, you followed up on every little clue.

Sometimes the smallest, random piece of information was enough to piece together and be the break in the case you were looking for.

Lucy followed a marked van out of the gates and headed back in the direction of Tom's house.

CHAPTER TWENTY-ONE

David waved goodbye to Natalia, her daughter, and the teenager whom he'd overheard Natalia offering a lift home. He wished the woman had offered to take him home. He'd spent most of the day catching his breath every time he caught sight of her. It was him and Jan left now, and she was on one, moaning about the state of the hall. He slammed the door shut and went back inside; it was a lot better than he'd expected.

'Come on, why don't we call it a day? Go home, get a Chinese takeaway, open a bottle of wine or two, put our feet up and sort the rest of this out tomorrow. It can wait.'

She stared at him, her small eyes narrowing even further. 'What about Margaret? She hasn't been in touch. We better call at her house and make sure she's okay. I feel bad in case she's ill or needs help.'

He'd forgotten all about her. 'You go home and have a bath; I'll order the takeaway, then go and check on her while it's cooking.'

'Are you sure?'

'Yes, you've worked hard today, dear. I have to show my appreciation somehow.' He'd ideally like to show her his appreciation by wrapping his hands around her chunky, short neck and choking her until she could no longer breathe, but he couldn't. Instead he would let her stuff herself, and drink all the wine: she'd fall asleep.

After placing his order at the Chinese takeaway he drove the short distance to Margaret's house and was surprised to see a police community support officer standing at the gate with a clipboard in her hands. He pulled up into the nearest parking space and got out of his car, striding towards her.

'Good evening, officer, is everything okay?'

He beamed at her; she squirmed and managed some kind of smile in return.

'Yes, no, not really, Father.'

'Oh, I'm sorry to hear that. I've just come to check on Margaret; she's one of my parishioners and she lives here. I haven't heard from her today; she was going to help out at the church fair. I'm a touch worried about her.'

He was pointing to the house that was all in darkness behind her.

'I'm really sorry. I can't tell you anything except Margaret isn't here. Well, I can tell you there's been a serious incident involving her.'

His frown was just enough concern with a touch of frustration. 'I understand you have to do your job but can you tell me if she's okay?'

He felt a twinge of excitement watching her face turn from pink to deep red.

'I can't tell you anything. I don't really know myself. If you ring 101 and ask for Detective Inspector Lucy Harwin, she might be able to tell you a little bit more than I can.'

Reaching out he patted her arm. 'Of course, I'm sorry. I know you can't tell me anything. I'll ring the station. Thank you.'

He walked back to his car, his interest piqued. What had happened to the old busybody? Whatever it was must be pretty serious to have a uniformed officer standing guard outside her decrepit garden gate.

CHAPTER TWENTY-TWO

February 1990

He lay in bed, his teeth chattering so loud the noise filled the room. His breath floated into the air, where the smoky white plumes looked as if he was smoking. He wasn't; he'd tried it once, and it made him puke so hard his stomach had cramped for hours. He never tried it again. There was no heating in this house and his body was cold despite the numerous blankets he'd dragged out of the linen cupboard and thrown over his bed. He could hear his dad downstairs. He was drunk and talking far too loudly. His father's voice echoing below him, he was quoting the Bible for the first time since his mum had died and the words filled his mind with terrible memories. His stomach was churning knowing what was coming next. The Bible quotes had stopped after his mother's death, which had been the only good thing to come of losing her. He had heard the giggling when they'd first come in, so loud it had woken him up. Then there had been the moaning and for the first time he'd heard the all-too-familiar sound of his dad's knuckles as they'd hit the woman's face or body. She'd screamed, calling him a cocksucker amongst other things. This had made him smile; he didn't think his dad was one of those. On the other hand, he was partial to being the one on the receiving end, so this was a bit of a change for him. He felt sorry for the woman: he knew this was going to end badly for her. Shit he knew it was going to end even worse for him, because if he didn't satiate his rage when his father beat her, he would drag him out of bed and finish it off on him.

The front door slammed so hard he felt the house vibrate and he steeled himself for what he knew was coming next, turning onto his side and squeezing his eyes shut. The heavy footsteps began to climb the stairs. He thought about picking one of the heavy brass bookends up and smashing it into his father's skull. He could take him by surprise, hide behind the door then bury it into his brains. Before he could move, the door flew open and he heard his heavy breathing as he stood in the doorway. He lay still, trying to keep his breathing shallow so he thought he was still asleep.

The covers were dragged off him and his eyes flew open. He scrambled off the mattress to get away from him. His feet got tangled in the multitude of blankets and he crashed to the floor in a heap. Regretting ever trying to think he could escape the bastard and his fists of iron, he braced himself. Waiting for the first punch, but it never came. There was hammering on the front door, it was opened, and he heard a deep voice shout: 'Police.'

He looked up at his father, who didn't look so mean and angry now, instead he looked shocked. He couldn't help it and grinned at him; despite knowing that he'd pay for his insolence later it was worth it. Even louder footsteps came running up the stairs and before his father was able to get out of his room two of the biggest coppers he'd ever seen were standing there, filling the doorway. Staring at the sight of the pale skinny boy lying on the floor curled up with his arms above him to protect his head. The older of the two men lunged for his father and he watched in slow motion as his fist shot out and punched his dad square on the nose. The crunch was satisfying. What was even better was the cry of pain his father emitted.

'Did you see that, Mickey, he went for me? That was self-defence; he'd have had me if I hadn't hit him first.'

'I did, he's a dangerous fucker. Likes hitting women and kids, his sort needs a good kicking.'

The copper didn't hit his dad again; instead he shoved him against the wall and dragged both of his arms behind his back, handcuffing him. Then he was being dragged out of the room and down the stairs, the whole time protesting his innocence.

The other copper walked over to him and leant down offering his hand.

'Come on, son, he won't hurt you again. I'll make sure of that. Now how old are you?'

'Eleven.'

'Do you have anyone you can stop with? Is that your mum who phoned it in?'

He shook his head. 'I don't know her; she comes home with him when he's drunk. My mum's dead.'

'Sorry to hear that. The thing is if we don't have someone you can go and stop with, you'll have to come back to the station with us and the social will come and get you. Have you not got any aunts or uncles, family friends? Someone we can take you to tonight until we've sorted this mess out?'

He racked his brains, he didn't really have anyone. No one bothered with them because his dad was a Bible-bashing, wife-beating, alcoholic.

'The vicar, I could go to his house. He's all right.'

'Which vicar?'

'Father Vincent, from the church a few streets away.'

'Right, well you get dressed and we'll take you there. See if he can keep an eye on you until we've sorted out this mess. I'm sure he won't mind, being a man of God and all that. It's what they do, isn't it? Help out people in their hour of need.'

He watched from the safety of the back of the police car as his dad was bundled in handcuffs into the back of a big blue van. The woman with the big earrings was holding some toilet roll to the cut above her eye as she told the coppers what had happened. She was still chewing gum, the whole time she was wailing and throwing her arms up in the air. The nice copper who'd spoken to him climbed into the front of the car.

'Blimey, she's loud, isn't she? She's enough to wake the dead that one?'

He nodded, she was, especially when they were doing the stuff grown-ups liked to do. He hadn't really known an awful lot about sex before she'd started coming around. Now he knew everything there was to know and then some. He'd watched them do all sorts of things, some of them she liked and some of them she didn't. Once when he'd snuck down, she was on all fours on the carpet with his dad ramming himself into her. She'd looked over and seen him peeping through the door. His heart had almost stopped, and he'd thought she'd scream at him. Instead she blew him a kiss and ran her tongue around her lips, moaning even louder.

'Does your dad hit you often, son?'

He shrugged. As much as he hated him he didn't want to end up having to live in some kids' home; lately he hadn't really battered him as much.

'Not really, he was drunk tonight.'

'Does he drink a lot?'

'No.'

Finally, the woman left, the blue van drove away and the other copper got into the driver side of the car.

'Right then, we're taking him to the vicar at St Aidan's. Then we'll go back to the station and deal with Rocky Balboa.'

CHAPTER TWENTY-THREE

Finishing the dregs of her vanilla latte, Lucy knew she needed to go home and eat. She hadn't slept for days. If he didn't turn up soon she'd be falling asleep at the wheel of her car. A car began to slow down to turn into the dead-end street, and she jumped out and ran across the road. There was a loud screech of brakes and she closed her eyes wondering if the impact of Tom's heavy car would be enough to kill her. It stopped inches from her, and she opened her eyes.

'You bloody idiot, have you got a death wish, Lucy?'

Before he could do anything she ran around to the passenger side and climbed inside.

'We need to talk and I don't think you want us to have this conversation in front of Alison and the boys.'

The animosity he'd been wearing like a mask slipped away and he shook his head.

'Christ, what a mess. Talk about what?'

'Yes, it is a mess. Tom, I need you to be honest with me. You know fine well that it's my job to ask you where you were last night.'

'I left work and went home, Alison can tell you that, Lucy.'

'You left work at six. I know that because I followed you out of the gates.'

'Did you follow me to Sainsbury's as well?'

'No, sir, I didn't. I went home.'

'Well after I'd been shopping so did I.'

'You spent ninety minutes in Sainsbury's? That must have been a big shop.'

'Fucking hell, Lucy, I didn't murder my mother. Why would I? So you can drop this bullshit now.'

'I know you didn't but I have to ask and you know that. You'd be the same if it was me. I'd hope that you'd be the same if the tables were turned.'

He shook his head, not speaking, and she got out of the car. He sped off towards his drive, and she got back into her car. As much as it made her feel like a bitch she needed to get hold of the CCTV from the supermarket. Although she didn't think he'd killed his mum she did think he was lying to her and she wanted to know the reason why; she'd never pegged Tom as one of those men who slept around. He'd always come across as a decent guy, a family man. Maybe she was wrong and he wasn't who she thought he was, which would be a huge blow to her because she liked and respected him a lot.

Lucy could feel her insides simmering, this wasn't good. Her phone rang and she answered it hoping that hearing George's voice would soothe her frazzled nerves. *It always used to do the trick before he ran away with a woman half his age and left her alone.*

'Can Ellie come back home to sleep? I don't know what's wrong with her.'

Lucy laughed. 'It's called being a teenager. What's she done now?'

'Called Rosie a slut and a whore.'

At this Lucy's voice filled her car as she laughed even harder.

'I should have known you wouldn't care, forget it.'

'George, come on. I'm sorry, that was childish. Have you punished her?'

'If you mean have I grounded her and taken her phone off her, yes, I have. Do I think it's going to make any difference? Not really, she doesn't care. She's too much like you; too stubborn for her own good.'

'Ouch, thanks. You've brought this on yourself, George, maybe if you'd kept your hands to yourself we wouldn't be in this fucked-up mess. I have a serious case on. Tom's mum was found murdered last night and another victim the night before. I can't really look after her at the moment; I haven't been to bed for two nights. I'm exhausted.'

She knew he would be shaking his head with frustration at her. He didn't get her dedication to the job. He never had, their arguments were always about how she sacrificed her home life to catch the bad guys.

'Why am I not surprised? I'm sorry to hear about Tom's mum, but come on, Lucy, wouldn't it be better for someone else to deal with it? Your daughter needs you, she's still alive.'

Lucy spat out her reply. 'My daughter needs me? Or is Rosie cracking under the strain of having to look after a kid not much younger than herself?'

The phone went dead, and Lucy threw it onto the passenger seat where it bounced off and landed on the floor. She knew she should go and see Ellie, bring her home with her, but George could go and fuck himself. She'd end up arguing with all of them if she went there; instead she drove home, leaving her phone where it had fallen; she didn't care if there was another murder tonight. If she didn't get some sleep, she wouldn't be any good for anything. George could deal with their daughter. It must have been quite a shock for him to hear his little girl speaking like that. Welcome to the real world, George, this was what being the parent of a teenager was really like. When they were all one big happy family he worked late, had weekends off and was only there for the good parts. He always missed the bad parts, letting her be the parent that laid down the rules. Well she was glad he was finding out for himself how bloody hard it was. Was he that foolish that he didn't realise how upset Ellie was, under all her teenage bravado? She'd never admit it, but Lucy knew that she wasn't as tough as she liked to make out. She knew this, because she wasn't either.

Inside the house which was so silent it was creepy, Lucy set about turning on lights. She pressed the button on the remote to bring the TV to life. She loved this house, but not living here alone. It was far too big; she'd put an offer in on a semi a few streets away. It didn't need anything other than a coat of paint and some new carpets – three bedrooms with a small front garden and a good sized back garden. She would make some vegetable beds and get them planted up; she'd always wanted to grow her own. George wouldn't let her dig up the back gardens of this house that he'd paid a fortune to get landscaped. It looked nice but it wasn't very practical. The thought of having a place of her own put a smile on her face. She couldn't wait to tell George he could shove this house where the sun didn't shine. No doubt he'd move Rosie in with him; she didn't care. At least that's what she told herself. The sharp pain which stabbed her in the chest told her otherwise.

Putting a microwave meal in to cook, she took the extra-large gin glass out of the cupboard and filled it to the top with wine. When the microwave pinged she put her spinach and ricotta lasagne on a plate and carried her wine into the lounge. The television played in the background while she wrote notes for what she needed to do tomorrow. The top of that list was to locate that bloody dead cat that Browning had managed to lose and to secure the CCTV from the supermarket. She just hoped that in the meantime their killer decided to have a night off and let her get some sleep because, otherwise, she was going to struggle to remember her own name, never mind anyone else's. That couldn't happen; if she dropped the ball it would spell disaster for them all. She needed to prove Tom's innocence. He was a good man, and even though Lucy knew good men could act in the most heinous of ways, she didn't believe he was like that at all. Tom was an even better boss, and she owed him big time for believing in her and pushing her to go for the promotion to DI. She knew he was a mess, grief affected people in different ways, but she didn't like to see him falling apart like this. Once she'd taken him out of the equation she could focus on catching the sick bastard who liked to crucify women, kill their pets and display them in public places for the world to see.

CHAPTER TWENTY-FOUR

Lucy opened her eyes and pressed the home button on her phone to see what time it was; she had to look twice and then it died. How could it only be six a.m.? She'd expected to wake up late, not early. Tossing and turning she tried to force herself to go back to sleep, but her body was having none of it. She was wide awake. As she lay there, her head a jumbled mess of thoughts, she realised she needed to do something to clear it. If she'd been a runner, she'd have laced up her trainers and run herself into oblivion. She was no runner; she liked walking though, so she got out of bed and pulled on her joggers, a hooded sweatshirt, beanie hat and a pair of reflective trainers.

Grabbing her phone she plugged her earphones into it and left the house; she shivered. The air was damp and chilly. Her head down, she began to power-walk towards the seafront and the pier. That was the thing she loved about this town, the fresh sea air, the smell of the salt. There was something soothing about watching the sea as it came into the bay; whenever she was stressed she'd come and walk along the seafront – the sea breeze guaranteed to blow the cobwebs away and clear her mind. As she reached the part of the promenade that looked onto the dilapidated pier, she stopped and leant over the railings. The sea was swirling in the bay, the waves crashing against the wooden struts of the rotting pier. She stood on the first metal bar of the railings to get a better view. As she stared out at the roaring, blackened waves she couldn't help wonder how she was going to solve this case without fucking up her own life in the process.

A hand grabbed her shoulder and she fell backwards as a loud screech left her lips. Swinging round she saw a man in his best running gear standing behind her with his hands up.

'I'm so sorry, I didn't mean to scare you. I was a bit worried. I've been running along the prom and saw you from a distance staring out at the sea. When you climbed on the railings, I almost had a heart attack. I had to run so fast to reach you.'

Lucy realised that he thought she'd been about to jump into the murky water below her and felt her cheeks burn. 'Oh God, I'm sorry. You thought I was going to jump in? I wasn't, I couldn't sleep. I wanted to clear my head and I love watching the sea.'

He patted his chest. 'Thank God for that. I'm a great runner and a terrible swimmer. Sorry for scaring you, I had to make sure you were okay. You are okay, aren't you?'

She laughed. 'I'm okay, I promise. Thank you for asking, I'm sorry for scaring you.'

He grinned. 'Phew, you're welcome. Have a great day and stay clear of those railings.' He winked at her, and she smiled back.

'I will, you too.' He lifted his hand and waved, then turned and began to run once more.

Lucy felt foolish. She also wished there were more people in the world like that man. He was a complete stranger and he'd bothered to come and check she was okay. How many suicides could be prevented if more people took a moment to ask a stranger if they were okay? She began to head back to her house; she might as well get showered and go to work. She had a killer to apprehend.

She walked into the CID office and headed straight for Browning, who was on the phone. He ended his call, and she smiled at him.

'Did you find that cat?'

He nodded. 'Sort of.'

'What does *sort of* mean? It's vital; it's evidence in a murder investigation.'

'I know, I'm sorry, Lucy. I left it in the boot of the car I was driving. Whoever got in it next must have binned it.'

She bit her tongue, because she didn't want to start the day off by biting off his head instead.

'So do you have a sample of the cat hair or not, Browning?'

'I thought we could get CSI to go in and get a sample of it. Margaret's house is still under scene guard. It was searched last night by task force. They didn't find anything to suggest it was the primary scene. She treated that cat like royalty; there will be cat hairs everywhere. On the sofa cushions, the bed – it had its own cat bed by the fire.'

He had a point. 'What colour was the cat anyway?'

'Black and white, mainly black.'

'Any grey?'

He shook his head.

'Right, you go with Amanda and see if she can find some samples for Catherine to send off for comparison. If her cat was black and white, the hairs on Margaret were grey.'

'It wasn't her cat then, boss.'

'If it wasn't her cat, it means our killer could have a grey pet at home. Locard knew what he was talking about when he said that *every contact leaves a trace*. Let's hope this is the one and not some stray cat that just happened to rub itself against Margaret while she was hanging there.'

Browning grimaced at the thought. 'If a cat had been near her, wouldn't it have had a go at, you know.'

'You know what?'

'Well wouldn't it have had a nibble? Did the doc mention anything?'

'No, thank God. She didn't.'

Lucy walked towards her office to retrieve her mug. Today she wanted to kick ass and without coffee it wouldn't happen.

She plugged her now dead phone in to charge; nothing could have happened last night because they'd have sent a response officer around to knock her up. It had happened many times in the past, in the days before such amazing technology that meant they could trace you at the touch of a button.

*

Instead of going down to the briefing room, Lucy waited until her team were present and then told them to meet her at the conference room on the top floor. Though she trusted every one of her team, she didn't know most of the response officers, therefore she didn't trust them not to gossip. When they were all sitting down, she stood up at the front of the room.

'You might be wondering why I've brought you up here instead of down to the usual room. Things are a little bit sensitive – what we discuss is between ourselves. I've spoken to the boss and I need to clarify the timing of him leaving the station on the night of Margaret's murder and the time of his arrival at home. As you can appreciate this is highly sensitive. If I so much as get a hint that response are gossiping about this, I'll know it's come from this room, and when I find out which of you it was you will be facing a disciplinary.'

A murmur went around the room.

'Do I have your word on it? We need to rule him out so we can concentrate on catching the killer. He's a little bit preoccupied at the moment, so I want Col and Rachel to go to Sainsbury's as soon as I've finished. I need the CCTV footage from Friday night; the DCI finished work at 18:00 hours, and told me he went straight there. I have no reason to doubt him, I just want the proof on DVD so we can cover his arse.'

Col leant forward. 'If you have no reason to doubt him, boss, why are we seizing the CCTV footage?'

'Because it's crucial. There is a slight discrepancy between the timings he's given me and what his wife says. I don't know what's going on, but it's our job to find out. This is strictly confidential; I don't want to hear any of you gossiping about it. Do you understand?'

Their heads nodded in unison.

'Browning and Amanda are going to go back to Margaret's house. The doctor found some pet hairs on Margaret's trouser leg. I need comparison hairs from her cat – Browning left the cat decomposing in the back of a div car which has since been disposed of.'

There were groans and laughter; Browning was glaring at her, but she didn't care. After dropping the bombshell about Tom, she needed to lighten the mood, even if it was at his expense.

'Margaret was heavily involved with organising events for St Aidan's, so I want to speak to the vicar and his wife. Mattie, you can come with me. Col, when you finish at the supermarket can you come back and run comparisons with the Sandy Kilburn case? I want you to check the records for cat killings, see if they're the precursor for any violent crimes. I don't think Sandy was his first violent attack; I think he's probably been attacking animals and people for some time while trying to pluck up the courage to take it one step further. He's finally done it, and now he's crossed the line he's not going to stop. I'll see if Leanne has finished inputting everything in to HOLMES. That should pick up any similarities, but Col, we all know you're a hundred times better than that computer programme. Thank you, let's kick some arse today and get some hard evidence and a suspect we can bring in for questioning.'

CHAPTER TWENTY-FIVE

They filed out of the conference room, and Rachel whispered to Col: 'You know what they say, don't you? Most murders are committed by family members. Do you think he did it?'

Lucy, who was behind her, slowed down, letting the comment go. Rachel was right; they needed to get Tom out of the picture, because it often was a family member. She hoped to God the footage showed him browsing the aisles and leaving sixty minutes later with a giant trolley full of food. She went to her office to retrieve her phone. Mattie followed her.

'How did you find out about Sainsbury's? Have you spoken to Tom?'

Lucy could detect the hint of disbelief in his voice. 'Yes, I had to. He's lying about where he was and I need to know why.'

Mattie shook his head. 'God, you're so anal at times. I'm telling you now, he's probably trying not to tell the whole world he's having an affair. He's protecting his family the best he can.'

'Why are you so fucking sure of that, Mattie? What, are you and Tom best friends now?'

Mattie shrugged. 'No, but I'm putting myself in his position and it's the only explanation.'

'Well you can talk to him next time if we need to, he might open up to you. You can tell him all about your latest conquest and compare the notches on your bedposts.'

'Sometimes you can be a real bitch, Lucy. If you want to know I haven't got a latest conquest, she left me for the pizza delivery guy because she said she sees more of him than me. I'll wait for you in the car.'

He turned to walk out of her office, and her stomach lurched as her mouth filled with stale wine and regret at what she'd just said. Mattie was her only real friend, she needed to stop being so mean to him. None of this was his fault; her fucked-up life was her problem not his and she needed to stop taking it out on him.

Mattie parked in the small car park outside of the church hall; they'd driven there in silence and Lucy felt terrible. He turned to her.

'Are you okay? How are things at home?'

'Bloody awful. George rang up asking me to have Ellie because she's been a cow to Rosie. I said no because I was too busy with the case. I'm so crap at this parenting thing. I'm sorry about…' She was wracking her brains trying to remember his last girlfriend's name.

'About what, Jody? Don't be, it wasn't serious. I'm a bit sensitive today, must be my hormones.'

He winked at her, and she nudged him in the side. 'Very funny, what a pair we are. Neither of us can keep a relationship going.'

'You speak for yourself, I'm not that bad. At least I don't marry them. I'm more of a love them and leave them kind of guy. Come on, let's get this over with; I hate churches and vicars. You can speak to him, I'll take his wife.'

'You might regret that when you see her. I get the impression she's an angry little thing.'

They got out of the car, harmony restored.

Lucy hammered on the vicarage door and let out a sigh. The door flew open and the woman on the other side glared at them.

'What are you trying to do, wake the dead?'

Lucy held up her warrant card. 'DI Harwin and DS Jackson, we need to speak to you about Margaret Crowe. Can we come inside?'

The woman studied her badge then stepped to one side to let them in. She pointed to the door to the left of them. Lucy walked into the large lounge, where the vicar was on the phone talking loudly to the person on the other end. He looked at her and smiled, ending his conversation.

'Well this is a nice surprise; it's Ellie's mum, isn't it? What brings you here?'

'I'd like to say it was a social visit, unfortunately it isn't. We need to speak to you both about Margaret.'

'Oh dear, is she okay? I've been phoning and haven't been able to get hold of her. Has she had an accident?'

Lucy didn't look at Mattie. She nodded and pointed to the sofa, where the vicar's wife was hovering and looking uncomfortable.

'I think it might be better if you both sit down.'

They did, but not together. He sat on a chair and she sat on the sofa, as far apart from each other as they possibly could be. Lucy and Mattie both sat down on the two-seater opposite them.

'I'm sorry to have to tell you that Margaret's body was found in the early hours of Saturday morning.'

The woman's hand lifted to her mouth as she let out a gasp. The vicar tried his best to look shocked, when in reality he didn't look in the least bit disturbed, which Lucy found very interesting. His wife, on the other hand, looked genuinely distressed.

'What do you mean *her body*, is she dead?'

Lucy nodded. The woman opened her mouth and let out a wail, making Lucy jump. She hadn't expected that reaction.

The vicar stared at his wife, shaking his head. 'Jan, for the love of God shut up and let us listen to what the police have to say.' He turned to Lucy. 'She's not very good at coping with death when it's someone she knows. Are you, dear?'

He was glaring at his wife. She clamped her mouth shut and looked at Lucy.

'I know this must be a bit of a shock for you both but I need to ask you some questions. We need to piece together her last movements so we can get a clearer picture of what happened.'

There was a slight nodding of both their heads.

'Can you tell me when you last spoke to Margaret?'

He answered. 'At the church hall; she'd helped us to set up for the winter fair two days ago. In fact it was her idea to have it in the first place. We left her there and went home. She said she was doing some final checks before going home herself.'

'What time was that?'

'I don't know, I'm not sure. What time was it, Jan?'

She shrugged.

'Did she say where she was going? Did she have any plans to meet up with someone?'

'No, I assumed she was going home. I don't think she went out much; the church and her cat were the most important things to her.'

'Did she tell you about her cat?'

He nodded. 'All the time.'

'No, I mean did she tell you about it being killed?'

Jan finally spoke, her voice a whisper. 'She told me, it was dreadful. Who would want to kill an old person's pet cat?'

'You never told me this. I wondered why she wasn't herself.'

'You never bloody listen, David, I did tell you. If you weren't disappearing all the time and paying attention you'd know this stuff.'

Lucy held up her hand before their bickering got out of hand; the last thing she wanted was for them to have a domestic in front of them.

'We're going to need to take a brief witness statement from you both. Do you want to come to the station or should we do it now?'

'I'm very busy this afternoon – I have thirty minutes before morning service. Can you do it now? How long will it take?'

'Not long, David, if I speak to you in here. Mattie, can you take Jan into the kitchen and speak to her in there?'

Mattie smiled at the woman and stood up. 'Of course, do you want to show me the way to the kitchen?'

She stood up and led the way, leaving Lucy alone with the vicar.

*

'This must be a terrible shock for you; but can you tell me what happened the last time you spoke to Margaret?'

He nodded. 'Well I remember she was walking around with that bloody clipboard tucked under her arm and worrying about the running order of the fair.'

'Did you get on well with Margaret?'

He stared at her, a slight pink blush began to spread across his face. 'Of course I did, I mean she was a lovely woman and very dedicated to helping out with the various groups the church run; her fundraising efforts were amazing.'

'I see, it's just you said a moment ago "that bloody clipboard": what did you mean by that?' She smiled at him.

'Well, I don't want to sound as if I don't care, because I do. I'm terribly upset to hear that she's dead.'

'But?'

'But she could be a bit of a pain in the arse if I'm honest; oh Lord that sounds horrific. She was bossy and had to list everything down, and then check it off her list. It could be very annoying. I'm more of a go with the flow and let everything follow its own course person.'

'I see, did you fall out with her over this?'

'No, I'd never do that. I'm very grateful to her for her help. I feel terrible I didn't know about her cat, and now she's dead. Who would do such a thing?'

'That's what I intend to find out. Did anyone else speak to Margaret? Did she fall out with or try to boss others around? Do you think she could have upset someone enough that they'd want to kill her?'

He shook his head. 'No, not at all. Jan and I left her to it. She locked up the hall.'

'Did you go out again that night or did you stay in with Jan?'

'I stayed in of course, I'm a vicar. I don't go out of an evening unless it's something to do with the church. I assumed that she'd get the bus home. She normally does. Where was she found?'

'Basterfield House.'

'She must have decided to walk home; the bus doesn't go anywhere near there. Why didn't she get the bus or knock on my door? I'd have given her a lift, and we wouldn't be here today, would we?'

He buried his head in his hands, and Lucy couldn't decide if he was genuinely anguished or doing it for her benefit. He was pretty hard to read. There was one thing she did know about him though, and that was she didn't like him. There was something about him that didn't sit right with her; he gave her the impression he was trying to give an award-winning performance and she wasn't sure if it was because he was a vicar or if it was his personality.

'It's hard to know under these circumstances what could have happened. If she'd been picked out as a victim by the killer, he would have got to her either way. It's all terribly sad.'

*

Mattie came back into the room. He stared at the vicar with his head in his hands, and Lucy nodded. Standing up she smiled at Jan, who was staring at her husband.

'Thank you both for your time. I'll be in touch if I have any further questions. If you can think of anything that you might think could be relevant in any way, shape or form then please ring 101 and ask to speak to me.'

Lucy wondered what was going on between the vicar and his wife, they didn't seem particularly close. In fact, they seemed to bicker more than they talked, which of course wasn't unusual for couples who had been married a long time. But could they really have been responsible for Margaret's horrific death – or was she way out of her depth?

CHAPTER TWENTY-SIX

March 1990

He'd been here for three weeks now. Father Vincent had told the police he could stay as long as he needed to. He'd been kind to him, he hadn't asked too many questions, and he fed him better than he'd been fed in a long time. The only rules were he wasn't to go into Vincent's bedroom, or David's, the trainee vicar's. He could use the library; he was allowed in the church as long as he didn't mess around with the stuff in there, and he had to do all of his homework before he could eat his tea. As far as rules go he could cope with them; it was nice knowing that he wasn't going to get a good hiding if he looked the wrong way or said he was hungry. David was a bit weird though; he watched him a lot, and he'd catch him staring. He wasn't very old and when Vincent wasn't around he didn't stay in the same room as him. All he did was talk about God and lick his lips. It was repulsive, and he reminded him too much of his dad. He didn't ask after his dad. He'd heard Vincent telling the housekeeper that the social were trying to get him a permanent placement. He didn't know what it meant; he didn't care really. Anywhere away from him had to be better.

Climbing out of bed he began to shiver. This house was freezing until the heating kicked in and that was only when it felt like it. He dressed in his school uniform, tugging the jumper down as far as it would go. He'd grown since his mum had bought it for him and needed a new one but he didn't know who to ask. The bathroom was huge and even colder than his bedroom. Brushing his teeth he looked up into the mirror and jumped to see David watching him.

'Sorry, will you be long? I'm late.'

Spitting the foamy mouthful of Colgate into the sink, he shook his head. Expecting him to turn around or something, he was shocked when he stepped inside and shut the door. Crossing the room, his shadow blocked out the light.

'You've had a terrible time; there's no need to be scared of me. I want to help you. If you need to chat about anything, your mum or even your dad, then you can always talk to me.' He reached out his hand and brushed his fingers against the soft skin of his cheek, and he yelped. Slapping the hand away from his face.

'Don't touch me.'

Shoving the much bigger man as hard as he could, he ran past him and out of the door, downstairs to the kitchen.

Vincent was stirring the contents of a pan on the stove, humming along to the radio. He turned around and smiled at him.

'Porridge for breakfast, young man, there's nothing like it on a cold morning to set you up for the day. Sit down and have some before you go to school. We don't want your stomach growling all morning before dinner time, do we.'

Shaking his head, he went and sat at the table. He was starving. That weirdo upstairs wasn't going to put him off his breakfast. With a bit of luck he wouldn't come down here until he'd left, but he was going to have to be careful around him. Vincent placed a huge bowl in front of him, and he began to shovel sugar into it to make it taste half decent. Vincent never said anything, just smiled and turned around to make a pot of tea.

'So, I'm going to be working a bit later tonight than I usually do. It's the monthly pensioner's quiz night in the church hall, so you can either stay here with David or come and help me once you've finished any homework. It's up to you, I don't mind. They normally have homemade pie and peas halfway through the quiz, which I must say are the reason I don't mind being the quizmaster. They're very tasty, throw a few onions and some beetroot on and you'd think you were at a pub somewhere.' He turned back to face him. 'What do you think? I know you might not want to hang around with the oldies.'

'I'll come.'

'Oh, that's good then. You didn't have to think about it, they'll love you. The old dears will be fussing around you.'

'It's okay, I'd rather do something than be stuck in here.'

He didn't tell him that being here alone with that weirdo, David, was the last thing he wanted to do in case it caused any trouble and they sent him home. Although the social worker had told him he wouldn't be going back home, he didn't believe them. He could avoid David in this huge house, but he couldn't avoid his dad or his fists in their tiny two up two down.

CHAPTER TWENTY-SEVEN

The door shut behind them, and Lucy was glad to be outside in the fresh air; the house was too stuffy and filled with far too much dust-gathering crap for her liking. She liked her space clear and clutter free, no cheap pot ornaments filling every surface. Jan must have spent years rifling through the rubbish that was donated to the church for jumble sales and fairs to amass such a collection of crap.

Mattie whispered, 'What did you think of those two then?'

She didn't answer, in case they were watching from the windows and her body language betrayed her. As soon as they were inside the car she spoke.

'I don't trust him. I get the impression he wasn't very fond of Margaret. He said she was too bossy, although I don't know if it's a good enough motive for murder. She's like a fiery little ferret.'

Mattie laughed so loud she turned to him and frowned.

'A fiery little ferret. That's a good one, Lucy.'

Driving out of the small car park she put the window down and breathed out. 'I got the feeling he was getting a bit antsy when I was questioning him.'

'About what?'

'His whereabouts for one, said he was at home with Jan – and he may well have been for some of the time. He started out relaxed, then when I started asking him more details he was blinking far more than he had been since we'd come in. He kept scratching his cheek; these are all signs that someone is lying to you.'

'Bloody hell, Lucy, do you analyse everyone you talk to?'

Shrugging she laughed. 'Not all the time, only when I'm interested in whether they're a person of interest or not to my investigations. Body language is a fascinating subject, the FBI use it all the time.'

'You need to get out more.'

She glared at him, and he turned to look out of the window.

'I didn't mean that, it's good that you read up on all this stuff. That's what makes you a great detective. I suppose it's better than playing on an Xbox in your spare time.'

'Yeah, well I've always liked reading. It's my equivalent of playing a games console. Let's go get a coffee then go back to the station to figure out where this is all going.'

'Do you think he could be good for this?'

'Whoever it is has some fucked-up problem with God or the church; he's a vicar, which kind of makes him an obvious choice, and what about Sandy? I'm pretty sure there's a connection somewhere along the line. We just need to find it. He could be harbouring some dark desires to kill, and trying to cover them up with his choice of job?'

'That's one sick bastard if he is. But at least it gets the boss off the hook.'

Lucy carried her coffee up to her office, glad to see both Col and Rachel sitting behind their desks. She waved them over and both of them stood up, following her into her office. Col shut the door, and she felt her heart sink.

'How did you get on?'

'Not that good to be honest, boss. We watched the footage, which clearly shows Tom going in and coming back out.'

'What time did he leave?'

'He entered at 18.11 and came back out with a bunch of flowers and one carrier bag of shopping at 18.20.'

Leaning forward she buried her head in her hands. 'Shit.'

'What should we do now?'

When she moved her hands away from her face, Col frowned. 'Lucy are you feeling okay, you've gone white.'

She nodded. 'Fine, thanks. Right, well I guess I need to go and speak to him again. Can you make me a copy of the footage with the timestamps on?'

He passed her a pen drive. 'Already done.'

'Thank you, for now this is between us. I don't want any gossiping; I still don't think he has anything to do with this, but I do need a proper explanation for the missing time.'

They left her alone to drink her coffee and massage her aching temples. Taking out her notepad she wrote down, *seventy minutes, what were you doing, Tom?* She needed to speak to him as soon as possible; she also needed to ask him if he'd ever heard of Sandy Kilburn before her body had been discovered.

CHAPTER TWENTY-EIGHT

Jan stood in front of the kitchen sink, tears leaking from the corner of her eye. Poor Margaret, what had she done to possibly make someone think she deserved to die? Sensing her husband standing behind her, she didn't need to turn around – he was very good at sneaking around. Then again she was very good at pretending not to notice; he thought she was oblivious to his night-time outings when it was the complete opposite. She was very good at faking sleep, at faking love, hell she could fake an orgasm with the best of them – only it had been years since he'd tried to sleep with her, so she didn't have to bother much with that particular skill. He had his secrets; she'd followed him a couple of times then decided she didn't want to know. All she'd ever wanted was a happy marriage, children and a home to call her own. When she first met David, he was a dashing young man whose love of God and helping people had been the thing to make her fall head over heels in love with him. She'd always been a bit on the chubbier side with very few friends due to her lack of self-confidence and would spend her spare time helping out at the church, rarely speaking. Shyness had crippled her teenage years, bitterness and anger her adult years. She knew he was waiting for her to speak, but she didn't have the energy.

'Well this wasn't how I expected this morning to turn out.'

Turning around she stared straight into his eyes. 'Excuse me?'

'Poor Margaret, you never know when your time is up, do you? I suppose the family will want her service here. I wonder if they'll want a full burial?'

'She was murdered; you're making it sound as if she was hit by a bus, crossing the road. Some bastard killed her and you're wondering if she'll be having a burial? What about who would do such a thing, why her? I don't understand. You're such a heartless prick at times.'

'I didn't mean that. Of course it's terrible, and who would want to murder her? I was just trying to make conversation, Jan. Break the silence. Do you ever give it a rest? Don't you ever get tired of being so angry all the time?'

Glancing at the heavy marble rolling pin on the draining board, she wondered if she would have the nerve to pick it up and smash him over the head with it.

'Where were you that night?'

'What do you mean? I was here with you.'

Her eyes narrowed as she stepped closer to him. 'Yes, you were until I went to bed. I heard you leave. I got up to go to the toilet and I checked your bedroom. You never even got into bed before you snuck out of the house like some teenager who wasn't allowed out after ten.'

His face turned ashen. 'I went for a walk. I wasn't tired. Unlike you I can't lay my head on the pillow and fall asleep within sixty seconds. I have a lot to think about.'

'So where did you walk to?'

'What are you accusing me of, Jan? I went out for some fresh air before bed. That's it; I didn't go anywhere near Margaret's house. Why the fuck would I? What did you tell the police?'

'That you were tucked up in bed like the good man of the cloth you pretend to be.'

The look of relief that crossed his face only made her more suspicious.

'That's all right then, you know what coppers are like. One sniff of a clue and they're barking up the wrong tree. They arrest more innocent people than guilty; you and I both know that. I'm sorry for shouting at you, sweetheart, we need to stick together at this tragic time not be tearing each other apart.'

He crossed the room and pulled her close, and she let him. Only because she didn't know who the hell he was anymore or what he was capable of.

'I'm sorry, too, it must be the shock of it all.'

'Well you sit down and I'll make us a nice pot of tea. We can have some of that banana cake Margaret made for us and pray for her together.'

The scandal of the popular vicar being a murderer would be the end of them both and bring back all the gossip and taunting of her teenage years that she'd worked so hard to forget. It was up to her to make sure that this didn't happen. Her life might not be perfect, but it was better than she'd imagined it would turn out to be. Now she was going to have to do everything she could to keep it that way. She took her marriage vows very seriously and for better or worse meant that she would stand by him, even if it was only to save herself the embarrassment of having people point fingers at her for being so naive.

CHAPTER TWENTY-NINE

Lucy knocked on Tom's door. His car was in the drive, but Alison's wasn't, which was ideal. She'd been hoping he would be on his own. The door opened and she took a step back, shocked at his three-day stubble and pale complexion.

'Lucy, come in.'

She followed him inside the pristine house, pushing down her feelings of envy for Alison, who pretty much lived a perfect life – or so it seemed from the outside, although Lucy now knew that to be untrue.

'Stupid question, but how are you doing?'

He shrugged. 'Been better if I'm honest. Excuse the mess; Alison has gone to visit her parents for a few days and has taken the boys with her.'

He led her into the kitchen, and she realised that he wasn't doing too well judging by the empty wine bottles stacked up on the side. There was an open bottle of Jack Daniel's on the kitchen table next to an empty glass.

'When was the last time you ate?'

'Yesterday, I think. Can't remember, not really hungry.'

'You're thirsty though? Look it's none of my business, but you have to take care of yourself. You can't let yourself go off the rails, you need to keep it together. *I* need you to keep it together.'

She walked across to the huge American fridge and pulled open the door, grabbing an assortment of things and a pack of bacon to make him some sandwiches.

'Yeah, help yourself, Lucy. I'll never eat it, and I don't know when she's coming home.'

'It's not for me you muppet, it's for you. Sit down, I'll make you some food and then we need to talk. But not until you've eaten something, you look like shit.'

'I feel like shit.'

'In fact while I'm doing this you could go and have a quick shower, change of clothes, have a shave and brush your teeth. It will make you feel better.'

Lucy wondered if she'd overstepped her mark, but hoped she hadn't. They had a deeper relationship than colleagues; she was his friend and he had been her mentor from the day she'd joined the CID department. He'd pushed her to go for the role of detective sergeant, helping her to prepare for the interview, then he'd done the same when the inspector's rank had opened up. Lucy smiled at him, then Tom pushed himself up from the table, saluted at her then turned and headed towards the stairs.

She exhaled the breath she'd been holding and began to clean the kitchen side. Gathering all the empty bottles she took them outside to the recycling container, then after washing down the marble worktops began to make him some food to keep him going.

By the time he came downstairs the kitchen was spotless and there was an assortment of sandwiches wrapped in bags inside the fridge. There was also a stack of toasted bacon and egg bagels on the table along with a pot of coffee. Tom walked across the room and kissed her cheek.

'You'd make someone a great wife, thank you, Lucy.'

She blushed; laughing, she pushed him away. 'Yeah, I did. Only he didn't think I was great enough to keep around. He traded me in for a much younger model.'

Tom's cheeks burned. 'Oh shit, Lucy. I'm sorry, I didn't mean that how it sounded.'

'It's okay, it's a true story and I know you didn't. Here, eat something.' She pushed the stack of bagels towards him, and he took a couple, pushing the plate back towards her.

'Only if you do; have you eaten today?' He raised an eyebrow at her, and she shrugged, grabbing a bagel from the plate.

They ate in silence; when the coffee was poured she reached out and grabbed hold of his hand.

'You're not going to like this but I had to do it. I need you to be brutally honest with me, and I don't care what the answer is you give me. You're still my friend, no matter how good or bad it is, and I will do everything I can to help you. You know that you can trust me, don't you?'

He nodded, squeezing her hand. 'Yes, of all the people I know, you, Lucy Harwin, are one of the very few I would ever trust.'

'Good. Now I need to know where you were when you left Sainsbury's at 18.20 hours on the night your mum was murdered.'

He gulped down the mouthful of coffee he'd just swallowed. 'I went to see my lover.'

Lucy let out the biggest sigh of her life. 'Thank fuck for that. Why didn't you tell me before?'

'It was a bit delicate should we say. What were you going to think of me when I told you I left work and went for a quick shag before going home to play happy families?'

'I think it's a whole lot better than you telling me you went and killed your own mother, Tom. I have no idea what your home life is like, I wouldn't judge you.'

'I know, but with George leaving you and everything else I thought you'd be angry.'

She threw back her head and laughed. 'I'm angry with George, yes. It doesn't affect how I deal with anything else. Your life is your business and nothing to do with me.'

He let go of her hand and sat back. 'Alison demanded I tell her where I'd been because she started thinking I was some kind of closet serial killer. I told her I'd been seeing another woman. She went mental, hit me a couple of times, packed a suitcase and took the boys away. So, there you have it, my life's gone down the drain in less than five days and it's all my own fault.'

'It's not your fault that your mum is dead though, is it? I'm sorry, but I need the name of your lover to confirm this and then it's all over with. I can concentrate on catching the killer before he strikes again.'

'Sara Cross. She isn't going to be happy that you know about us. Do you think he's going to strike again?'

Lucy knew that name, but she couldn't think from where. 'Yes, I do. I think he killed both your mum and Sandy Kilburn; I just need to figure out what links them. Do you know if there was any connection between them? Had you ever heard your mum mention Sandy?'

He shook his head then wrote down Sara's address on a piece of newspaper and tore it off, before handing it to her. Standing, Lucy took it from him. 'Thank you, now there's food in the fridge, and before you sink any more of that bourbon, why don't you phone Alison and try to smooth things out? Speak to the boys, it will make you feel better.'

'Thank you, I will. I've dug myself into a huge hole this time. I'm glad you're here to pull me back out.'

This time it was Lucy who bent down and brushed her lips against his much smoother, woody-smelling cheek. 'If you need to talk, about anything, phone me. Don't sit and drink yourself to death, I haven't got the time to add another unexplained death onto my caseload.' She winked at him, and he grinned.

Walking back to her car she felt a whole lot better knowing where Tom had been, even though she didn't approve. She'd get Browning to pay a visit to Sara Cross to get Tom's alibi signed off and then they were good to go. Now she'd been fed and had coffee it was time to go home and do some research on the good Father

David Collins, because at the moment, in her eyes, he was looking good as a suspect. She needed to find out if Sandy Kilburn had any connection either to him or his church.

CHAPTER THIRTY

April 1990

He sat staring at the grass under which his mother was buried. The sun was warm on his face today. He'd bunked off school to come and say goodbye to her. He couldn't go without telling her why he wouldn't be visiting anymore. He didn't want her to think he'd just abandoned her. It wasn't as if it mattered now anyway. This was his last day at the vicarage: the social worker had found him a foster home in Manchester. He didn't know whether this was a good or a bad thing, as all his life he'd never really been anywhere other than Brooklyn Bay. David had stopped being weird around him after that day in the bathroom, so he'd rather stay there with Vincent, who was the only person to ever be kind to him since his mum had died, but he knew that he couldn't. His dad had started to come around to the vicarage when he was pissed up and give both Vincent and David a hard time. The police had arrested him a few times, and he hated him now more than ever. He was sure it was because of this that they were making him leave; if he'd kept to himself they wouldn't be rushing to move him away to a strange city. Saint Aiden's Church cemetery was quiet, just him and the dead people – which suited him just fine. His mum's grave was around the back of the church, hidden from view, so it was a pretty good place to skive off school without getting caught.

He heard the familiar high-pitched laugh and froze. It was her. Even though he hadn't seen her since he'd been taken away from home that night, he couldn't forget that laugh. There was some muffled talking and more laughter, this time it was much quieter. He crawled forwards on his hands and knees, wondering if his dad had brought the woman here – nothing would surprise him. The door at the side of the church ten feet away creaked open then slammed shut, and he held his hand against his chest to try and stop his heart from hammering so loudly against his ribcage. He'd thought this was it, that he was going to have to run as fast as he could to get away from them before his dad pummelled him to death. Once he'd calmed down, his interest got the better of him and he stood up, creeping towards the church. Why would he want to bring her here of all places? He placed his face against the lead windows and cupped his hands across his forehead so he could see inside. It was far too dark; he could see shadowy figures moving around, but he couldn't see his father or her clear enough to see what they were doing in there. He looked at the heavy oak door which had slammed that hard it had bounced back, not shutting itself properly. He knew this was a very bad idea, but he had to see them one last time for himself.

Squeezing himself through the small gap he felt the cold air envelop him – churches were always freezing cold. He'd been to this one that many times in the past couple of months he could wander around it blindfolded and know where he was. This door led into the vestry and from there to the vicar's office, where he kept all the communion wine and holy wafers. He listened; he could hear her voice although it was much fainter. So he knew it was safe to go inside. They were either in the office or the church itself. Stepping inside the vestry the talking had stopped, replaced by the all-too-familiar moaning she liked to do whenever they were having sex. A tingle of excitement swept through his body, even he knew this was wrong. Dirty and wrong, you didn't do it inside a church; his dad must be really losing it to be doing that inside his beloved place of worship. Tiptoeing across the cold, tiled floor he reached the office door, which was closed.

There was a keyhole with no key, so he bent down and pressed one eye against the small keyhole. The breath caught in the back of his throat – it was her all right. There was no mistaking the bleached hair. She was bent over the desk, her denim miniskirt pushed up to her waist and her black lace knickers around her ankles. It wasn't his dad who was standing naked behind her, though. It was David. He was shocked; he'd thought he was a weirdo who liked little kids. He hadn't expected to see him giving it to her. There was a loud slapping noise, and he looked back through the keyhole to see him slapping her bare bottom, while she squealed with delight.

Feeling sick, he stood up and ran back the way he'd come in. She was a bad woman, he had no doubt about that. Then again, surely the vicar wasn't supposed to be having sex inside the church? He highly doubted it, the church was supposed to be a special place of worship. Outside in the fresh air he ran back towards the vicarage; he didn't know what to do. He shouldn't have looked in the first place, but he couldn't help it. What did his mum used to say, 'curiosity killed the cat'? It served him right for being a peeping Tom in the first place.

As he ran through the back door to the vicarage, Vincent was sitting at the kitchen table with a man and a woman who were looking at various hymn sheets which were laid out on it. All three of them looked up at him.

'What are you doing here, shouldn't you be at school?'

He shook his head. 'Sorry, felt sick. Teacher said I could come back here and see you.'

Vincent smiled at him. 'Get yourself a drink of milk and some biscuits, then take them upstairs. There's a good lad. I'm working.'

He did as he was told, spilling milk all over the worktop his hands were trembling that much. Carrying the glass and three digestives up to his room, he used his foot to slam the door shut. He didn't know if his hands were shaking with excitement over what he'd just seen or whether it was because he'd been sure he was going to have one final showdown with his dad one last time. He did know that the woman wasn't a good person and the vicar was even more of a pervert than he was. But where was his dad? He wouldn't be happy to know what his girlfriend was doing with the vicar, would he? He'd probably beat the crap out of him and her if he ever found out.

He lay on his bed trying to imagine what it would be like to be the one giving out the punches to the people who deserved them, instead of being the one on the receiving end for a change. He knew that when he was old enough he was going to come back and do the same to his dad. He might think he'd got away with beating up him and his mum, but he hadn't. One day he'd be standing over him, punching, kicking and spitting on him to see how he liked it. When he'd finished with his dad he'd find the woman because she'd been going with his dad when his mum was dying and that was unforgivable. Then letting every man she knew do stuff to her... she was a dirty slut. Like his dad, she deserved everything that was coming her way.

CHAPTER THIRTY-ONE

Lucy sighed when she drove up the street and saw every single light was on inside the house. It meant Ellie was there and, as much as she loved her angry teenage daughter, she was too tired for any drama tonight. Walking in through the unlocked front door she had to grit her teeth – no matter how many times she told her to keep the house secure when there were no adults home she didn't. Anyone could walk straight in, steal anything of value and be gone before Ellie, whose usual attire included a pair of earphones permanently stuffed into her eardrums – blaring out whatever her music of choice – even noticed. Although Lucy wouldn't have a clue what to do with the Spotify that she paid for every month without Ellie setting up her playlists for her.

'Ellie?'

No answer, but she could hear footsteps upstairs. Lucy kicked off her shoes and ran up just in case it wasn't her daughter and she was being burgled. Ellie walked out of the bathroom and jumped to see her.

'Christ mum, you gave me a fright.'

'Evening to you too. Why was the front door unlocked?'

Her daughter rolled her eyes, making Lucy bite her tongue.

'I forgot.'

'So, to what do I owe this pleasure? Have you upset Rosie again?'

'No, she's a bitch. She's even moodier than you. I wanted to come home and ask you if it's okay if I babysit for Natalia and her husband.'

'Natalia?'

'The lady from the church with the really cute kid. She said she hasn't got a regular babysitter and if I wanted to help her out she'd pay me twenty quid each time. She's nice, and her husband has the Italian off the high street.'

'What did your dad say?'

'It was okay as long as you were happy.'

Ellie stared at her, arms crossed waiting for her reply. Lucy didn't know the family, but she knew the restaurant and as far as she was aware there were no issues.

'I suppose so. I want you to give her my mobile number, then she can ring me if there's any problems. Promise?'

'Really? Thanks, and of course I will. She wants me to babysit tomorrow night while she helps at Street Saviours. As soon as Tony comes home I'll get a taxi back.'

'What's Street Saviours? I've never heard of it.'

'It's where they open the church hall late on a weekend night. They go out with flip-flops and lollipops, hand them out to the drunks to stop them fighting. If people are really hammered they take them back to the hall, give them a bacon bun and coffee to sober them up.'

Lucy could feel her mind begin to whir into action. Maybe Sandy Kilburn had been there or helped out, and she was pretty sure Margaret would have helped out with it. This could be their connection to the church and David Collins.

'It's a good idea, though I find it hard to believe Natalia spends so much time helping out at church when she has a busy restaurant to run. Have you eaten?'

Ellie laughed. 'Yeah, but I'm starving. Can we order pizza? I haven't stopped thinking about it since I knew Nat owned the Italian.'

Lucy smiled. 'Already have some on its way.'

Her daughter walked across the room and high-fived her. 'You know when you're not cranky I love you.'

Wrapping her arms around her, she hugged her and whispered, 'Yeah, same here, kid.'

*

They sat on the sofa staring at the two huge pizza boxes; Lucy was stuffed and happy. Nothing made her quite so happy as a meat feast with extra cheese. Ellie stood up, groaning.

'I think I'm about to explode, is it okay if I get a bath and go to bed?'

Lucy, who was already showered and in her pyjamas, nodded. 'I'm knackered, I'm going to bed soon. Night, Ells.'

As Ellie ran up the stairs she shouted, 'Night, Mum.'

When she heard the bath taps begin to run, she dragged her laptop towards her and waited for Google to load so she could begin to check out David Collins: she needed to know as much about him as possible before she let her daughter anywhere near him again. For all she knew he could be their killer. Of all the places on the list from school to volunteer why did Ellie have to pick that church? She would have thought she would have run a mile from a church, it just showed how much she didn't know about her own daughter. Tonight had been a rare example of how their relationship should be – tomorrow, when she told Ellie to keep away from there, it was going to cause a major shitstorm. Knowing her daughter, she would do the complete opposite of what she was told, so she might have to go about it a different way. Starting tomorrow, Lucy was going to be keeping a very close eye on David until she had some concrete proof to bring him in for questioning.

CHAPTER THIRTY-TWO

He took the small gift box that her birthday present had come in from the back of the drawer and sat on the dining room chair. Placing the box on the table in front of him, he stared at it. The excitement of just knowing what was inside, it made his heart race. He knew it was wrong to have it here, in his home, but he didn't know where else to keep it. He wanted it close; no, he *needed* it close, so he could touch the contents and look at them whenever he had the chance. The house was peaceful for a change, no noise, no television or radio blaring and no raised voices. It was him and his Pandora's Box. Opening the lid, he stared at the white, plastic, vulgar button earrings. Wondering why she'd chosen to wear these or a different coloured variation of them every single day of her life. Whenever he'd seen her being screwed by one man or another she'd had a pair of them in her ears. They were vile, gaudy and cheap, which he supposed was a good description of her because she had also been vile, gaudy and very cheap. A voice in his head whispered *did that mean she had to die*? Shaking his head from side to side he had to get rid of his inner voice of reason because it spoke far too loudly some days. Yes, she had to die, he reassured himself. The minute he set eyes on her again that night, when she'd been helped into the church hall a drunken, sobbing mess, he'd realised who she was. Sandy Kilburn's earrings had sealed her fate. He'd never before seen anyone else stuck in an eighties time warp and still wearing them. She was full of dirty secrets that he didn't want exposing to the world, so he'd had to silence her. The only problem was, when he'd finished and realised what a work of art he'd created, he'd known that there was no going back to how his life had been. The thrill of killing her had been the biggest excitement of his life when he'd stepped away from her bloodied, bleeding body. Killing his father had been a murder of necessity, something that he'd had coming. Portraying to the world the image of a pious, righteous man was the biggest fuck you to God he knew of. Then home, behind closed doors, sleeping with anything in a skirt and beating his wife and son until they were bruised and bleeding. The man had been the biggest hypocrite that he knew, leading a double life until the day he'd finished it. There was something his dad had taught him well: how to live two lives without anyone raising an eyebrow or even having an inclination about it.

Killing small animals had been a hobby of his as he'd got older and angrier at the shit life he'd been cursed with. They'd filled the gap, the yearning inside of him quite well. His first murder when he was fifteen had been one of necessity; the old bastard had deserved it and had it coming in every sense. Expecting the guilt to kick in after he'd walked away, it hadn't. The guilt never came, the same as it did with the animals. Cats were the easiest, the streets were full of them. Especially after dark – there were too many to choose from. Not once in the following years did he ever ask himself if they deserved to die, so why was this happening now? He'd done a pretty good job of keeping the doctor's appointments and medication hidden from her over the years. But he'd thrown it all away a couple of weeks ago, flushed it down the toilet. He didn't need it now; he was the strongest and felt better than he'd ever felt since he'd been that sad, angry loner of a teenager. His life had turned out a lot better than he'd imagined it could. He didn't touch the earrings, afraid he might catch some disease from them, but he did pick up the delicate gold crucifix. Lifting it out of the box he held it up to the light; there were a few dark spots on it, and he knew they were blood. He needed to clean it properly: when he was next alone he'd drop it into some Coke to soak, that stuff pretty much rotted everything.

Movement upstairs made him drop the chain back into the box. Snapping the lid shut he pulled open the dresser drawer. Pushing it down at the back, pulling some papers and letters in front of it. He stood up and went into the kitchen. It was time to pretend everything was good in his life. He had to make sure she thought he was the same man she'd married. If she got a whiff of the change in him she'd be suspicious – he wasn't sure of what, but she would definitely pick up on the change in his demeanour. He had to carry out the act of his perfect life, so he could carry on doing what he really wanted to do. Kill.

CHAPTER THIRTY-THREE

Lucy arrived at the station the same time as Mattie, and he waited for her to park her car into the smallest, last space available – this was why she loved her tiny car.

'Morning.'

'Morning, Mattie, I spoke to Tom.'

'What did he say?'

'You were right – but this is just between us. He's having an affair – or was; I have no idea if it's all done with now, because Alison has found out and left him.'

He stared at her. 'Christ, as if he needed that on top of everything else.'

'It wasn't my fault, I had to know the truth. I'd rather it was this than us dragging him in for questioning as a suspect.'

'I suppose so. Poor bloke, I bet he's in a right state.'

Lucy bit her tongue. She didn't condone what he'd been doing because she knew what it was like first-hand to be the partner of a cheating spouse, but it was none of her business, and she wouldn't let how she felt influence their friendship or working relationship. She felt sorry that he'd lost his mum under such horrific circumstances, but there wasn't one ounce of sympathy about his marriage situation; in her view, if you play with fire you're going to get burnt.

'Yeah, his life is a mess at the moment. I'm sure he'll get it back on track. I was going to ask Browning to go and speak to this Sara Cross who he's been sleeping with to confirm his alibi, but I'd rather you did it.' She handed him the ripped piece of newspaper.

'Now, if possible, and you can bring me back a bacon buttie, please, smothered in tomato sauce and butter.'

'Because you asked so nicely, I will. I'm not moving my car though, I'll never get parked again.'

Walking in through the double doors to the corridor where the car keys were all hanging on white boards he grabbed a set and turned around. 'I suppose you want a vanilla latte to go with it?'

She fluttered her eyelids at him. 'Yes, please.' She threw a £20 note in his direction. 'Get yourself the same, my treat.'

'You're far too kind.'

*

By the time he came back she had typed up a list of everything that needed doing and gone through the intelligence system to see if David Collins was on there. He wasn't, and she'd been more than a bit disappointed, as she'd been hoping to find something on him. Mattie sat in the chair opposite her, pushing her breakfast towards her.

'You will be very pleased to know that Sara Cross – after having a major fucking shit fit – did confirm that yes, he was with her for an hour after he left work. She hasn't seen him since; he hasn't even phoned her to tell her about his mum and Alison leaving him, so she's pretty pissed off with him as well. I think I might have to give our Tommy a lesson on keeping up with his love life and how to handle women. It's basic rules: you don't ignore the woman you're having an affair with, do you? I mean if she gets too arsy she could turn up at his house and make it a thousand times worse than it already is.'

Lucy couldn't help roll her eyes. 'How kind of you, what a thoroughly decent person you are. Thanks for that, at least we can leave him alone now to grieve. Not sure how he's going to sort his love life out; though, to be fair I don't care. It's his mess, let him clean it up himself; the last thing you want to do is get involved.'

'You know this is my last shift, don't you? I fly early hours; but if you need me to stay and work the case I can cancel.'

She felt her heart sink. She'd forgotten all about his impending holiday. 'Don't be daft, I can manage without you for a couple of weeks.'

'Sure about that? Because I'm not. Promise me you'll at least try and keep yourself out of trouble.'

'Positive, you have a great time. I want you to drink lots of cocktails for me. I'm not sure I'll be able to get my own breakfast though, I'll probably starve to death and be dead by the time you come back.'

He laughed. 'You better not, as much as you're a pain in the backside I'd rather work for you than anyone else. So what's the plan for today? You might as well use and abuse me before the end of my shift.'

'Today I want to find out as much about David Collins as possible. We need to go back and speak to the lovely couple about a project they run from the church hall. Have you heard of Street Saviours?'

He nodded. 'Aren't they the God squad who go out helping the piss cans of a weekend?'

'Why has everyone heard of them but me? Ellie told me about them last night. I think if we can link Sandy Kilburn to them and Margaret we'll have our connection to the vicar. Then we can bring him in for questioning.'

'You really think he's good for it?'

'I think he's up to something. I don't trust him. I'd like to get him in for interview and ruffle his feathers. See how he reacts when he's questioned.'

'Risky, he's a pillar of the community. His ferocious ferret of a wife isn't going to be too happy about it either. You could cause uproar, not to mention upset his loyal parishioners.'

'Tough, I don't care about his reputation. I care about finding the sick bastard who killed Sandy and Margaret. Up to now we haven't had any other leads, so it's better than nothing.'

Mattie left her to finish her breakfast in peace. Lucy needed to get things moving and fast before it happened again.

CHAPTER THIRTY-FOUR

October 1994

The streets were filled with little kids dressed up as ghosts and witches, running around screeching and knocking on doors. He'd never really celebrated Halloween. He'd always wanted to, but his dad wouldn't let him. Said it was against God's wishes and it was like celebrating the Devil's existence. How he'd had the cheek to dismiss Halloween because of his 'religion', yet beat up his wife and child was beyond him. He hadn't had a lot of friends to go out with anyway; there were none his father approved of, and each year he'd watch the kids wearing cut-up sheets from his bedroom window. It was different now; the costumes were much better. More and more kids were out walking the streets while trick or treating; it was the perfect cover for what he had to do.

The train had taken longer than he'd expected to get back to Brooklyn Bay; he had to be back at the children's home by ten. The foster parents he'd lived with had told the social worker they couldn't cope with his unruly behaviour and he'd been sent to a home. He couldn't afford to be late; he needed to do what he had to do then get back there so they didn't wonder where he was. As he turned into the street with his coat zipped up to his nose and the black beanie hat on, the only things you could see were his eyes. He felt his heart hammering inside his chest, a combination of fear at facing his dad for the last time and excitement that he was finally going to give the bastard what he deserved making it hard to keep calm. As the house came into view, his house, where he'd spent most of the time a quivering wreck, he paused. Staring at it, he noticed a single light bulb was burning in the upstairs bedroom. He reached the front gate which wasn't shut because it was hanging off its hinges. The house looked even more run-down and shabby than when he'd lived there, which didn't surprise him because his dad hadn't maintained it when his mum was alive. After she died, he didn't even bother replacing light bulbs that burnt out. Checking the street until he was satisfied that no one was paying any attention to him, he crossed the road. The only people around were a bunch of young kids knocking on doors further up, laughing and screeching as they shared out with each other the crappy sweets they'd been given.

He had the back door key clutched in the damp palm of his left hand and hoped that the tight-fisted git hadn't changed the locks. The front door was the same as when he was last here, so he very much doubted it. He went around to the back where the rotted wooden gate was pushed shut but not latched. He opened it enough to squeeze through and was in the back garden. The kitchen and living room windows were all in darkness, too; just to make sure he crept along from the side and peeped inside. The last time he'd done this his father had been having sex with that cheap whore he brought home when he was drunk. He wondered where she was, and if she'd ever let him fuck her again after that night he'd hit her and got himself arrested. Not that he cared about her; she was nothing compared to the woman his mother had been – he missed her so much. Reaching the back door, he was relieved to see it was the same one, although it wouldn't have mattered if it wasn't. He'd spent the last four years thinking about this moment and nothing was going to stop him: he would have found a way to get inside one way or another. Pushing the key into the Yale lock, he turned it, holding his breath. Then he pushed it open and stepped inside.

His nose wrinkled at the stench: it was vile and smelt as if someone had already died in here weeks ago. Waiting for his eyes to adjust to the dark, he blinked a couple of times and pulled on the black leather gloves he'd stolen along with his boots from the charity shop. The worktops were covered in stacks of filthy pots and takeaway cartons. The table was covered in empty bottles of vodka and whisky, so he'd really lost it. He was nothing more than a sad, lonely alcoholic. His feet remembering the way led him to the stairs, where he listened for any movement. A loud snore filled the air, but it didn't come from the direction of the bedrooms. He turned to the living room, where the door was open and he could make out his dad's figure slumped in the armchair in the corner. A smile spread across his face, this was even better than he could have hoped for. He stared at the heavy maroon bible on the sideboard – he still kept it there after all this time. He wondered if he bothered to read it anymore; Vincent had long stopped bothering with him after his abusive tirades outside the vicarage when he was stopping there. Taking it from its resting place he felt the weight, passing it from one hand to the other. It should be enough to do some serious damage. What would you call it? Divine retribution?

Then he stepped inside.

The first blow stunned the man, whose eyes fluttered open, trying to make sense of what had just happened. Not hesitating for a second, he lifted the book and brought the spine of it crashing down onto the bridge of his nose. The hot spray of fresh blood covered his hands, as a low groan came from the man in the chair as his hands flew to his nose. Before he could push himself to his feet he hit him again and again. Dragging him from the chair and throwing him to the floor, he began to kick him with the heavy Dr Martens he'd stolen especially for this moment. When his dad was a bloodied pulp he leant down and shook him hard to make him listen.

'Long time no see, eh Dad? You must have known this day was coming. How long have you been waiting for me? Sitting in this chair by yourself, day after day. Drinking yourself to death. I hope it's been a fucking long time, you piece of shit. Where's your God to save you now? I don't see you quoting the Bible; let's see, what was your favourite line? Ah, yes, I know now. Should I remind you and you can repeat it after me?'

The bleeding, semi-conscious man let out a small whimper, and he laughed.

'Funny how you don't seem to be enjoying it now the tables have turned. "If we confess our sins, he is faithful and just and will forgive us our sins and purify us from all unrighteousness." Isn't that right, isn't that what you used to shout at my mum when she was lying on the floor, bruised and bleeding, afraid of you? I'll give you one more chance. What happens if we confess our sins? You know confession is good for the soul, don't you?'

The man groaned, making no attempt to repeat the words. He knelt on the floor next to him, then lifting the blood-soaked bible as high as he could, he brought it down onto his windpipe, crushing it. Leaving the bible on his chest he stood up, watching to see if his chest would continue to rise and fall. It didn't and for the first time in a very long time he felt as if he'd satisfied the burning desire that had been eating away at him.

CHAPTER THIRTY-FIVE

Armed with several photos of Sandy Kilburn, Lucy drove to the church hall and parked on the street opposite, where she could watch the comings and goings. She would have to come back later on to speak to the volunteers who helped run Street Saviours, which she'd learned was on tonight. For now, she was content enough to speak to David and his wife Jan again, show them the pictures and see if it jogged any memories. What she desperately wanted was for him to show her some kind of reaction. That was why she'd picked the post-mortem photos to show him, see if there was any shock, remorse, a flicker of recognition, anything. Mattie had stayed behind to catch up on his paperwork before finishing up for his holiday, though she could have brought someone else with her. When she'd looked around the office there'd been only Browning and Rachel, both of them managing to look busy and not in her direction. She'd rather be on her own anyway, it gave her time to think. As she got out of the car she heard her name being called and looked across the road to see Jan Collins walking towards her with an M&S carrier bag in her hand.

'Are you coming to speak to us, Detective?'

She crossed the road towards the woman who seemed a bit friendlier today.

'Yes, is David in?'

Jan shook her head. 'No, he's out visiting parishioners. You can come in and talk to me though, I might be able to help you.'

Lucy followed the woman the short distance to the vicarage and waited for her to open the front door then followed her inside.

'I like your car, I always wanted one of those. I love that green colour, it's so pretty.'

'Didn't you get one?'

'No, David said it wouldn't look very good turning up to funerals in a car that looked like a huge spearmint. I told him not to be so bloody ridiculous. I mean you turn up at all sorts of horrible things in it right? Has anyone ever commented that it's inappropriate to you?'

'No, to be honest it's not something I've ever thought about before. The colour of my car doesn't stop me from being a professional and doing my job. In fact it has nothing to do with it.'

'That's what I told him, but he wouldn't have it. He's full of what he thinks is right, but sometimes he doesn't know shit. Listen to me going on, when you must be really busy. What did you want?'

Lucy couldn't help wondering why the woman was much more amiable now than her previous visit, then thought that it might be because her husband wasn't here. She wanted to ask her about David but didn't want to put her in a bad mood. However, she needed to know if she knew Sandy Kilburn.

Jan, who had been busy packing away her purchases into the fridge and cupboards, turned to face Lucy, her face serious.

'I just needed to ask you if you knew or recognised this woman.' She passed her a picture of a living and breathing Sandy Kilburn which Col had taken off Facebook.

She took it, studying it for some time then shook her head. 'No, sorry. I can't say that I recognise her. Should I?'

'Not really, I was hoping she might have been a volunteer at the church or a parishioner.'

Jan glanced down at it again then passed it back, shaking her head. 'Sorry I can't help you, but David might know of her. You can ask him later; he'll be back for his tea about six.'

'Thanks, I'll do that. What time does the street helper's thing start?'

She laughed. 'You mean Street Saviours? We normally meet in the hall between ten and eleven on the night it's open, get the tea urns on and the grill hot for the bacon. It's quite an entertaining night if you can put up with drunks and the chance they might be sick on you. I didn't think it was going to work at first and I told David that, but he didn't listen. He never does, always thinks he knows best. Well this time he was right; the first few times we had the odd person. Now it gets quite busy. If you're not doing anything we could do with some extra volunteers to help out. Especially now we're down a volunteer. Poor Margaret was such a good help, so kind to the drunks and patient with them. I did ask David if we shouldn't open this week, you know as a mark of respect to Margaret. Do you know what his answer was? He said that we owed it to Margaret to carry on, it's what she would have wanted.'

Lucy tried not to grimace. She couldn't think of anything worse than volunteering for Street Saviours. It was bad enough dealing with the aftermath of the pissed-up arguments and domestics on a Sunday morning and getting paid for it. There was no chance she'd do it for free on her nights off. Her spare time was very precious, not to mention she was in the middle of two massive murder cases. She also had a feeling Margaret wouldn't give a shit whether they opened or not.

'I can't, it would be too much with work. Sorry, did Margaret help out a lot then?'

'She did, bless her, in fact she loved it. She had a bit of a soft spot for the young lasses who'd get so drunk they couldn't tell you their names or where they lived to get them a taxi home. She'd sit with them, hold their hands and talk to them.' Her eyes filled with tears that she tried to blink away.

'Sorry to have upset you. I'll leave you to it. I need to speak to David. Can you ask him to call me when he gets in? I can always nip back and then that's another box ticked off my list.'

'I will.'

Lucy handed her a business card.

She walked back to her car wondering if she should leave it and speak to him later on. Jan didn't seem as angry when she was on her own, maybe she was being protective of her man when they were together. This made Lucy smile to herself as she got back into her car. She'd never thought that it might not be appropriate when she turned up at crime scenes in her little Fiat, who even thought like that? Lucy was gutted that tonight was Mattie's last shift before his holidays. She was going to have to ask Browning to help her out more, but she wasn't going to take him to the church hall tonight; she wanted to speak to David there and put him on the spot – just to let him know she was wanting to speak to him, to make him sweat a little. She didn't need Browning, and neither did she want him complaining about not getting paid for working overtime and huffing and chuffing at the drunks.

CHAPTER THIRTY-SIX

Ellie knocked on the door to the semi and smiled as she heard a loud screech from inside and pounding footsteps come running towards it. The door opened and Bella grinned at her. 'I thought you were never coming; Mamma is in the shower. Daddy is coming now.'

'Bella, who's at the door? You know never to open it unless someone is with you, what have we told you about talking to strangers?'

'It's okay, it's Ellie. She's babysitting me so that doesn't count because I know her and she's my friend.'

The door opened wide, and the dark-haired, handsome guy who Ellie assumed was Bella's dad smiled at her.

'Sorry, I didn't know you were coming, Nat forgot to tell me. Please come in. I'm Tony and you are?'

He held his hand out, and feeling stupid she took it and shook it.

'Ellie, I said I'd babysit while Natalia helped out at the church tonight.'

A dark frown crossed his face. 'She never said she was going there tonight, I'm sorry. I have to go, but make yourself at home. Phone numbers for us both are on the fridge if you need them. Good luck with this one, she'll talk your head off all night. When your ears are aching send her to bed.' He bent down, kissing his daughter on the forehead.

'Be a good girl for Ellie.'

He went out of the front door, and Bella grabbed her hand, pulling her along to the living room where it looked like a toy shop had exploded all over the floor.

Natalia came down and smiled to see the teenage girl playing Barbies with her daughter.

'I'm sorry, she was so excited you were coming I had to say she could stay up for an hour. I hope you didn't mind?'

'Course not. Oh Natalia, my mum, who is always on duty and never gives it a rest, wants you to have her phone number, in case there's a problem and you can't get home or something.' Ellie stood up and dug out the scrap of paper she'd written her mum's number on.

Smiling, Natalia took it from her and pushed it into her pocket.

'What do you mean she's *always on duty*?'

'She's a police detective; when she's not at work she still thinks she is. She's crazy about catching the bad guys. Sometimes, well actually all the time, she's a bit overprotective.'

'I never knew that she worked for the police, what an exciting job she must have. I think if I saw what your mum saw I would be the same. I'll probably be like that when Bella's older anyway. No matter how old your kids get, you'll always be our kids and we have the right to drive you mad. Your mum sounds like a very wise woman.'

Ellie shrugged. 'Yeah, don't let her hear you say that. She's always telling me she knows better, and I should listen to her more.'

'Where is she tonight?'

'Dunno, probably at work. She works late all the time, that's why my dad got so fed up with her and left.'

Realising she'd probably said far too much, she shut up; if her mum found out she was telling her private business to anyone she'd go mad.

Natalia smiled. 'There are plenty of snacks in the kitchen and there's a huge dish of lasagne if you're hungry in the fridge. The downside to owning an Italian restaurant is that you eat Italian leftovers for ever. It's not good to your waistline when you have a passion for pasta.' She laughed and patted her slender tummy.

'I'll be home by midnight, I'm tired tonight. I said I'd help for a couple of hours because they're a bit short of volunteers. Any problems ring me. Bella, bed by nine, you have to do what Ellie tells you, okay?'

Bella nodded. 'Yes, Mamma.'

'Good girl. See you both later.'

The front door closed, and Bella stared at Ellie. 'I'm hungry, can we have some nachos?'

'You can have what you want, kid, if it's in the cupboard.'

They went into the kitchen and began to prepare a huge dish of nachos; Bella poured the salsa and almost a whole packet of mozzarella onto the tortilla chips. Ellie decided that babysitting for a kid with such good taste in junk food might just be the best job in the whole of Brooklyn Bay.

CHAPTER THIRTY-SEVEN

By the time Lucy got back to the station Mattie had long gone and she felt more than a little envious that he was going to be doing nothing more than lie on a golden beach soaking up the sun. She was going to book a holiday for her and Ellie as soon as she had this killer in custody, a break would do them both good. Forget about horrific murders, cheating husbands and how her life had turned to shit overnight.

Browning, despite his grumpiness and reluctance to do anything at more than a snail's pace, was still at his desk. He looked up at her. 'It's like a sinking ship in here today, there's only us two left. Do you need anything doing, Lucy, or are you going to call it a day?'

'I don't think there's anything now; did the PCSOs finish the house-to-house enquiries around Basterfield House do you know?'

'They did and believe it or not nobody heard anything. There are a couple of houses with private CCTV systems, and they've been checked for footage. They only cover the front of the properties but there's nothing of any note on them either.'

'One day in the not-too-distant future, we'll get a break. Someone will have a camera which captures the whole, terrible thing in glorious technicolour with the assailant's face as clear as day on it.'

He laughed. 'One day we will, not sure which year though so don't go holding your breath. I see the golden boy is off to Greece, lucky bugger.'

Lucy nodded. 'He is indeed. I think I'm going to call it a day, you should too. I'm hoping to bring David Collins in tomorrow, so it might be a long day.'

'The vicar?'

'Yes.'

'Makes sense, religious murders; who else is there to blame but the vicar?' He winked at her.

'It's a start, have you met him?'

'Not had that pleasure yet.'

'That gives you something to look forward to tomorrow then.'

She went into her office to get the file she'd copied. Ellie was babysitting then sleeping at George's. That meant she could sit down with a glass of wine, finish the left-over pizza, study the case files up to now and have a snooze until it was time to go back out and question the volunteers at the church hall about Sandy.

Lucy groaned when her alarm finally penetrated the deep sleep she was in. Turning it off she wondered if she shouldn't just leave it until tomorrow. Get a list of the volunteers and go and interview them at home. Pulling the fluffy throw up to her chin, she'd almost talked herself into it, when she realised that it would waste hours trying to chase them up. She had no idea where they lived, if they worked, or what the hell they got up to in their own time. It would be far easier to speak to as many as possible tonight and then, fingers crossed, there would only be a few to follow up on tomorrow. Her eyes opened wide, and she pushed herself up off the sofa. Picking up the plate and empty wine glass off the coffee table she took them in the kitchen and went upstairs to freshen up.

Dressed all in black she parked the unmarked car that she'd gone to the station to swap with her own across the road from the church hall. This way she looked far less obvious, and if she wanted to follow David for any particular reason she wouldn't stand out. She had a hunch there was something going on with him. It was tough; this was much harder than she'd ever imagined her first case as lead investigator would ever be. She felt terrible for Tom and the horrific way he'd found out his mum had been murdered. Mattie had escaped on holiday leaving her here on her own, and Lucy wasn't afraid to admit, at least to herself, that she was terrified it was all going to shit. They had nothing on Sandy's killer apart from the possible connecting cat hairs. And Mattie would be furious with her, she knew. Here on her own, this late at night with no backup. It was just as well he wouldn't know, so it didn't matter; at least she'd had the common sense to pick up her radio, cuffs and CS gas, just in case.

People were beginning to trickle into the church hall, mainly women, which didn't really surprise her. A couple of guys had gone in earlier, but no more since then. She recognised Natalia, who had walked in and immediately been ambushed by the vicar. He was a letch, at the very least, although that wasn't really an arrestable offence, unfortunately. Ten more minutes and she'd make her entrance, piss him off a little. Probably piss his wife off a lot more if she thought she was becoming a nuisance. But they knew very little about Sandy; her Facebook account was pretty run-of-the-mill, she had a few friends, none of them local. She lived on her own in a small flat on Bridlington Court; her neighbours said they'd only just moved in so didn't know her. So it was crucial she got as much information about her as she could from the volunteers: she needed someone to recognise her so she could get some kind of background information on her lifestyle. Failing that, she was going to have to put a request for information about her in the press, which she'd rather not unless she had to. It would mean losing more members of her team to answer the phone calls and follow up on enquiries which would more than likely have no value to the case whatsoever.

He was watching the church hall waiting to see how many turned up to tonight's God squad meeting. He despised them, pretending to be nice humans when most of them were sinners, not saints. His fists kept clenching, and his brain didn't seem as clear tonight, it was as if his thoughts were having to swim through murky water to form. He felt as if he needed to do something only he wasn't sure what. He wanted the vicar. But he couldn't go in there because he didn't know how he'd react. It had taken him a while to realise he was the same one from when he was a kid, the creep who liked to fuck whores in the church. He doubted that he'd changed over the years and would bet anything that he still fucked whores. He couldn't blame him when he looked at his wife though. She scowled most of the time, making her look as though she was in a permanently foul mood.

About to get out of his car, he stopped when he saw the woman a couple of cars ahead of him get out of hers and cross the road. He knew her, but couldn't place her. Where had he seen her? This made him even angrier because usually his memory was impeccable and never let him down. She had something in her hand that she was trying to shove into her trouser pocket. He leant closer; *she's a fucking pig, that's a police radio.* He wondered what she was doing there. His paranoia kicking in, he turned the key and drove away, wondering why a copper was going into the God squad and why she wasn't in uniform; *what was she doing on her own?* The plain-clothes coppers he saw were always in twos. What was going on? His heart began to race even faster, he needed to get away from here now. She might be onto him; she might know that he was waiting for the vicar to come out.

He drove off, and parked a few streets away and got out of his car. He needed fresh air to clear his head. He also needed to know what was happening, so he began to walk back towards the church hall. He would find a dark corner to hide in and watch her, needing to see what she was doing on his territory. If he had to take her out, he would, without a second thought. There was no way she was jeopardising everything he'd worked hard for.

CHAPTER THIRTY-EIGHT

November 1994

He didn't like living in the children's home very much, but he supposed it could have been a lot worse. He did like where it was situated on the outskirts of Manchester, a huge house with its own secluded gardens and small woods at the bottom. He had his own little pet cemetery in the woods where he spent a lot of his time. It was his secret place; it was where he buried the cats, chickens, and rabbits that he'd killed. He enjoyed watching them bleed to death when he'd cut their throats; however, he could only kill them when he knew he could get back inside the house without getting caught covered in blood. Sometimes it got messy; if he had to he'd break their necks instead. It wasn't as much fun though.

He was getting ready to sneak outside when he heard Angela calling his name. He was always respectful and kind to the staff. It wasn't their fault he was here, and he didn't want them to think he was anything other than normal. He left his room and ran downstairs to see what she wanted. Standing either side of her were two men in suits, and he knew they were either social workers or coppers. His stomach dropped and he wondered if he was being moved from here. Well if he was, he wasn't going without a fight. He smiled at Angela, and she reached out to take hold of his arm.

'Come on, sweets, these police detectives need to talk to you. We'll go into my office.'

His blood ran cold and he wanted to pee so bad, his mouth was dry. How did they know it was him? Had he left some kind of evidence behind? The wave of nausea that filled his stomach made the colour drain from his face, and a voice inside his head whispered *don't freak out, act normal.*

He followed her inside the office; the coppers followed him. She pointed to the chair by the desk and told them to sit on the sofa opposite. Angela perched herself on the desk next to him, and he smiled at her.

'I'm afraid they have some bad news for you, pet, but I'll let them tell you. Is that okay?'

She had hold of his hand. Normally he would have shrugged it away. This time he let her hold it; he could feel her soft, delicate fingers entwined with his and he liked it. He also wondered what it would be like to crush them between his much bigger hands, snapping her fingers one at a time.

'I'm Detective Peters and this is Detective Andrews, I'm afraid we have some very bad news about your father. He was found dead this morning by the vicar who said he hadn't seen him around for some time. He was concerned for him and went to pay him a visit.'

He wondered how he should react; shocked was probably the best way to go. Lifting his hand to his mouth he shook his head. 'Dead? How? What did he die of?'

The men looked at each other and then at Angela, who nodded. 'I'm a big believer that honesty is the best policy, there is no point trying to sugar coat it, is there? He needs to know.'

It was Peters who nodded in agreement. 'We believe he was murdered. His body has probably been there a couple of days judging by the decomposition.'

'But why, who would want to kill him?'

'That's what we have to find out. Don't worry, we will find who did this to him. I need to ask you some questions if that's okay, son. I know this is probably all a bit of a shock for you, so take your time and think very carefully.'

'Okay.'

'When was the last time you saw your dad?'

He shrugged. 'I think it was about four years ago, when he came to the vicarage I was stopping at one night. Pissed up, demanding to see me, but Vincent, the vicar, didn't let him in, and he was shouting and threatening him. Vincent had to ring for you lot, and they dragged him off in the back of a van.'

'And you haven't seen him since?'

He shook his head. 'No, I didn't want to. He used to hit me and my mum before she died.'

Angela squeezed his hand. 'I'm afraid he wasn't a very nice man, but surely you have all that on record?'

'We do and no, he wasn't. Have you been back to see him recently or had any chance meetings with him? We understand if you have and it brought back a lot of bad memories; it can't have been very easy living in that house, never knowing what was going to happen next. It must have been horrible not being able to protect your mum.'

'No, I hate him. Why would I want to see him again? I'm not even sorry that he's dead. When you find out who did it tell them thank you from me. He ruined my life and killed my mum.' A loud sob escaped his chest, and he buried his head into his hands to hide the tears.

'I think that's enough now. If you need anything else you can ring me, and we'll do this once he's had time to process everything you've just told him.'

Peters nodded. 'Yes, of course. Thank you.'

Angela showed them out of the front door, and he kept his face buried in his hands; he couldn't stop the grin that filled his face. When she came back into the office and hugged him, he let her. She smelt nice, and he could feel her breasts pushing against his chest as he pretended to sob. When he finally broke away he had to put his hands in front of his trousers to hide his erection. Excusing himself he ran back to his room, slamming the door for effect. Throwing himself onto his bed, he buried his head into his pillow, stifling the laughter that was trying to erupt. Even if he said so himself, that was quite a performance.

CHAPTER THIRTY-NINE

David, who was laughing with Natalia, stopped and stared in horror at Lucy as she walked into the hall. He strode over to her, grabbing her elbow and steering her to one side.

'Jan said you wanted to speak to me; she didn't say it was in public. Can this not wait until tomorrow?'

Lucy shrugged her arm away from his grasp, anger threatening to fill her veins at the fact that he'd dared to touch her like that. 'Actually, I want to speak to all the volunteers, not just you.' Pulling the mortuary headshot of Sandy from the inside of her coat pocket she passed it to him and watched his face, hoping the horror of what he was looking at would give her the reaction she wanted.

'Do you know her, recognise her?'

He took it from her and stared at it. 'Is she, you know?'

'Dead? Yes, very much so. Has she ever volunteered here? Maybe she's been here when she was drunk for some of your help. I need you to think because it's very important.'

His head shook from side to side. 'I don't think so, she definitely hasn't been a volunteer. I know all of those, though I can't say if she's been here when she was drunk because I imagine she looked a little different when she was breathing.'

Lucy reached into her pocket, pulling the living, breathing image of Sandy out, and passed it to him.

'No, I definitely don't know her, sorry. I wish I could help.'

She took them both from him. 'Thank you, I'll just ask the others while I'm here. I don't expect you can remember every drunk who sets foot through the doors. I know I wouldn't be able to. One of the volunteers might know.'

'If you insist, but please don't upset them by showing them the picture of her you showed me first. These are nice, kind, gentle people. I don't want them upset when they're already grieving for Margaret.'

'I do insist; my team can't spare the man hours by interviewing them all at home, but of course I'm not going to purposely upset them. I do have a job to do though, and if they find it hard answering my questions then there's not much I can do about that. You want me to find Margaret's killer, don't you? This could be related. I must also insist that you give me a list of the volunteers who normally help but who aren't here tonight. I need to speak to them all.'

He walked off in the direction of the kitchen, where, no doubt, Jan was, and she began to introduce herself to the various volunteers dotted around the hall. None of them recognised Sandy, and Lucy could feel herself getting more despondent by the minute. She'd been sure she'd have found a connection between the murder victims and the work in the church hall.

Natalia walked out from the kitchen and smiled at her.

'Ellie's mum?'

Lucy nodded, smiling back. 'Guilty as charged.'

'Thank you so much for letting her babysit Bella, she's such a lovely girl. I'll take her home after I've done a couple of hours here. Tony should be home by then.'

'That's nice to hear, and you're welcome. I suppose she's told you we don't always see eye to eye and that I'm a right old dragon.'

'No, not at all. Tell me one teenager who isn't a nightmare for their own parents. I was horrible to mine.'

Lucy warmed to the woman in front of her. She was nice and very diplomatic. She could understand why her daughter would like her, so that made her one of the good guys in Lucy's books. There weren't many people she liked knowing so little about them.

'What brings you here?'

Lucy passed her the 'nice' photo. 'I'm working; I desperately need to know if this woman has ever volunteered here or was ever here for help.'

Natalia studied the photo. 'I'm not sure, she kind of looks familiar, but I couldn't say. We get so many and usually they're not in the best of states, as you can imagine. People look completely different when they're dressed up to go out than they do every day. Sorry.' She passed it back, and Lucy smiled.

'Don't be sorry, it's not your fault. I guess I was clutching at straws. Thank you.' She turned to walk away to find Jan, to see if she had a list of absent volunteers for her, when she heard Natalia shout.

'Lucy, can I have another look?'

Lucy passed the photograph back, and also passed her the mortuary one. Natalia studied them both, looking from one to the other. 'I think I do recognise her, though her hair is normally bigger and curly like they used to wear back in the eighties. She always has big plastic button earrings in. I don't know if you're old enough to remember, but back in the day they always wore these huge, brightly coloured earrings. She isn't wearing the earrings in these photos, and her hair isn't as bouncy. I wonder where her earrings are? She's been in a couple of times, always plastered. Loud and funny, but I get the impression she's a big drinker.'

Lucy wanted to kiss the woman in front of her. 'You're sure?'

'Definitely, I thought I recognised her. If she'd had the earrings in I'd have known straight away; they must be antiques by now. She's the only woman I've ever seen still wearing them.'

'Do you keep records of the users who come in here?'

Natalia shook her head. 'No, it's hard enough to get a name or an address for a taxi to take them home. We don't usually bother.'

'It's okay, thank you so much. You've been very helpful.'

'You're very welcome.'

Lucy went to the kitchen, where Jan and David were having the world's quietest argument.

'Sorry, am I interrupting?'

'No, what do you want now?'

Jan was back to her normally feisty self. 'Do you have that list of volunteers who aren't here?'

She tutted. 'Why didn't you ask me that this afternoon? I could have got you the complete list and saved you the bother of coming here tonight, upsetting everyone and being a pain.'

'I'm here to try and find out who would want to murder an innocent old woman, or had you forgotten about Margaret? Now if you could get me the list I can leave you all in peace.'

Lucy folded her arms and smiled at Jan, who was clutching a pair of tongs in her hands as if they were an offensive weapon. If being married to a vicar made you this angry and defensive, she'd get a divorce. The woman turned into a different person whenever she was in close proximity to her husband, and it wasn't as if he was that good-looking. Lucy wondered why she acted this way. Slamming the tongs onto the worktop, Jan stormed off, returning five minutes later with a printed sheet of paper that she thrust into Lucy's hands.

'These are the names and addresses of all the volunteers. I've ticked off the ones who are here tonight, so you don't go bothering them again tomorrow when they're at home.'

'Thank you, that's very kind of you. Have a nice evening.'

Trying not to smile at the woman and upset her even more, Lucy headed towards the doors, where the first of the night's casualties was being led in, the woman complaining loudly that she felt sick and didn't know why because she'd only had one bottle of wine. David came into sight carrying a red plastic bucket which he thrust under her nose while grimacing. Lucy wondered if he actually enjoyed this or if it was all some kind of show. He didn't take his eyes off her, and she didn't let him know it bothered her. She was glad to be out of there before the girl began to puke her guts up – there were far better ways to spend your nights than holding sick buckets for complete strangers. Thanks to Natalia, at least she knew that Sandy had been here a few times. She had something to build upon now, and God knew she needed to catch a break with this case.

CHAPTER FORTY

The briefing room didn't seem the same without Tom or Mattie there, both of them an integral part of her team and her closest allies; Lucy checked the rest of her staff were all present.

'Right, last night I had a bit of success trying to find out if Sandy Kilburn had ever accessed the Street Saviours. One of the volunteers recognised her after some time; she said whenever she saw her she always had huge plastic, brightly coloured button earrings in. When she was booked into the mortuary, I need to know if she had earrings with her. They weren't on her body; I just want it double-checking. I'm pretty sure the answer is no, so if not where are they? The same for Margaret Crowe. I spoke to Tom and he told me that his mum always wore a gold chain with a small crucifix around her neck. I don't recall seeing one on her at the scene or during the post-mortem, so someone check with CSI if they found one on a sweep of the crime scene. If not I have a feeling that our killer is taking trophies away from the scenes. As terrible as it sounds, it would be pretty good for the investigation, because when we identify who he is, if the earrings and necklace are in his property when we search it, then we will have him bang to rights.'

'When we find him,' Rachel muttered.

'We'll find him, have a bit of faith. I'm not denying this isn't a difficult case, because it is. We've had two brutal murders with no motive that we know about yet. I do believe they're linked, and Catherine should be able to give us the hard evidence to confirm this theory. I want to concentrate on David Collins today; Browning and

Rachel, you can have first watch. Let's see what he gets up to. He told his wife he was out visiting parishioners yesterday afternoon. I want to know if he was, but if he wasn't, then where was he? Up to now we have a volunteer and a service user dead, and both women have connections to his church. Both murders have a religious element to them, too. Collins swore blind he didn't recognise Sandy, but if she's been there and she was as loud as Natalia said she was, then I think he's lying. I'm also not convinced by his wife's alibi. I get the impression she would lie to stick up for him, despite them having what looks like a strained relationship. You know how it is, some people don't believe their loved ones can be capable of such violence, when we know the bitter truth. It seems that Sandy liked a drink, so can we have the pubs nearest to her home address checked to see if anyone knew her or if she was a regular in any of them? Browning and Rachel, if you do the day shift I'll take over later on. Col, you concentrate on the pubs. Hopefully by the end of the day we should be in a much better position to bring him in for questioning.' She was already feeling more positive about the cases.

Her phone rang and she answered it.

'Good morning, Lucy, I have some interesting results for you. Do you want them over the phone or would you like to meet me at my office in ten minutes?'

'Morning, Catherine, I'll come to you. I have no one to make my coffee.'

The pathologist laughed. 'Good job you have me to look after you then. See you soon.' Lucy hung up and turned to Browning. 'I'm going to see Catherine Maxwell, I'll ring you later and see where you are. Be careful and try not to let him know we're watching him. Or he might go to ground.'

Catherine's office was situated along the corridor before the mortuary, and Lucy could smell the fresh coffee as soon as she walked through the double doors into the corridor. Knocking on her door, she waited for her to open it. Lucy did a double-take; how did she manage to look so damn glamorous this early in the morning?

'Wow, you look amazing.'

Catherine laughed. Her cheeks flushed pink. 'Lucy, this is why I love working with you. You always say the nicest things. Thank you, I'm in court this afternoon and have no pms this morning. I thought I'd make an effort. You, my friend, look tired, did you sleep last night or the night before?'

She shrugged. 'I'll sleep when I catch the bastard who is murdering the women in this town.'

'You work too hard; I don't know how many times I have to tell you this.'

Catherine poured a large mug of filter coffee, added some fresh cream and passed it to her.

'It's not a vanilla latte, but it's good quality caffeine.'

She took a sip. 'It's beautiful, that's what it is. So what have you got for me? Please say you have a DNA match for someone on the system that I can go and arrest right now before anyone else has to die.'

'Ah, I wish I did. It would be nice to catch a break now and again, wouldn't it? Those television shows make it look all too easy, even I get annoyed with myself because I'm not solving the cases as fast as they do.'

Lucy nodded. 'A girl's got to dream.'

'They certainly have. Now for something different; the hairs collected off both victims were cat hairs; you remember the hairs recovered from Sandy Kilburn's nightie? I've sent those along with the cat hairs found on Margaret Crowe to an old university colleague of mine at Leicester. He works on the cat DNA database in the forensic science department. Do you remember the groundbreaking case of David Guy back in 2012?'

'No, was it local?'

'No, this was in Hampshire. His dismembered body was found wrapped in a curtain which contained eight cat hairs. The suspect had a cat called Tinker. The cat hairs were sent to California for analysis, and the mitochondrial results showed there was a genetic match with the suspect's cat, and no matches among the 493 cats on the American cat database. They also created a UK cat database, using a random sampling of 152 cats, to show how rare it was that the cat DNA matched the hairs found in the curtain, as cat DNA has fewer variants than human DNA, and is not as accurate as a genetic marker.'

'I had no idea.'

'Well this is where it gets interesting for you. The cat hairs taken from the clothing of both victims have an identical genetic make-up, which would appear to confirm it's the same killer.'

'Or both victims came into contact with the same cat.'

'Possibly, but I think it's unlikely. The hairs taken from Margaret's cat are not a match. So, when you find your man or woman, if he has a cat, which I'm pretty sure he has or someone very close to him has, we can send a sample off for testing against the hairs we already have, and if they match you'll be able to link him or her to both crime scenes and the victims' bodies. Case closed.'

Lucy tried to process the information. 'Wow, that's clever stuff. There's only one problem with it, I just need to find my killer. Thank you, it helps a lot, I think.'

'You know me, I've always been a geek. Hopefully you'll catch a break soon and when you do this will definitely help you to secure a conviction. It's all added evidence that places him at the crime scenes.'

She finished her coffee and stood up. 'I'm sure it will. Good luck in court.'

Lucy left feeling hopeful; things were coming together in a roundabout way.

CHAPTER FORTY-ONE

Browning was eating his third sausage roll, while Rachel was still nibbling away at the first half of her cheese and tomato sandwich.

'Here we go, he's finally come out to play.' He pointed his grease-stained finger at the man leaving the vicarage.

'Thank God, my arse is going numb sitting here.' Stuffing her sandwich back in the box she turned the engine on.

'Erm, Rachel, he's on foot. Can't exactly follow him in a car, can we? It might look a bit too obvious.'

'Oh, yeah, sorry. I didn't think of that. Go on then, you can follow him and radio me when you want picking up.'

He looked at her. 'Sod that, age over beauty. You're fitter than I am, my knee's giving me a bit of gip. You follow, and I'll pick you up.' If he had to listen to Rachel moan about her boyfriend's lack of domestic skills and what to wear on Saturday night much longer he might have committed murder by sausage roll when he shoved his last one down her throat to choke her.

She got out of the car muttering under her breath, and he grinned. He didn't care; she looked a lot less obvious walking behind him talking on her phone than he would. He waited for her to faff around, then she swung her bag over her shoulder and walked off, sticking two fingers up behind her back for him to see. It made him laugh out loud. He had no idea what the boss was on; he didn't think the vicar had the balls for the killings – although sometimes people surprised you when you least expected it. She might be right for all he knew. She had been in the past, and at least they were doing something productive.

The vicar headed the short walk into town, towards the promenade. Rachel wished she'd wore her trainers today instead of the
short heels. Bloody Browning was a lazy pig. He had flat shoes
on, he'd have been able to walk better than she could if he hadn't
just consumed half of Greggs. The vicar was in a hurry, walking
faster than she could. It didn't matter, there weren't many people
around and he wasn't hard to pick out from the crowd with his
black shirt; he'd removed the dog collar when he got out of his
street, stuffing it into his pocket, and then he'd carried on walking
until he reached the flats on Bridlington Court. This was a bit out
of his way. Surely he didn't have any parishioners that lived here?
These flats were well known for being full of druggies, alcoholics,
and prostitutes or at least unofficial prostitutes.

Pulling out her phone, she began an imaginary conversation
when he stopped sooner than she'd expected and knocked on a
ground floor flat. He turned around scanning the area and looked
at her. She ignored him, talking loudly into her phone.

'I'm here now, babes, what number did you say? I forgot. I've
got something to cheer you up.'

The flat door opened, and he stepped inside. It shut quickly
behind him.

'Bridlington Court; get your arse here now. I'm freezing, and
my feet are bloody killing.'

When the car pulled into the street, she jumped inside. 'He's
in that flat, number twenty. He clocked me before he went in, but
didn't take any notice. You better park down there so he can't see
us when he comes out.'

Browning did as he was told, parking behind a battered old
Corsa with one wheel missing. Rachel got her radio out and asked
the control room for an address check. Browning was on the phone
to Lucy.

'Boss, he's gone into 20 Bridlington Court. Didn't Sandy Kilburn
live along here?'

'Yes, number thirty-three. I'm only around the corner, I'll be there in a minute. What's he doing there? It's a bit out of his jurisdiction. Can you go and peek through the windows, knock on the door and pretend you've got the wrong address? I'm on my way.'

Rachel shrugged. 'Whatever she said, I'm not doing it; I had to follow him here, and I'm done for the day. Now it's your turn.'

He got out of the car and began to stroll up the street. He knocked on a couple of doors away from the flat Collins had gone into. The blue door opened a crack, and Browning lifted his sleeve to cover his nose.

'Police, it's nothing to worry about just doing some enquiries. There was an incident in the street last night, did you hear or see anything?'

The man who reeked of stale, cheap booze and cigarettes shook his head then slammed his door shut. Browning continued knocking on doors until he reached number twenty, where he walked past the window; the blinds were almost shut. He pressed his face as near to the glass as he could, then stepped away as Lucy whispered in his ear. 'What's going on?'

He turned to her, red-faced. 'I don't know if you want to know, boss.'

Stepping aside to let her take a peek, he heard her mutter 'oh fuck.'

'Yes, what are we going to do?'

She stepped towards the front door and hammered on it, giving it her best open-up-it's-the-police knock. There was a lot of scuffling around from inside, and the door opened slightly.

'What the fuck do you want, knocking like that?'

'Police, we need to talk to you about an incident last night.'

'Well I'm busy, you'll have to come back later.'

Lucy put her foot in between the crack of the door. 'I can't, it's urgent. Let me in then you can get back to what you were doing.'

The woman with the bright red lips and see-through negligee opened the door wide, and Browning's eyes almost popped out of his head as his cheeks changed colour. She was naked under the flimsy gown for the whole world to see. She stood there with her arms open wide.

'No fucking respect you lot. I'm minding my own business and you just barge in.'

Lucy pushed past her, ignoring her. Browning stood there wondering where to put his eyes.

'That's it, darling, take a good look. I've got a space after this one, how would you like me to tie you up and whip you? I'll give you a discount for being a public servant.'

He shook his head and walked past, her laughter filling the air behind him.

Lucy was standing in the doorway to the bedroom, her arms crossed shaking her head.

'If it isn't the local pillar of the community. Is this some kind of religious practice, Father, maybe a new kind of confession? I needed to speak to you and look what I find when we're on house-to-house enquiries.'

Browning looked inside to the see the vicar tied to the bed, a rubber ball in his mouth. He was stark naked with red marks all over his body where he'd been hit or beaten.

'Holy shit.'

Lucy nodded. 'Untie him and read him his rights. I'll get a van.'

CHAPTER FORTY-TWO

By the time David Collins had been untied, dressed and handcuffed a police van was waiting outside the flat to transport him to custody.

'I know my rights, you can't do this. It's not illegal to pay for sex, let me go now, do you have any idea what you're doing? My solicitor will wipe the floor with you, fucking useless wankers.'

'Calm down, you'll give yourself a heart attack. You're not being arrested for paying for sex; if you'd listened you'd realise you're being arrested for the unlawful killing of Sandy Kilburn.'

'What the fuck? Who is she, I've never heard of her? You're fucking mad.' But his face which had been beetroot red turned a deathly shade of white as he stared at Lucy.

'I want a lawyer.'

'We'll sort that out in custody. All you have to do is answer some questions, truthfully this time, and we can get it all sorted out.'

Two officers arrived, and she handed him over to them. He was led out of the flat to their waiting van. One of the local drug dealers who was watching with great interest lifted his phone and snapped some photos of the guy getting walked out of slutty Sue's. Posting them on Facebook for the world to see, no doubt, and Lucy knew that within thirty minutes they would be picked up by the local paper.

Browning turned to Lucy as they watched the van drive off. 'I hope we're right.'

'So do I, but at least we can question him now without his wife interrupting or defending him. Clock's ticking, so who wants to interview the lovely lady?'

'Not me, I'm too old to have to stare at that. I almost had a heart attack when she opened the door.'

She turned to Rachel. 'Find out what she knows about him, how often he visits, if she knew Sandy, if he ever visited Sandy. We need to get back and speak to Collins.'

'Yes, boss.'

'Oh, and Rachel, make you sure you let her know how important her cooperation is. If she won't talk, arrest her for obstruction and bring her in.'

Lucy walked into the parade room and breathed a sigh of relief to see most of the task force team sitting around drinking coffee. 'I need you to do a search for me now, if possible, have you got anything on?'

They shook their heads in unison. 'Good, it's at St Aidan's vicarage. I've just arrested the vicar in relation to the Sandy Kilburn case. The main thing I'm looking for is a cat or any evidence of a cat, a pair of big plastic earrings and a gold crucifix. Of course anything that might be of evidential value to a murder will be bloody wonderful as well. If you find me anything of relevance, I'll take you all out for a slap-up meal. It's that important. Oh and I don't know if he'll have had the balls to phone his wife when he's been booked in, but if he hasn't she's a very angry woman, so you might have to use your powers of persuasion to get past her.'

Mitchell, who was the oldest out of them, laughed. 'I'm not in the mood today; I'll just cuff her and throw her in the back of the van for obstruction. Never had to search a vicarage before, Lucy, should be interesting to see what turns up.'

'Well, let's hope it turns out to be worthwhile. A lot depends on it.'

She left them organising themselves and grabbing kit bags. Now it was time to see if Collins had been booked in and a solicitor called. For the first time she wondered if she'd done the right thing:

was he good for it or was she clutching at straws? The fact that he was at the house across the road from Sandy's put him in the same area, and she had a gut feeling he'd lied to her about not recognising the woman when she'd asked him last night. Lucy always trusted her instinct because it had never let her down yet. Surely he would have known who she was if she was as memorable as Natalia said? It was time to find out just how much the friendly local vicar knew.

CHAPTER FORTY-THREE

He read the newspaper headlines on his phone, and didn't know whether to be angry or happy: the police were fucking clueless. He stood up and began pacing up and down, banging his fist against his thigh harder and harder.

'VICAR ARRESTED IN CONNECTION WITH MURDERS.'

This made it all the more interesting because the vicar was next on his list. He studied the photograph of the man in cuffs being led to the waiting van outside the flats. Everyone knew you went there for sex or drugs; it was unlucky for the vicar he was caught having sex so near to that slapper Sandy's flat. He could understand the police's reasoning; he recognised the blonde woman standing outside the flat. It wasn't a very good photo of her, a bit blurry, obviously taken from someone's phone camera. It was definitely her, the copper he'd seen going into the church the other night. If she wasn't in uniform, then she was CID, so she must be the one investigating his crimes. He wondered if she was good enough to catch him. She'd latched onto the religious aspects of his murders and gone for the person who had the most in common with them. He decided she was pretty good, but not that good or it would have been him in handcuffs and not that poor bastard. Now he was going to have to wait until he was released from custody – that might be tomorrow or today if they found nothing incriminating against him. Which they shouldn't; everything she had must be circumstantial. It had to be, because they had the wrong man. The vicar's biggest crime was being a sleazeball, God-loving, sex-addicted hypocrite, which was enough to put him on his hit list but surely not enough to charge him with murder.

The voices in his head were getting louder, and he wondered if he should have stopped taking his medication like that. After all he'd taken it for years and they'd worked, keeping him calm, happy, able to live a relatively normal life. He hadn't killed anyone since he was a teenager, since the day he stamped and bludgeoned his dad to death with his own bible. The desire to kill again had always been there, never really going away. It had just been kept at bay with the tablets. If he hadn't seen that old slag Sandy again it probably wouldn't have happened. Seeing her going about her business, looking the same apart from the wrinkles and slack jaw, had brought it all back to him. The way his father had spent more time with her than his wife, the way he'd beat him and his mum then take her drinking to the pub. He hated her as much as he hated him. It's funny, he thought, he'd lived here most of his life and not once had he walked into her in all these years. Then he'd seen her, drunk, loud and causing a fuss, going into the church hall. The vicar had looked at her in disgust, and he wondered if he remembered it was the same woman he'd screwed inside the church all those years ago. From the look on his face he would have said it was a big old yes. Did he regret it, he wondered? He obviously had a thing for whores. Following him the last few weeks had been quite an eye-opener: he visited the flat opposite Sandy's a couple of times a week. He'd seen him pick up one of the younger, better-looking prostitutes that hung around the pier in his car. Driving her to the back of the wasteland where she'd given him a blow job on the back seat. He'd never used them himself, he didn't need to, but he did like to watch now and again.

Putting the phone down he wondered if he should be paying special attention to the pretty, blonde copper. She hadn't done anything to upset him, as such, but she was likely to be the one to put a stop to all of this and he wasn't sure if he was ready for that. Killing was like an addictive sport, one he'd forgotten how much he enjoyed. Once he'd killed the vicar he might just have to start watching her; if she got too close then she would be next on his list. After the vicar he didn't really have a reason to carry on, but if he did, it would be because he couldn't stop. Tilting his head, he stared at her photograph, wondering what she'd look like hanging upside down from a cross with her throat slit.

CHAPTER FORTY-FOUR

Browning let Lucy leave the custody suite first: the interview hadn't gone very well. Collins's lawyer had stopped them at almost every question. Lucy waited until the heavy door shut and locked behind them, making sure they were out of earshot.

'He's going to walk unless the search has brought up anything.'

'At least we've had the chance to interview him, let him know we're onto him.'

The slight doubt she'd been having earlier was weighing heavy on her mind and she was regretting being so hasty.

'Yeah, well at the moment it looks like the only thing he's guilty of is being addicted to having sex with prostitutes.'

'Can you blame him, given his home life?'

She laughed. 'I don't suppose so. Fuck, I wanted him to break down and confess.'

'You and me both. Come on, we tried. It keeps the public's faith that we're doing something and the top brass from breathing down our necks.'

As they walked into the office, Col threw a printout from the online edition of the local paper at Lucy, who caught it. Her face paled, and she flopped down onto Mattie's empty chair. 'Oh shit, how did they get around to it so fast?'

He shrugged. 'There's always someone with a phone around.'

'But already, Christ, has Mitchell been back?'

The loud footsteps vibrating the spiral staircase answered that question.

'Did you call my name?'

'Please tell me you found a huge, fat, grey cat and a box with my missing jewellery?'

'Sorry, Lucy, it was clean. No cat, no jewellery that you described. There was a stash of some quite unsavoury porn mags in the garage. But there were no bloodstained clothes or objects. His wife went mental by the way. Dougie had to take her to the van and calm her down with his smooth-talking charm. She said she was going to sue you, the force, us and our cocksucking mothers.'

Leaning onto Mattie's desk, she put her head in her hands. 'This is a complete disaster. Thanks.'

He patted her arm. 'You win some, you lose some; if you didn't take the risk you wouldn't get anywhere in this game.'

She looked up at him and smiled. 'I know, thank you. I guess it's back to the drawing board.'

He turned and left, running back down the steps.

Browning looked at her. 'Should we release him?'

'I suppose so, there isn't anything to keep him for, is there? Will you do the honours? Tell him not to go anywhere though. He's not completely off the hook. I better phone the press office and get them to issue a release that he was only helping out with enquiries and that no charges have been made. Oh and please could you drop me off a copy of the interview notes when you've typed them up.'

She stood up; she was going home for a bottle of wine and an early night. This had turned into the worst day ever.

When she drove out through the station gates she was so tired she didn't see the car pull out after her, following at a slow distance. Her head was a mess and she was tired, all she could think about was drowning her sorrows and sleeping. She needed the wine to make her sleep, because after today's cock up, her mind would kick into overdrive the minute she lay down. The doubt swirling around in her head like some grey mist, convincing her that for all her bravado maybe she wasn't ready to take on a case of this magnitude. What were the top brass going to say? Whoever was replacing Tom might push her off it. Her mind had a habit of replaying every single scene from the day until the early hours, just so she could scrutinise her actions and make her feel even worse than she already did. Stopping off at the off-licence she bought herself a couple of bottles of wine, a family size bar of Galaxy, and the biggest bag of chilli Doritos she could find. If she was drinking, she was eating crap as well. God she hoped Ellie wasn't sleeping at hers tonight; she wasn't in the mood for arguing with her. The other day had been a rarity, the teenager was normally sullen and miserable. Snapping at her every comment. Before she set off again, she rang George.

'Can you tell Ellie I'm working late, it's better for her not to come around, please.'

'Is everything okay, Lucy, you don't sound yourself?'

She let out a high-pitched laugh. 'No, everything is not okay. How could you think that? You left me for a younger woman. Work is crap, and I'm beyond tired.' He paused, and she broke the silence. 'I'm fine, it's been a long few days that's all.'

'Do you need to talk?'

Christ she did, Mattie wasn't here to unload her spectacularly crap day onto. George was always such a good listener; she felt the familiar stab of pain in her heart that he was no longer her husband or best friend.

'No, I'm good. Just tired, if you can let Ellie know that would be great.'

She hung up before she got all emotional on him. Why did he have that effect on her? She should hate him for what he'd done to her, yet she couldn't. He was the first man she'd ever really loved and deep down, under all the hurt, she still loved him, and if he came and asked for her forgiveness, as stubborn as she was, she would probably take him back with open arms, and he knew that. Wiping her eyes with her sleeve she drove home, not daring to turn the radio on in case any soppy songs came on – because that would see her sobbing and snivelling for the rest of the night into her wine glass.

When she got home the house was in darkness, and she breathed out a sigh of relief. She loved her daughter but she was in no mood for anyone tonight.

Standing under the steaming hot shower she let the water soothe her aching muscles and her tired mind. When she finally stepped out she had to smother herself in body lotion her skin was so wrinkled. She'd almost finished one bottle of wine and the bar of chocolate; going downstairs in her clean pyjamas she poured the tortilla chips into a huge dish and carried them through into the living room. Placing it on the coffee table next to the almost empty wine bottle, she picked up her glass and finished the last mouthful.

A loud knock on the window made her jump, and she got up wondering who it could be. It was tough if it was work: she was off duty, full stop. She glanced at her phone to make sure there were no missed calls. Crossing the room she peered out through the blinds, but she couldn't see anyone. Maybe the takeaway guy had the wrong house, it happened. Turning to sit down again, a loud hammering started on her front door. Wishing she was dressed and not in a pair of unicorn pyjamas with a towel around her head, she opened the door a little and looked around. She couldn't see anyone and wasn't going outside to check. If those little bastards from a few houses down were playing knock a door run, she'd kneecap them when she got hold of them. She shut the door and was almost back at the sofa when someone pounded on the door again. Pushing her feet into her slippers this time, she strode towards the door and threw it wide open. She looked around, she had no immediate neighbours and no one ever knocked this late.

She walked down the front steps towards the front gate and heard the air whooshing behind her. As she turned, the cricket bat connected with the side of her head, sending an explosion of stars bursting through her mind, and she fell to her knees. The sharp pain and the combination of the wine made her stomach lurch. Opening her eyes to see who the fuck had hit her, Lucy heard an angry scream as the bat hit her again, sending her flying forwards. Dazed she hit the floor and lay there unable to move. Blinking her eyes she saw a short, round figure standing over her.

'You bitch, you've ruined my life. How dare you do that to me? You've made me a laughing stock and I won't have it.'

Lucy tried to fight her off, but her head was bleeding profusely, and her eyes kept trying to close. She lifted her hands to protect herself from further blows and felt the wind knocked out of her as the woman threw herself onto her chest. She tried to push her assailant off but couldn't; she was too heavy, and her lungs were on fire with the sudden pressure that was crushing them.

Then the weight was gone from her chest, and she heard Browning's familiar voice.

'You're under arrest for grievous bodily harm. Lucy, Lucy, can you hear me?'

She tried to say yes; instead, she felt a warm blackness begin to fill her mind as his voice became fuzzy and far away.

CHAPTER FORTY-FIVE

Browning had Jan cuffed and in the back of his car where she was kicking the shit out of the back of his seats. He threw open the door and grabbed her by the scruff of her neck.

'I've never hit a woman in my life, but so help me God if you carry on I'll fucking kill you.'

He slammed the door shut, running back over to Lucy's lifeless figure on the ground. She was out cold and bleeding everywhere. Her face was a mess where the heavy wooden bat had smacked against her, catching her eyebrow and eye, but at least she was breathing, even if she was going to look as if she'd been in a boxing match. He could hear the sirens in the distance and prayed they'd get here quick because he didn't know how much longer he could keep his hands from Jan Collins's throat.

The police van arrived first, and the two officers ran towards him; they took one look at Lucy but he pointed at the car. 'Get her in the back of the van now. I've arrested her for GBH until we find out how serious her injuries are.'

'Is that the DI? Oh God, there's an ambulance on the way. Won't be long?'

A second set of sirens filled the air. Browning, who wasn't one for public shows of affection, was kneeling on the damp grass next to her and had tight hold of Lucy's hand. 'It's okay, Lucy, the ambulance is nearly here. We'll have you sorted out and cleaned up in no time, you're going to be okay, kid.'

He looked up at the sound of the loud slamming doors and breathed a sigh of relief. Standing up he stepped away so the paramedics could work on her. He turned to watch the two officers who were fighting with Jan. They were trying to drag her into the back of the van, but she was kicking off big style. He was about to tell them to pepper spray her when the youngest, who hadn't been in service long, shouted out: 'Fuck this. Calm down, lady, or I'll spray you.'

She did her best to kick him in the shins, so he pulled out the gas canister and aimed for her eyes. This resulted in a barrage of screams and foul language as she launched herself at him.

Browning shook his head. 'She's crazy.'

The spray seemed to do the trick and all the fight left her as her knees sagged, so that they had to drag her the rest of the way to the van, screaming that she was now blind and would sue them all. He ran over to help them throw her into the cage, and the doors were slammed shut. All three of them leant against the back of the van, trying to catch their breath.

'Who is she and why has she battered the DI?'

'That's the vicar's lovely wife. I think she's battered Lucy because we arrested her husband who was tied to a bed at some prostitute's flat this morning.'

'Bloody hell, shouldn't she be full of forgiveness and understanding if she's a vicar's wife? I've had easier fights with men who are six foot and off their heads on steroids.'

'I guess you could say she's having a bad day, maybe she's not feeling the love of the Lord right at this moment in time.'

The paramedics had Lucy on a trolley and were putting it on the lift on the back of the ambulance. He walked over to them.

'Is she going to be okay?'

They shrugged. 'Hopefully; she's got a couple of nasty head wounds that will need stitching.'

'I'll follow you up; I'll just make sure the house is secure.'

He watched the ambulance drive away, glad she'd asked him to drop a copy of Collins' interview notes off. He didn't want to think what could have happened if he hadn't turned up. He went into her house feeling like an intruder. He would be the first to admit he wasn't particularly close to Lucy. They got on okay, but she was a lot younger than him and he had been pissed off when she'd got the promotion to DI and he hadn't. He wouldn't want to see anyone hurt like this though. He saw the empty wine bottle and the full one next to it, along with the untouched bowl of tortilla chips. He couldn't see any sign of a struggle inside the house, so he turned the lights off, picked up her phone from the coffee table and locked the front door. The crime scene was outside on the front lawn.

Another van had turned up, this one with an officer and the duty sergeant.

'What the hell happened here?'

'The vicar's wife lost her shit after we'd arrested him earlier. She must have followed Lucy home and lured her outside where she battered her with that cricket bat.' He pointed to the bloodstained bat which was lying on the grass next to a large puddle of blood.

'Jesus, that's mental. Is Lucy okay?'

Browning shrugged. 'Don't know; she's out cold. I'm going to the hospital. When she wakes up I'll get a first account from her. Have CSI been called out?'

'Yeah, on their way. I can't believe it; in all the years I've been on the force I've never known anything like this.'

'Me either. I'll update you on her condition when I get there; someone needs to contact her next of kin and let them know.'

'I don't know if you're aware – I checked it and she's still got George down. Do you think she'll want him there?'

'Bollocks, I don't know. Leave it for now, I'll see how she is then we can take it from there. Christ what a sorry mess this whole bloody thing is.'

Browning walked to his car shaking his head.

CHAPTER FORTY-SIX

Lucy didn't know where she was, except for the fact that she was lying flat on her back, being driven along the world's bumpiest road and her head felt like her brains had exploded inside her skull. She opened one eye and saw the green uniform of the paramedic who was staring down at her.

'It's okay, we're taking you to hospital. You've got a couple of nasty gashes on your head.'

She tried to talk and found her voice didn't want to make an appearance. Instead she blinked then shut her eyes again. Before long she was being wheeled into the brightly lit accident and emergency department, where the lights hurt her eyes, and she found she couldn't open them both at the same time anyway so squeezed them shut. Then she was on a bed in a cubicle and the paramedics were telling the doctor that she'd come off worst against a cricket bat. It all came back to her; that woman was even angrier than she'd ever imagined. She must have followed her home or got her address from someone. She had wiped her out with the first blow, the dirty fighter. If she'd come at her with her fists, she would have been able to get the better of her. She wondered if Jan was the killer, then remembered the search had brought nothing back from her house. So she was just pissed off with her, then.

The nurse held the curtain back for the doctor to come in. He began to lift her eyelids and shine a torch into them.

'I think we'll get her scanned just to be on the safe side. Lucy, can you hear me?'

She opened her eye.

'We'll get you sent down for a CAT scan to check there's no serious swelling inside your head. Once that's been done, hopefully we can glue your head back together. You'll need to stay in for twenty-four to thirty-six hours so we can monitor you though. Cricket bats are a lot tougher than skulls.'

He smiled, and she wanted to tell him to fuck off. She was well aware of that because she was the one lying here with her brains all turned to mush. Instead she smiled back at him, realising she better not piss him off or she might be here for days and she hated hospitals. He left her to it, and the nurse stepped forward.

'I'm going to try and clean you up, lovey, before you go for the scan. Make you feel a bit better.' The nurse disappeared, and she closed her eyes once more.

A few minutes later the curtain was pushed to one side, and she heard Browning's deep voice.

'That was a close call, how you are doing, Lucy?'

She looked at him. 'Been better, thank you for turning up when you did.'

He shrugged. 'It was nothing, right place at the right time for a change. I had a copy of those notes you asked for and I had a feeling I should check on you; bloody years since I've bothered listening to my gut. Glad that I did. I was only going to drive past your house and post them through the letterbox. I almost had a heart attack when I saw that crazy woman standing over a body on the front lawn with her cricket bat raised above her head. She lost it big style. I think she would have carried on hitting you until… you know.'

Lucy didn't want to know. Over the years she'd imagined the different ways she could die on the job. Death by cricket bat hadn't even been in the running.

'Did you lock my front door?'

He nodded, holding up the keys and her phone. 'Thought you might need these. Is there someone I should contact for you, next of kin? Andrews said George was still down and I wasn't sure if you'd want him here or not.'

'God no, I don't. Thank you, that's another favour I owe you. I'm okay, I don't need him here; they can sort me out and let me go home. I'm not staying any longer than I have to.'

The nurse walked in pushing a trolley with a bowl of water and various cloths on it. 'Sorry, you have to stay overnight. Doctor's orders; I'm going to wipe this excess blood off, so you don't contaminate the scanner too much and then we're going down there. It's your lucky night, it isn't busy at the moment. Everyone's in here with sprains and breaks for a change.'

'Are you up to giving me a first account?'

Lucy nodded then immediately regretted it. She began to relate the last hour to him, as the nurse continued cleaning the wounds and never said a word. When she'd finished, he closed his notebook.

'Do you want me to wait here with you?'

'No, thanks. I've taken up enough of your time. I'm fine on my own.'

'You're sure, I don't mind. The wife has gone to bingo, so I don't need to rush back.'

'No, there's no point in you hanging around. Thanks though.' Lucy was touched by the concern he was showing her. It had been a while since anyone had been so kind. Her eyes threatened to fill with tears.

'If you're sure.'

A porter appeared ready to wheel her down to the X-ray department, and she waved her hand at him. Then closed her eyes, the movement made her stomach lurch and she'd had enough of talking.

CHAPTER FORTY-SEVEN

The officer walked him from the custody suite to the glass door at the side of the building and opened it for him.

'Are you sure you have a lift because we can sort you one out? It's no problem.'

'I am, you lot have done enough damage. The last thing I need is to be dropped off at home in a police van. I'll phone my wife. She'll be here in a few minutes.'

The door shut behind him and he inhaled the cold, salty sea air. His stomach was a mess; he had the worst indigestion thanks to the rank microwave chilli con carne they'd given him an hour ago. He didn't know whether he would be better not ringing Jan. Right now seeing if the Travelodge had a spare room for the night seemed like the better option. How was he going to face her? All these years he'd put up with her for appearance's sake because he knew he could go and visit some hooker to satisfy his needs. Something his wife had never been able to do even before they'd got married.

He began the long walk back to the vicarage; the fresh air would do him good. He could have a think about his predicament on the way home. A police van drove past him, loud bangs and thumps coming from inside the back of the cage. He wondered who it was inside, they were certainly angry. He'd been mad on the way here, too, but not mad enough to make such a racket. His life as he knew it was now in tatters, and he walked with his head down against the sea breeze. It was certainly freezing cold tonight; if he'd known how today was going to end he'd have brought a jacket with him.

His dog collar was tucked into his pocket, along with the silver crucifix he usually wore. In all his life he'd never imagined that he'd be doing the walk of shame.

A car turned the corner and slowed down, the driver taking a long look at him. Then it sped off, and he wondered if it was someone he knew. Although he didn't know if he knew anyone who drove such a flashy Merc. *Dear Lord, don't let it be the press.* He walked faster, oblivious to the fact that his face had already been plastered on the front page of tonight's headlines. If he thought his life had turned to shit when he'd been led out of that flat in handcuffs this morning, it was about to get a whole lot worse. He carried on walking as fast as he could, deciding to go home and face his wife. He didn't have any money on him for a hotel and there was no point in postponing the inevitable. Better to get it over with; at least with a bit of luck she'd fuck off and leave him for good this time. He'd rather be alone than listen to her rub his mistakes in his face every single day for the rest of his life, like he knew she would. Then there was the church and his loyal parishioners – he'd let them down; the archbishop would probably find out. He supposed he should be lucky he'd managed to keep up the façade for this long.

Half an hour later, he was almost home. He'd expected the lights to be on, but the vicarage was in darkness. As he got closer he wondered if Jan had drowned her sorrows and gone to bed. He hoped that she had. At least he could sleep on the sofa before having to face her. Everything would be better in the morning, it always was. Whenever he'd spoken to people with suicidal thoughts, he'd always stressed to them that tomorrow was another day. What might seem like the end of your world right now, after a sleep and a fresh new morning, well it wouldn't seem so bad. The only trouble was now that he was in that position, he wasn't too sure if he was right.

He pulled the front door key from his pocket, letting himself in. The house was cold, that wasn't like Jan. She had the heating on whether it was summer or winter. He kicked off his shoes and realised he needed to shower, feeling dirty after his stop in the cells. He was going to have to go upstairs whether he wanted to face her or not because the bathroom was up there. He didn't lock the door behind him like he usually would, because he was too worried about facing his wife and her wrath. She wasn't above hitting him, not that she did it very often, but she had in the past thrown pottery at his head and once smacked him with a tennis racket so hard he'd needed stitches on the side of his head. If she lifted a finger this time he'd hit back, he was cold, hungry and pissed off.

Their bedroom door was pulled to, but not shut. There was no point trying to piss in the dark; she'd go even madder if he pissed all over the floor. Tugging on the pull string, the bathroom lit up and he began to pee. He figured if she was going to barrel out of the bedroom and lose her shit with him, now would be the time. He finished and flushed the chain, still no Jan. Washing his hands he dried them and went across the hall to their bedroom, flicking the light switch. The bed was empty, and his heart skipped a beat; did this mean she'd finally left him? Christ he hoped so, life would be so much easier without her hanging around his neck like a lead weight. He crossed to the wardrobe and threw open the door, gutted to see her dowdy clothes still hanging there. The suitcases were still on top, so if she had gone she'd taken an overnight bag. He checked the small safe they had hidden behind the shoe rack – it still had their passports and cash inside.

A noise downstairs broke his train of thought; he'd known it was too good to be true. Maybe they'd phoned her to pick him up from the station and he'd missed her. The mood she was going to be in if she'd been sitting there all this time waiting would be epic. He straightened up and let out a sigh, stuffing a wad of the cash into his pocket. He'd made up his mind: he was through with this life. He'd devoted enough time to the church and Jan; he wanted to spend the rest of his shame-filled years living the life he wanted to. Fuck them all.

He ran down the stairs ready to confront her, but she wasn't there. The front door was ajar and he wondered if he'd shut it.

'Jan, is that you?'

He went into the kitchen, which was in darkness. Flicking the switch it lit up and was empty. He went into the living room doing the same, and jumped to see a tall man dressed in black standing by his sideboard, holding the gold-plated photo frame that contained a rare photo of David and Jan looking happy. He couldn't believe the cheek of the local police. How did they have the audacity to just walk into his home when he'd been let out without charge?

'Oh, you're not my wife. Who are you and what are you doing in here?'

'I need to speak to you, it's important.'

'Christ, are you having a laugh? Not again. I've just been let out of custody. You lot have ruined my fucking life. It can wait until tomorrow. I'm tired and hungry. I'm not speaking to you now, get out of my house.'

The man began to laugh. 'Have you sinned, Father? Have you begged for forgiveness or mercy?'

David looked at the man; he looked familiar. He also looked like some kind of maniac, his eyes were wild-looking, they kept darting from side to side, and there was a fine film of perspiration on his forehead. He was staring at him, and a cold sliver of fear ran down David's spine. He didn't know what this was about, but he knew it wasn't good; maybe he was mentally ill and seeking solace, but at this time of night he just wanted to get him out, and fast.

'I don't know what you're talking about. Look it's very late and I've had a very long day. Please can you come back tomorrow and we can talk as long as you need to?'

The man nodded, turning to leave.

David let out a sigh of relief. After today he needed an entire bottle of Jack Daniel's to drown his sorrows. 'Thank you, good night.'

Placing his hand on the man's back, he ushered him out towards the front door.

He swung around so fast it knocked him off balance. Gripped in his hand was a huge butcher's knife which he swung towards him. David stumbled backwards, lifting his hand to stop the blow. The knife sliced through his fingers, making him shout out in pain. Blood began to run from the gashes, and he looked at the man, who was grinning.

'How many whores have you slept with this month? I wonder if your wife will be as forgiving of your little misdemeanours now that it's such public knowledge. I shouldn't think so, do you?'

'You're mad, get out of my house now. I'm phoning the police.' He ran for the living room and the phone inside – but he never made it there.

The knife sank into the side of his neck, and he felt the hot spray of arterial blood as it began to pump from the wound. Clasping his hand against his neck, David did his best to keep moving towards the phone, but his knees gave way and he fell to the floor. He could hear his attacker laughing behind him.

'Your filthy games are over. Do you remember me? I bet you don't, it's been a long time. Let me see, the last time I saw you in 1994 you were almost in the same position. Fucking that whore Sandy in the vestry. All these years later, and who's fucked now?'

David looked at the wild-eyed man who was covered in his blood; it was hard to concentrate. Everything was going grey. He tried to remember who he could have been back then, and it hit him.

'You're…' The words wouldn't come out; his teeth began to chatter. He'd never felt this cold as the blood drained from his body.

CHAPTER FORTY-EIGHT

Lucy felt the warm sun on her face and opened her eyes as best as she could, not sure where the hell she was until she heard the shouts from the old woman across the corridor, screeching to the nurses that her tea was too cold. *Shit* she said to herself, realising she was in hospital. After being woken up every two hours through the night to have her observations done, she'd finally drifted off. As she moved, her head felt as if it was too heavy for her shoulders. She needed the toilet and to have a look at the damage to her face in a mirror. No one had shown her last night and she hadn't really wanted to see, but she needed to get out of here, the sooner the better. Apart from a dull thud inside her mind and the fact that she could only partly open one of her eyelids she was okay. That bloody woman was a maniac. Who in their right mind would follow someone then batter them senseless with a cricket bat? She threw back the sheet and stood up. It hurt, but it was nothing a couple of co-codamol wouldn't make better. It just felt like the world's worst hangover. She supposed the bottle of wine wouldn't be helping either. She was in a private room, which was nice, one of the perks of working for the police. They tended to give coppers their own room, just in case any of the patients in the wards were former detainees.

She shuffled along to the bathroom, not locking the door in case she passed out. There was a small mirror above the sink; grasping hold of the sink, because the room was starting to spin, she looked at her reflection and shut her eyes. Bloody hell, she looked as if she'd been in a professional boxing match. Mattie would go mental if he saw the state of her now. She was tempted to take a photo and send it to him with some laughing emojis across the bottom, but she stopped herself. Knowing Mattie like she did, he'd panic and try and get a flight home – she didn't want to ruin his holiday, even though she wished he was here. She was missing him more than she'd ever tell him. Browning was good, but it wasn't the same. The conversation between them didn't flow like it did with Mattie. She felt her eyes well up. Good God that knock to the head had her feeling all emotional. What was wrong with her?

She went back to sit on the bed, and noticed on the chair next to her were her slippers. She had no T-shirt or jeans and realised that they must have taken her blood-soaked pyjamas for CSI to examine. Bloody hell, she was going to have to get someone to go to her house and get her something to wear. She was damned if she was going to ask Browning to rifle through her underwear drawers and wardrobes. She looked at her phone, picked it up and dialled George's number.

'Hi, can you do me a big favour, please?'

'I'm on my way to work, is it important?'

'Not really, but I have no one else to ask. I need some clothes bringing to the hospital. I'm on Ward Six, I think. I want to get out of here and I haven't got anything to wear.'

'Oh shit, are you okay, Lucy? What happened, are you ill?'

'No, I had a run-in with an angry woman. I'll explain when you get here. Please, George, I can't stay here any longer and I can't ask anyone else.'

'Give me fifteen minutes. Does Ellie know?'

'No and I don't want her to. Thank you.'

She ended the call, feeling even lower than she had before. It was a bit shite when the only person you could ask for help was your cheating, sort of ex-husband.

*

Twenty minutes later there was a knock on the door and it opened. George walked in with her overnight bag over his shoulder.

'Jesus, Lucy, what the hell happened?'

He came and sat down on the bed next to her, his fingers lifting to brush her fringe away from the wound on the side of her head. She wanted to push him off, and she also wanted to grab his hand and hold it against her cheek. She missed the way he held her, touched her.

'Angry woman with a cricket bat, she got the better of me. I'm fine, it looks much worse than it really is.'

'Are you sure about that because from where I'm sitting it looks bloody horrific.'

She pushed his hand away. 'Yes, I am. Thank you for bringing my stuff; you can go now.'

He shook his head. 'I'm not going to leave you, you can't just dismiss me, how are you going to get home?'

She hadn't thought that far ahead, so she shrugged.

'I'll take you. It's not a problem. Are you sure they've said you can go home? It's a right mess; you'd think they'd want you to stay in to keep an eye on you.'

Lying had never been an issue in their relationship, well not with her. She hadn't thought he'd ever lie to her either, but he had.

'No, they haven't. Look I can't stop here, I have too much to do. There's a killer walking free out there. I need to find him and stop him before he kills again. It's just a matter of time and I won't let there be another victim while I'm in here feeling sorry for myself. It's not an option.'

'It looks like you've already met whoever it is. You're not seriously going to work, are you? Come on, Lucy, you need to stop thinking there's only you who can deal with these maniacs. You let your obsession with catching the bad guys take over your whole life, over our whole life. When are you going to start living your life a little?'

'I haven't exactly got much life to live at the moment if you remember; I'm on my own with a part-time, angry teenage daughter and a husband who left me. I don't have anything else better to do than hunt down maniacs.'

He shook his head. 'I'm sorry, sorry for messing up your life. I'm sorry for leaving you… but I'm not sorry to leave the workaholic Lucy behind who doesn't even care for herself. I loved you, I still love you, but I don't love watching you work yourself to death or being on my own while you're out there doing it.'

He stood up. 'I'll wait outside then take you home.'

Closing the door behind him Lucy wanted to scream at the top of her lungs; instead, a quiet sob left her lips and a tear ran down her cheek. Was she even doing the right thing? She'd given up her entire life for her career and that wasn't going particularly well. There was still a killer walking around free; she'd almost been killed herself and had the bruises to prove it. She inhaled, deeply. *What choice do you have, Lucy? You've got nothing to lose now, you will catch this man and put him behind bars where he belongs, and then you can start to get your life back together again. It's not too late to start over.*

CHAPTER FORTY-NINE

Last night had been risky, far too risky. He'd crossed the line; he knew that he had. Then again it was done now; he couldn't have waited any longer. Luckily for him his wife had been that tired when she got home late that she'd fallen asleep and never even moved once. He'd stood there watching her for some time; a part of him loved her so much he couldn't imagine a life without her in it. Yet despite that he still couldn't stop the voices in his head and the desire to kill taking over his entire body; he couldn't stop even if he wanted to, it was so strong. After the news headlines, the vicar could have left the town and gone into hiding. He went into the garage where he'd stripped off the blood-soaked clothes and kicked them to one side last night. Anyone could have found them and then how would he have explained that? How he'd made it home without anyone calling the cops was beyond him, the man had bled a lot. It was everywhere, even the hallway had been covered in it. He'd had to step in it to drag him outside and it had been slippery, that meant there would be footprints in the blood. He'd seen the programmes on the television; they could match the footprint to your shoes. Sloppy, he'd been too sloppy and was going to pay for it. The fucking police would have a field day with all the evidence he'd left behind. Not only had he left bloodied footprints all over the house and outside, he'd cut himself and hadn't even noticed until he was undressing last night and felt the sharp sting of the slice across his right thumb. Of course, it was easy to pass off if questioned about it, anyone using a knife could cut themselves.

Muttering away to himself he grabbed the pile of crusted, vile-smelling clothes and carried them outside to the fire pit. Dropping them on the floor next to it he began to build a fire, throwing a full packet of firelighters onto the kindling and coals to get it hot enough. Leaving it burning while he went to find his shoes. He had no choice: he needed to burn them, all of them, because he couldn't remember which ones he'd worn last night and he hadn't left them in the garage. Inside the house he began to gather up all of his trainers; the only shoes he left were the expensive leather loafers he'd bought last year. He knew he hadn't worn those: he'd have broken his neck because the soles were too slippy. He left them in the hall cupboard and carried the armfuls of expensive trainers out to the back garden. The flames were roaring; first of all he dropped the clothes into the fire. The smell was horrendous, and he had to cover his nose; he hoped the neighbours weren't home, they'd wonder what the hell he was burning. Once they'd begun to sizzle, he began to throw one trainer in after the other. Nike, Adidas, Lacoste, Vans, Converse: they were all expensive. Not cheap ones, oh no, he had expensive taste. He sat there rocking back and forth, slowly feeding his shoe collection into the flames and praying that no one would come back and catch him. He could take the credit card and buy new shoes, it didn't matter. Getting rid of the evidence was all that mattered.

When the last pair had been thrown into the flames, he stood up and began to walk up and down his garden barefoot. He needed to do something, though he wasn't sure what. There were some loose ends, what were they? Was it over, had he finished or was there one left to go? He heard voices and ran into the garage; he didn't want her to know what he'd been doing. He had to pretend everything was okay, life was good, he had to go to work. Yes, of course that was it. He had to go to work and pretend everything was just the same as it was. It was safer that way, carry on as usual. Wasn't that what you did under these circumstances? He asked the white noise in his head if this was right. It didn't answer him, just kept on crackling and buzzing; it was driving him mad. He pushed his hand into his pocket and felt the stiff collar he'd taken from the priest's pocket. There had been a wad of £20 notes; he didn't want those. He didn't need money, he had money. He wanted a keepsake to add to the others. He would go in and put it in his little box of memories – lots of people kept memory boxes; he bet they weren't like his though. Special memories of the people he'd killed, to look at whenever he wanted to relive the moment. He needed to concentrate. If she knew what he'd been doing she'd be horrified and he didn't want to upset her; she was innocent in all of this. He was guilty of everything. He thought that he'd be able to stop once it was done. Now, he wasn't so sure he could. The compulsion to kill was stronger than the voice of reason inside his head.

CHAPTER FIFTY

Browning stared at the woman across the table. Jan Collins was glaring at him with a look of hatred so intense it was making him want to loosen his collar and wipe his brow. He'd thought a night in the cells to cool off and calm down would have made her less angry, but he was wrong. He wouldn't squirm in front of her. He was equally as good at playing hardball, but she was good. The duty solicitor had moved his chair away from hers when they'd first sat down, which was a bad sign if even they didn't want to get too close to the woman.

'Jan, would you like to tell me for the record why you followed DI Harwin home last night, lured her outside then tried to kill her?'

The woman shrugged. 'No fucking comment.'

The solicitor held up his hand. 'Can I have a moment with my client please?'

Browning spoke. 'For the purpose of the tape interview suspended at 9.21 hours.' He stood up and left them to it.

Stepping outside of the interview room he went to talk to the custody sergeant behind the huge desk, but hadn't even reached it before he was called back. He went in and the solicitor nodded.

'Jan is aware that there is an eyewitness to the assault. She is sorry for the injuries caused to DI Harwin and hopes she makes a full recovery.'

Browning glanced at the woman who was scowling so hard he wondered if she'd put permanent crease marks in her forehead.

'My client accepts full responsibility for her actions, which were completely out of character for her, and wants to help with the enquiry.'

*

Browning came out of the interview room and shook his head at Rachel.

'She's nuts, but she's having it. So we'll get her bailed and get her sorry arse out of here. I don't want to look at her another minute longer.'

'You're letting her go? After what she's done to the boss she should get remanded.'

'In an ideal world she would. However, we have to take into account the circumstances which led a local pillar of the community to lose her shit and batter a police officer, and the fact that the CPS gave the orders.'

'And they were?'

'The fact that yesterday we blew her whole world apart. Before we found her husband tied to the bed in slutty Sue's she was having a nice day at the mother's union. In the space of an hour she'd found out that her husband is a creep who was arrested for murder and she lost it. It's not good publicity for the force if we go to town on her after yesterday. She didn't know he hadn't been charged with murder when she was following Lucy.'

'But she could have killed her.'

'She didn't though, thankfully. Lucy won't want a massive fuss. She'll be happy that her bail conditions state she's not allowed anywhere near her.'

'That's bollocks.'

'That, Rachel, is life, you know how the CPS works. They'll say it's not in the public interest to make it an even bigger deal than it is. I'm going to check on the boss; you can get her bail cons sorted and release her. Whatever you do make it clear if she so much as enters the same street as the boss that she'll be locked up and the key will be thrown away.'

'Can I make her cry?'

'If you can make that cry, I'll buy you a breakfast in the morning. Just scare her enough so she won't repeat the assault. Is that okay?'

She nodded. 'Fine, by me.'

Browning parked the car and got out just in time to see Lucy and George walking out of the same doors that she'd been rushed through last night. He jogged after her.

'Boss.'

She turned around and smiled. 'Were you coming to see me?'

Out of breath, he nodded.

Lucy turned to George. 'Thank you for waiting for me, I'll get a lift back with Browning.'

George frowned at her, and Browning got the impression he wasn't impressed.

'Lucy, you need to go home and rest.'

'I'm quite aware of that, Browning will drop me off. I've made you late enough for work as it is. Thanks again.'

With that she grabbed the overnight bag from his hands and began to walk towards Browning. He reached out, taking it off her and she didn't complain, which was a first for her. She got into the car, put her seatbelt on and let out a huge sigh.

'You have no idea what good timing that was. He's done nothing but go mad since he got here.'

'I can sort of understand that, boss. Are you supposed to be going home, by the way, they said twenty-four hours minimum? It hasn't been that long.'

'Don't you start, I've had enough of that off him. Yes, I've signed myself out. I need to go home get dressed properly, then get back to work. Where are we up to? What did you do with the feisty ferret?'

He laughed. 'She's been charged and bailed not to go anywhere near you. Is that okay?'

'I suppose so, we did kind of push her over the edge.'

'Rachel is going to make her cry then let her go.'

'That makes me feel a little bit better. Can we stop off for some food? I'm hungry and I need a coffee.'

'You must be okay if you still want to drink coffee.'

'Nothing comes between me and my coffee, you should know that. I wouldn't want to be David Collins when she gets home. We'll probably end up getting called out and arresting her for battery when she gets hold of him. All those years they've been married and she never suspected him of visiting prostitutes to get his kicks. Makes me feel better that I never suspected George would ever cheat on me, I suppose.'

'People have secrets, sometimes they're very good at keeping them. Sometimes they're not. I'm never going to complain about my missus again after seeing Jan Collins in fine form. It makes you appreciate what you have coming across women like that. You don't think she could be our killer, do you? She's certainly got the temper for it.'

Lucy shook her head. 'I contemplated that last night. The search team didn't find anything of evidential value in the house. Regardless of which of them could have done it, we're still missing a cat, and the trophies from the scene. No I think she's just a frustrated, angry woman.'

'What if the vicar had been sleeping with Sandy and Margaret though? I mean he's not fussy, is he?'

'Oh God, did you have to put that image in my head? I think he was lying about Sandy. I don't see how he wouldn't have noticed her when she came into Street Saviours, and maybe he was sleeping with her. We need a full sweep of the street, house to house, again; a mugshot to see if anyone can place him going into Sandy's. I think we're going to have to be very careful with our observations of him unless we can come up with something concrete. As much as I'd like it to be him, hell I want it to be him, I don't think it is because there's just no forensic evidence that links him to both murders. What we have is circumstantial and that won't hold up in court.'

He glanced at Lucy who had her head against the headrest and had closed her eyes. Driving to her favourite Costa on the retail park, he left her dozing while he went inside for her coffee. Then he went into the Subway next to it and got her a bacon roll smothered in tomato sauce. She needed some fuel inside her because he had a feeling she wouldn't stay at home and put her feet up like he imagined the doctors had ordered. She'd be showered, changed and ready for work in less than thirty minutes, and there was no point in arguing with her because she didn't listen to anyone, and he respected her for that. He was glad he'd been there to save her last night.

CHAPTER FIFTY-ONE

Jan Collins was let out of the same side door of the police station that her husband had been twelve hours earlier. That stuck-up little snotty bitch of a copper had been horrible to her, and she'd had to take it and bite her tongue or they wouldn't have let her out. Having to nod and agree with it all, solemnly promising not to go within a one-mile radius of that fucking cow, Lucy Harwin. She remembered last night in its full technicolour glory, how heavy the bat had been to swing. The loud crunch when it had hit her head, the blood and the satisfaction of watching her hit the ground like a sack of shit. She hadn't meant to hurt her that much, but the anger and frustration that her average life was now turned upside down for the whole world to scrutinise had taken over. The anger over her wasted decades of being married to David had exploded from her through that bat. Yes, she knew he was a creep and a pompous prick, and she'd known all about the whores. What did he take her for? And yes, at first she'd been devastated. She'd thought that he loved her and that she was enough of a woman to satisfy his every need, and she'd really tried their first year of marriage. He'd swept her off her feet; she'd been over the moon that he'd even taken an interest in her when she knew she wasn't much to look at. It hadn't made a difference to him no matter how hard she tried and then she'd realised that it meant she didn't have to sleep with him. Which could only be a bonus because now he turned her stomach. The thought of him wanting to have sex with her when God knows what diseases he could have picked up from the women he picked up on street corners made her shudder.

All she wanted was an easy life and she'd thought being married to a vicar would be just that. No huge mortgage to pay because of the free house, spending all day organising fundraisers or helping the pensioners out suited her just fine. It meant she didn't have to find a job and go out to work. Well that was all gone, the church wouldn't want him after this. They were going to lose their home; their livelihood and any respect they might have had within the community was long gone. All because he couldn't keep his dick in his trousers and, to top it all off, they had accused him of killing some woman. Christ he might be a pervert, but he wasn't a killer. For one thing he didn't have the balls to kill anyone, and how did she know this? Because during all the arguments over the years and the times she'd hit him, he'd never, not once, hit her back. When she got home she was going to pack her suitcase, take the wad of cash he had stashed in the safe, and go stop with her sister in Blackpool. She'd had enough of this stupid sham of a marriage. The pretence had gone on for far too long – it was over.

The taxi pulled up and she got inside, glaring at the driver and daring him to make a comment about her current predicament.

He didn't. 'Where to love?'

She gave him her address, watching his face to see if a hint of scorn crossed it. He didn't even blink; obviously he'd seen all sorts if this was the regular firm the police used to pick up criminals and take them home. She shuddered. The shame was awful, and how was she going to face David? She should have waited for him and got him with the fucking cricket bat first, teach him a few lessons before going for the copper.

When the taxi stopped outside her address she pulled the crumpled £5 note from her pocket. He took it, giving her some loose change.

'You keep that, thank you.'

Not at all in the mood for a huge argument, which no doubt he was expecting, drained of everything, she decided she was having some toast and tea then going to the train station. She would let him stew. She wondered if the church hadn't already sent someone around to tell them to get out.

As she approached the vicarage, she noticed that the front door was ajar, swinging back and forth in the biting wind. As she walked up the path she could see a dark smear of something on the freshly painted pale green door. As she'd spent ages sanding the door down and repainting it, her anger began to bubble, until she pushed open the door and inhaled the metallic, earthy smell. The house was so still, not what she was expecting, and a cold shudder shook her whole body. Jan stared not quite understanding what her eyes were seeing, and she blinked a couple of times. The beige walls were covered in spots of dark red: it was sprayed everywhere. As she stared at it, then the big puddle of black, congealing liquid on the floor, she realised what it was and let out a high-pitched howl, shaking her head from side to side.

'David.'

Afraid to go inside because it resembled a slaughterhouse, she stepped away; pulling her almost dead phone from her pocket she dialled 999 and began screaming down the phone to the call handler.

'Blood, there's so much blood. You need to come now.'

CHAPTER FIFTY-TWO

Lucy and Browning were sitting at the breakfast bar in her kitchen, bacon rolls consumed and sipping coffee. 'That's better, I feel almost human now. Just need a couple of painkillers then I'm good to go.'

She'd come in, showered got dressed and wrapped her hair in a bun before eating. She'd thought about putting some make-up over the worst of the black eye, but the cut above her eyebrow was smarting and she didn't want it to get infected. So she'd left it. Browning had grimaced when she'd sat down.

'I really think you should take the day off, boss. One day won't hurt. Your head must be hurting, it's a mess, it's hurting me just looking at it.'

'I can't sit here on my own all day worrying about what everyone is up to, it will drive me crackers. We're already down Tom and Mattie, and if I go down, too, you'll be on your own and I can't do it to you. They'll call in another DI to take over, and I don't want to be pushed out because my face might upset a few people.'

'Hey, believe it or not I'm capable of managing for one day.'

'I didn't mean that. Of course, you are, you've been doing this longer than I have. I mean I don't want to leave you doing all the work. Besides I'd drive you mad phoning you every hour for an update.'

'Yeah, I know you would. Look if you start to feel dizzy or begin to talk crap I'm bringing you back here. No arguments. George would go mad if he knew you were coming into work.'

'It's got nothing to do with him. He lost the right to an opinion when he left. I only rang him this morning because I didn't want you having to find my clean underwear.'

He laughed. 'Thank God for that; I'd have died of embarrassment. I've never looked through Wendy's underwear drawer and we've been married thirty years.'

His phone began to ring. 'You're kidding me, how long ago was this? Okay be on my way soon.'

'What's that about?'

'More fun and games at St Aidan's vicarage. You can wait in the car, boss – Jan Collins has a restraining order not to come within a one-mile radius of you. Apparently, she's phoned 999, hysterical and screaming about blood on the door.'

Lucy stood up, her stomach doing backflips. 'Oh God, now what.'

'Let's go and find out. I really hoped I'd seen the last of that vile woman.'

The police car skidded to a halt at the entrance to the small car park, and the two officers jumped out. The control room operator had just warned them that the caller was violent and had only recently been released from custody for grievous bodily harm of the DI and to approach with caution. Both Adam and Tess were fresh out of probation; this was the first serious call they'd attended on their own. Adam had his hand resting against his taser, as he looked at Tess. 'You do the talking and I'll be ready to fry her if she gets out of hand.'

Tess smirked. 'Deal, make sure you don't fry me by mistake though. You're not a very good shot, are you?'

She looked around the deserted car park outside the front of the church hall. It was so peaceful. The large house, which must be the vicarage, would have once been impressive, but it was shabby now. The painted exterior walls had seen better days. It must have been so lovely living in such a grand house in the shadow of the church. Tess had always loved visiting churches; she'd been here a few times in the past. She walked towards the woman who was standing in the corner of the tidy front garden, shivering and sobbing.

'Now then, Jan, what's the matter?'

She lifted her finger and wailed, pointing to the house. 'Blood, so much blood. I don't know where David is.'

'You wait here, and we'll go take a look.'

Tess motioned to Adam, and he joined her. Pulling on a pair of latex gloves she pushed the front door open and heard him balk behind her.

'Oh shit, I hate blood. Can't go in, sorry.'

Shaking her head, she stepped inside, shouting, 'David, it's the police, we're here to help you.' Expecting to hear a grunt or a groan she was greeted by silence. She turned to Adam. 'I'll go check the house; you better get a duty sergeant here and a DS. This isn't good.'

She stepped inside, breathing through her nose so she didn't get the full stench of the blood. It was everywhere: the walls, ceiling, even the light shade had red drops covering it. She could see inside the kitchen and living room – they were empty. There was no blood going up the stairs, so she didn't think anyone was up there, but she needed to check in case he'd managed to get himself up there and died on the bathroom floor. Her heart pounding in her ears she called out again. 'David, it's the police. I'm coming up.' She ran up the steps, checking all three bedrooms and the bathroom. Then shouted down to Adam. 'It's clear, there's no one here and no sign that anyone has been up here bleeding.' She ran back down and carefully made her way back outside; whatever had happened here it would need to be documented by CSI.

Jan asked, 'Is he in there? Did you find him?'

'No, it's empty. He can't have gone far, bleeding like that.' She looked at the church hall and the church. Then whispered to Adam, 'Had we better go inside and check them out?'

He shrugged. 'Dunno, better wait for the sarge to get here.'

'Don't be a dick, what if he's bleeding to death inside?'

'Go on then, you do the honours.'

She rolled her eyes at him but walked towards the church hall, which was nearest. She looked down on the floor and saw big splotches of blood leading towards it and a couple of smeared footprints. Nodding her head at the blood, Adam looked down and realised what she was saying. He took hold of Jan by the elbow.

'Come on, let's get you inside the van. It's cold out here and you're shivering. I'll put the heater on for you, and we'll wait for backup to arrive, so they can help do a search of the area. We'll find your husband, he won't be far.'

Jan let him lead her to the van, and he opened the sliding door for her; he didn't trust her sitting in the front. Going by her previous unstable behaviour she might throw a hissy fit and steal the van. Putting the keys in the ignition, he left it running with the heater turned on. 'I'm just going to help my colleague do a quick search. You wait here. Is that okay?'

She nodded, wrapping her arms across her chest and closing her eyes so she didn't have to watch what they were doing.

Tess turned the black iron handle on the huge wooden door and pushed it open. There was more blood smeared in here – it looked like drag marks. Avoiding stepping in them, she pushed the interior door open, checking the floor so as not to stand in the blood. The feeling she was being watched came over her and she sensed him before she saw him. Lifting her eyes from the floor she looked towards the huge cross that was hanging from the wall. She'd been in here before, had her kid's birthday parties in here. Now, the cross had been turned into a living crucifix. Her eyes met with David Collins's glassy eyes and she let out a scream, her hand lifting to her mouth.

CHAPTER FIFTY-THREE

Adam gripped hold of Tess's arms. 'What's up?'

She took a deep breath. 'He's inside.'

'Is he?'

She nodded. 'Oh God, I don't think I'll ever get that out of my head for the rest of my life. He's dead, his neck, there's blood. Too much blood, whatever you do, don't let her come in. It's really bad.' She pointed to the van, but the woman inside was rocking back and forth, her eyes were still shut.

Adam spoke into the radio which was clipped onto his body armour. 'Control we have a confirmed foxtrot, we need a DS soon as possible.'

'Who has confirmed, 2819?'

'It was 2822, injuries sustained are incompatible with life.'

He looked across at Tess; she noticed that the skin on his face had taken on a green tinge. 'Bloody hell, what a job for our first one on independent patrol. I knew we should have taken those shoplifters at Tesco.'

Tess couldn't agree more; she would never again complain about going to a grade two job ever if this is what happened on a grade one.

Browning parked behind the van which was blocking the entrance to the church hall. 'Wait here, I'll find out where the Rottweiler is.'

Lucy did as she was told. He spoke to the two officers standing next to the van and gave her the thumbs up. Walking back towards the car, she got out and he went to the boot.

'He's dead.'

'Suicide?'

'Not unless you can cut your own throat, drag yourself into a church hall, undress yourself and then hang yourself upside down from a cross before dying.'

'Oh shit. Not another?'

'We better go check it out. Do you want to sit this one out?'

'No, I can't.'

They both began to rip open the plastic packets and then dress in the protective clothing inside of them, Lucy aware that at least it would hide her identity from Jan. She didn't want things to escalate, but she had no choice – this was her investigation. She needed to take control and do her best to find out what had happened. When she'd fastened the leg covers around her calves she stood up straight and looked at Browning.

'Ready?'

'As I'll ever be, come on. Let's get this over with.'

She looked on as he took hold of the scene guard log from one of the officers and signed them both into the scene. When he passed it back, she ducked under the blue and white police tape and, watching the ground to make sure she wasn't standing in any evidence, made her way once more towards the church hall. Her heart was racing; she hadn't expected this. Never in a million years would she have thought that David Collins would become victim number three. She'd had it completely wrong, and she wasn't afraid to admit it.

As she stepped into the hall she looked up at the life-sized crucifixion and inhaled sharply. This was bad – in some ways it was worse than Sandy and Margaret because she didn't know either of them. They were complete strangers and it was easier to detach yourself from the terrible tragedy when you didn't know the victim. His entire chest was covered in deep slash wounds. The previous victims had cut throats, but no other injuries. This was horrific, and her mind began to fill with guilt. Had she caused this, by arresting him and bringing him to the killer's attention? Or had he been on the killer's list all along? She had been so sure he had something to do with it. She heard Browning swear behind her and knew he would be feeling pretty much the same.

He muttered, 'Definitely not suicide. How did he get him up there, he's a big guy? That must have taken some strength. I don't think I'd have been able to lift him up.'

'For a terrible moment I wondered if Jan was the killer, but he looks as if he's been here some time. When was she released from custody?'

Browning checked his watch. 'About an hour ago, so she's definitely out of this. Oh crap, who's going to tell her? You can't go anywhere near her, and I don't know if I'm brave enough.'

'I think she already knows; did they say the primary scene was the vicarage?'

'Yeah.'

Lucy took one last look at him, turning around. 'Let's go check out the house. We can't do anything until Catherine gets here.'

She cautiously made her way back out, followed by Browning who closed the door to shield the body from prying eyes. Lucy looked at the bloody smear on the vicarage door, then pushed it open, glad to have a face mask on, shielding some of the strong smell. She didn't need to go inside and contaminate the scene more than it already had been.

'I think we need the Chief Super; he was in custody less than twenty-four hours ago. It's going to need investigating above our level. What a mess, I didn't expect this. Never in a million years.'

'It's not your fault. You were doing your job; he was a genuine person of interest. There were valid reasons to bring him in for questioning. I would have done the same in your position and so would any other officer in charge of the investigation. So, don't go getting all morbid on me.'

'It doesn't make me feel any better though, does it? You know they're going to kick me off the case, don't you? They'll say it's a conflict of interest because of Jan, which it is. I won't be allowed to investigate this one.'

'No, you won't. Officially. Unofficially it's a different matter. We'll keep running it, but out of the loop. It would be foolish to remove you after everything; no matter what they say or do you're the lead, Lucy.'

'Thank you, I appreciate it. This one feels different though, it's sloppy. The others were like military operations; there was no dead animal this time either, that we know about. Although he didn't need to add any shock value to this, did he? They didn't own a pet, so why did he kill Margaret's cat? It doesn't make any sense.'

'Maybe we're getting to him, and he's losing it. This is far worse than the other two, and I didn't think I'd ever say that. He's taking more risks, perhaps he's becoming unhinged.'

She thought about it for a moment. 'I think you're right, I think he is losing it or he might have lost it completely. Let's hope he's left more than a cat hair behind this time; some nice human DNA would be good, even better some prints.'

She walked back towards the car, needing to sit down for a little bit. She was afraid to tell Browning that her legs felt as if they didn't belong to her; her head was spinning and she felt as though she was about to pass out.

Oh, God. This is all my fault; if I'd caught the killer he wouldn't be dead.

CHAPTER FIFTY-FOUR

Lucy was watching Browning. He was speaking to the officer keeping a close eye on Jan, who was still inside the back of the van. He looked back at Lucy, and she pointed. He nodded, he knew what she meant. They had to get Jan away from the scene and somewhere safe; as much as she disliked the woman it wasn't fair for her to watch the circus that was about to take over the area. The officer got inside the van, and she let out a huge sigh. Breathing deeply to restore the balance in her mind, she knew she had limited time to work this scene before someone from above realised she shouldn't be here and told her to leave. Watching the van drive off she waited until it was out of sight then got back out of the car, determined to give David and Jan Collins her best, despite the difficult circumstances. The worry that a more experienced DI wouldn't have done what she'd done and arrested David was weighing heavy on her heart.

The officer left guarding the scene looked like she felt: her face was almost as white as the paper suit she was wearing, she looked shell-shocked. She walked towards her.

'I'm Lucy, the DI. I don't know if I introduced myself before.'

'Tess.'

'Tess, can you walk me through the scene, from when you arrived to when we arrived?'

She listened to her account, interrupting with questions.

'How did you get inside the house?'

'The door was already open. I asked Jan and she said it was ajar when she got here.'

'Did you touch anything? Don't worry if you did. It happens, I just need to know before CSI go in?'

She shook her head. 'Nothing, I had gloves on.'

'Good, that's excellent.' Lucy looked at her collar number, poor kid was fresh out of training.

'You're doing really good. Aren't you just out of company?'

'Yes, I never expected anything like this. I mean I know it happens, but you don't expect your first job to be this gruesome, do you?'

Lucy smiled. 'No, you don't. To be honest with you this is probably one of the worst jobs you'll ever attend, so you're doing really well. Everything else will seem a breeze after this.'

'I hope so.'

'Did you notice if the lights were on, were all the windows shut?'

'The hall light was on; the rest of the house was in darkness. I didn't check the windows, and I haven't closed any, so they must have all been shut.'

'Good, that's really good. Last question, when you went into the church hall did you touch the body to see if he was breathing?'

'God no, I'm no doctor but even I could tell that he'd been dead some time.'

'Thanks, Tess. You've done an excellent job.'

The CSI van pulled up, and Lucy waited for Jack and Amanda to get suited and booted. When they'd signed themselves in, she briefed them on the situation.

Jack turned to Amanda. 'Your choice, body or house?'

'I'll take the house, I don't know if I'm ready to see a mutilated vicar not long after eating my breakfast.'

Jack smiled at his wife, pulled the heavy case over his shoulder and walked towards the church hall. Lucy pointed out the blood spots and footprints, and he took the little fluorescent numbered markers out of the case, dropping one by each of them. He looked at Lucy, and she nodded. 'It's really bad, Jack.'

'Aren't they all?'

'This one's worse than any of the others, than any I've attended, and I've been to some awful deaths over the years.'

'Great, I'm going to stop being such a gentleman and giving Amanda first choice.'

This made Lucy laugh.

Browning shouted her name, and she turned around to see a large group of PCSOs standing on the other side of the police tape. She walked towards them, smiling. They were life savers, not only would they do the house-to-house enquiries far more efficiently than response officers – who hated it – they would also take over the scene guards, which was a huge help. Now if she could get Catherine Maxwell inside the scene and get her opinion before she got shafted everything would be much better. She felt better knowing that Jan wasn't watching her every move and judging her; no matter what the outcome was, she was always going to blame Lucy for David's death.

But Lucy didn't need her to do this, because she would spend the rest of her life blaming herself.

CHAPTER FIFTY-FIVE

Catherine Maxwell couldn't have timed it any better. Jack had just informed Lucy he'd done the initial documenting of the scene inside the hall and she could go inside as soon as she arrived. Lucy waited for the doctor to dress in the protective clothing. She ducked under the tape with such grace that Lucy felt a twinge of envy towards the woman who seemed to do everything elegantly.

'Lucy, we really need to stop meeting like this. Maybe we should go out for cocktails some time instead.'

This made Lucy chuckle. She didn't have many female friends, so it would be nice to hang out with Catherine out of work.

'I think that's a great idea, you can count me in. I can't remember the last time I went out without the rest of CID.'

'That's a date. Now, tell me what you have?'

Lucy gave her a brief explanation. 'I think you need to see it for yourself, to appreciate the full horror.'

'Oh, great. There's nothing I love more to get my day off to a great start.' She winked at Lucy then stepped inside the church hall. Lucy followed her.

'Oh, crap. I've never seen anything like this, in all my years.'

Catherine turned to Lucy. 'This is overkill? If we are assuming it's the same offender then I would take a guess and say that it looks as if he's regressed into a classic, disorganised offender. This is much worse than the first two. They were organised, methodical, clean – this is messy. He wasn't killed here though, there isn't enough blood.'

'No, the vicarage is the primary scene. He was dragged or carried here. There's blood everywhere in the hallway of the house.'

'I'll take a look at that after I've finished here, but for what it's worth, I'm going to stick my neck out and hazard a guess that he's probably gone into psychosis. If he already had a psychotic personality it might have been under control with medication. I think he's stopped taking it and it's escalating; the good thing is there's more chance of him leaving evidence behind. He won't be thinking straight. His contact with reality will be impaired. Of course this is just my opinion. But if you want a professional diagnosis you'll have to speak to a psychiatrist.'

For the first time Lucy felt a glimmer of hope. If Catherine was right, and the killer was off his meds, he was going to be acting strange, out of character. If he was married or had a job, the people around him would notice the change in his demeanour. If they issued a press release, it might make people sit up and take notice. There were so many possibilities. She stood back and watched as Catherine began to take a cursory look at the body. Lucy stared at the crucifix; he was sacrificing his victims, but for what? What did it mean to him? What personal vendetta was he on?

'Where are his clothes?'

'In the house in a bloody pile.'

'I need them, to check if there's any damage to them which correlates to the wounds. Judging by the lack of blood, I think the slash wounds were done post-mortem. She looked at his neck; there were two deep wounds to the left side. 'These stab wounds are the cause of death. Underneath them are the major blood vessels. The carotid artery and the jugular vein. This would have caused massive haemorrhage; the arterial spray would have been something. The offender didn't get out of this one without being covered in blood; in fact he would have been saturated, depending on the proximity he was standing to him. The pattern of injury suggests to me that his motive was to kill the victim; he didn't want to just injure him.

Which, in my opinion, is premeditated murder. How am I doing? I bet you already had that figured out?'

'I kind of guessed he wanted him dead. I didn't know the rest of the stuff though. You're doing good.'

'Of course, I'll be able to give you the full results at the pm, but for now it's something.'

'What about time of death? He was in custody until his release at 21.25 last night.'

Catherine lifted a half-closed eyelid. 'Eyes are cloudy, which is a good indicator he's been dead at least eight to ten hours. He's in complete rigor which sets in eight to twelve hours after death. I would hazard a guess that time of death is somewhere between ten and midnight.'

'Considering he was attacked in the hall and that was the only light that was on, while the rest of the house was in darkness, I think he was followed home. Or it happened pretty much as soon as he got home; so either someone knew about him being released or they were waiting for him in the hope of him coming back soon.'

'He has defence wounds on his fingers, so he tried to defend himself. He's quite a tall guy, so the killer must be at least his height. I mean how did he get him up here?'

'No idea. I've heard that people having psychotic episodes can exhibit superhuman strength.'

'That's true and it would explain this.' She pointed to the body.

'I'm afraid that's all I can give you for now, the rest will come out in the post-mortem. Lucy, I know you already know this, but there's a chance he might strike again. Sooner, rather than later. We don't know for sure he is having an episode, but it would explain the difference between the crime scenes. You need to be very careful. I'll finish up here and see you at the mortuary. I'll push everything else back and wait until you're happy for him to be released from the scene. Once I've got everything I need it's your call.'

'Thank you, I don't know what we'd do without you, Catherine.'

'The feeling is mutual, Lucy. By the way what happened to your face?'

'I had a run-in with the good vicar's wife after I arrested him at a prostitute's house and brought him in for questioning about the previous murders.'

'Ouch, does she have an alibi?'

Lucy nodded. 'Yes, she was in custody for GBH, and she was only released this morning. This whole investigation is a right mess, Catherine.' The look etched across the pathologist's face confirmed Lucy's last statement. They needed to find whoever was killing these people and fast. She was glad she got that list of volunteers for Street Saviours from Jan before the shit hit the fan, because everyone who had a connection to St Aidan's Church was going to have to be warned to be extra vigilant – that included her own daughter. Ellie had only volunteered there a couple of times but it still put her at risk. She needed to figure out a way to tell her to keep clear of the bloody place until they'd caught the killer, something which she'd been going to do before she got attacked. There was no way of guessing who was next on his list but she could guarantee it would be someone who had dealings with the church.

She walked out of the church hall, relieved to be in the fresh air. Catherine followed her on her way to speak to Amanda, who was standing outside the house. It was time to go back to the station and decide where to go from here. And to find out if she was being pushed off the case… because at this point she didn't see how she could stay on it.

CHAPTER FIFTY-SIX

As Lucy walked into her office and looked around she sighed. She would have given anything for Mattie to be here. As it was, Browning had stepped up to the mark and was doing a really good job; she couldn't fault him in that respect. It just wasn't the same though, she felt more comfortable with Mattie. The office was full; her team were waiting for her to give them their tasks. Her head was aching before she'd even got to the church hall, now it felt like it was going to explode. She couldn't tell anyone though, because they'd sign her off sick and send her home. Up to now she'd done a pretty good job of dodging the Chief Super, but she knew it was only a matter of time before he caught up with her and told her she couldn't work the case. She closed the door and shut the blinds, hoping it might give her a little more time. There was something about these murders – revenge or hatred were the most common motives when it came to religious crimes. What had Margaret done though? She could understand someone hating David Collins: he'd abused his power by using prostitutes. God knows what else he got up to behind his wife's back, when all the time he was putting on an act of being a servant of God. Sandy, from the information given, was a big drinker, always had been. She lived in Bridlington Court, which potentially connected her to Collins. She read the latest email from Rachel; she said that Sandy Kilburn in the past had been known to sleep with anyone who bought her drinks and showed her a good time. She didn't imagine that Margaret had slept with Collins; although who was she to rule that out? He might like older women. Sandy had been introduced to the church through her attendance at Street Saviours, so did that connect her and Margaret? She was writing the names and connections down on an A4 sheet of paper. They needed to interview the male volunteers, speak to them and see if any of them were cagey. She'd be able to spot someone who was off their meds, as they'd be acting strange.

A sharp shooting pain across the side of her head made her close her eyes as a wave of sickness washed through her. She was finding it hard to concentrate. There was so much to do and it was only a matter of time before they removed her from the case.

Going into the communal office she perched on the end of Col's desk. Browning was still at the scene, hopefully keeping the Chief Super busy and buying her a little more time.

'Right, we have a tremendous amount of work to do today. I've printed off a list of the volunteers for the Street Saviours. I want to go and interview them all; they need to be warned they could be at risk. So, Rachel, you can come with me and we can get this boxed off as soon as possible. Col, I need you to run some background checks from way back in the day. I'm pretty convinced Sandy Kilburn wasn't the first victim.'

'How do you work that out, boss? We haven't had any similar murders or attacks flag up on HOLMES.'

'I'll call it a gut instinct. There's a connection. I think whoever is doing this has killed before. There was no doubt about what he was doing with Sandy. He just jumped right in and killed her in the most shocking way he could imagine; the doc said there was no hesitation on the wound to her neck. I want you to go back as far as you have to. Any cases – be they assaults, sudden deaths, murders which have a religious aspect to them. I need this now, if possible, because I have a feeling I'm going to get pulled from the case and we're so close.'

'Why?'

'Because of Collins being in custody. The Super will be panicking and thinking about all the bad publicity. You know what's going to happen: he was killed a matter of hours after being released. They will be treating it as a death following contact with the police.'

'That's ridiculous, you didn't have anything to do with his death. That was his bad luck, why should you have to step back?'

'Because that's how it works. They'll want someone to blame in the press to make them look good. Come on, Rachel, let's get going. We have a few names to cross off this list, and I want to get out of here. If the Super comes looking, you have no idea where I am; I want to hold off the inevitable as long as possible. Col, ring me if you get anything, I don't care how tenuous the link. If it mentions anything to do with God, a church, a bible or even that they were wearing a cross, I want to know about it. Thanks.'

Turning to leave, she reached the stairs, as Rachel stood up grabbing her jacket from the back of her chair and followed.

CHAPTER FIFTY-SEVEN

May 1995

He sat feeling the warmth of the sun as it filtered through the trees, warming his face, and staring at the dead rabbit. It had been a close call. That slag Sharon had asked him what he was doing by the rabbits. She hated him, and he didn't like her either, always calling him names and teasing him. Last year the pet rabbits had mysteriously disappeared, and Angie had sworn that someone had stolen them. She'd even phoned the police, who'd come out and spoken to her about it. Nothing had happened; they weren't interested in two missing rabbits. He was pretty sure they had much more important stuff to be investigating. Angie had been sad they'd gone, and for a while he'd felt bad and had made himself a promise not to do it again. He hadn't for some time; he'd concentrated on his school work and behaved like the perfect kid. It was hard though; the police had come back to speak to him another two times about his dad. Each time he told the same story: he hadn't done it. They'd questioned him longer each time until Angie or Paul had stepped in and told them if they needed anything else to make it official. Both times they'd left, he could tell they were frustrated with him, but he wouldn't crack. If they were waiting for him to make full confession they'd be waiting the rest of their lives. He didn't care: he felt worse about killing Angie's rabbits than he did about his waste of space dad.

He had to bury this rabbit and hope that he could stop himself from doing it again. At least Angie was on holiday, so she wouldn't know about it. He should have broken its neck and left it in its hutch. They might have thought it had just died then; but it was a bit hard to blame it on natural causes when its head was no longer attached to its body. He heard the whispering in his head and shook it hard; the voices came when he least expected them. It made it hard to concentrate in school, as the teachers thought he was being disrespectful, but he was trying to shut them out. Sometimes he'd see things that weren't there, and he didn't like that. He would walk into the school canteen and everyone would turn to stare at him, sometimes they laughed. Then he'd shake his head or blink, and everyone would be busy eating, chattering, laughing and taking no notice of him. They had no idea who he really was; he was the teenage equivalent of Superman: he could fly if he wanted to. He just didn't want to because he was scared of heights. He knew he could take every kid on in this school and kill them all. The teachers wouldn't be able to stop him, he was that strong. He'd stopped talking to the few friends he did have and now they kept their distance. It was okay with him, he didn't need them. He didn't need anyone.

He heard his name being shouted, breaking him out of the trance he was in. Paul, one of the support workers, who wasn't soft like Angie, would want to know where he was and what he was doing. He looked down to make sure his clothes weren't covered in rabbit blood and guts. They weren't, so he jumped up and rushed back through the overgrowth to get to the big house.

He rushed inside to see Paul standing there, arms folded across his chest and Sharon standing next to him, glaring.

'Where's the rabbit?'

'What rabbit?'

'You fucking creep, where is it? I saw you take it out of the run.'

'Shh, Sharon.'

'I took it out to play, and it ran away.' He could feel the panic beginning to rise inside his chest. He'd fucking slit her throat if she carried on. He'd never liked her, always mouthing off and bragging about what she'd nicked from the shops or which boy she was shagging.

'He didn't, the freak has hurt it. Just like he did the last two; he's a weirdo, he wants locking up.'

'Right, that's enough. Sharon you go to your room; you come in the office with me.'

She stamped all the way up the stairs and along the landing. As she reached her bedroom she shouted, 'I want a fucking lock on my door; he might come in and kill us while we're all asleep.'

Paul grabbed his arm, pushing him into the office and shutting the door behind him.

'This is a serious accusation, do you understand that? Tell me you let the bloody thing go by accident again, because if I think for a minute that you've killed it I'm going to have to phone the police.'

'I did, I swear. I only took it out to stroke it, and it jumped out of my arms and I've been searching for it ever since.'

He had his fingers crossed behind his back; he was going to get her back for this.

'I hope so, I know she doesn't like you and I also know how good she is at making horrible stuff up about people when she isn't getting her own way. So listen to me, this time I'm going to believe you. When Angie gets back you tell her that you accidentally lost it, and if I so much as hear anything different I'm going to drag you to the fucking police station myself. Am I making myself clear?'

Nodding his head up and down so fast he almost gave himself whiplash, he whispered, 'Yes, Paul. I heard you. I'll go back out and look for it, might come back with a bit of luck. I'm sorry.'

'Yeah, if you had a bid for freedom what would you choose? To be stuck in a smelly, old hutch or running free?'

He thought that pretty much summed up his current situation. 'I'd want to run free.'

'Wouldn't we all. I'll talk to Sharon. Don't let me hear of any more weird stuff going down, do you understand?'

'Yes.'

'Right, sod off and go make a token effort to look for the bloody thing so I can tell Angie you tried.'

He turned and walked out of the office, his cheeks burning. He'd almost been caught. The last thing he wanted was for Paul to go to the coppers. They might figure out about his dad. He decided after this wake-up call, he wouldn't do anything else. At least not until he was well out of here, that would be at least another two or three years and then he'd be free to do as he pleased.

CHAPTER FIFTY-EIGHT

Lucy snuck back into the office using the fire exit stairs and not the usual spiral staircase. She needed to see if Col had anything for her. Peering through the glass she couldn't spot the Super and opened the door. Col was at the printer, which was across the hall from the boss's office, so she waited for him at his desk. He crossed the room towards her, smiling, which made her feel slightly better.

'Anything?'

'Not a lot, but something. I found a murder from October 1994, a sixty-year-old God-loving alcoholic who lived on his own was bludgeoned to death with his bible and stamped all over. His body was discovered a couple of days later.'

'Did they apprehend anyone?'

'No, they had no prime suspect apart from his son, who had been taken into care a few years earlier after being abused and beaten by him. The kid at the time was taken in by the local vicar until they found a placement for him. Police interviewed the kid several times, said he hated his dad, but denied killing him. There was no forensic evidence and he had an alibi. There were stamp marks all over the body, but they were a shoe size eleven. The kid was a size nine.'

'Where is he now? It's too much of a coincidence. He was abused as a child, put into care, lived at a vicarage for some time. Our killer has a strong hatred of everything religious, and he's taking out people for whatever reason. We need to find him.'

'I'll see what I can do. I've run the usual checks and there's no trace of Darren Sharp. Well there are lots of Darren Sharps, but none with a matching DOB or the right age.'

Her phone began to ring. She looked down relieved to see it was Browning and answered.

'Boss, has the Super caught up with you yet?'

'Not yet.'

'Good, I need the go-ahead to remove the body from the scene.'

'You're satisfied everything's been done, twice.'

'Yes.'

'Good to go then.'

'I'll meet you up at the mortuary, Lucy, be there in the next thirty minutes. The undertakers have been on standby for the last two hours. God knows how they're going to get him in the bloody body bag, his arms are as stiff as a board.'

Lucy shuddered, she didn't want to think about it. 'Thanks, I'll see you there.' She looked around; all she had to do was to get back out of the station before the Super, Simon White, clocked eyes on her.

Col nodded at her. 'If he asks, you've gone to an emergency doctor's appointment. It's the truth, sort of. I'll run Darren Sharp and all the associated aliases through the system. Do you want me to take Rachel and go visit the children's home he was in? They might still have some records of what happened to him, if he was adopted out or whatever?'

'That would be amazing. I'm not sure Rachel will be much help though. She's in weekend mode already.'

He shook his head. 'There's a surprise, when isn't she?'

Lucy smiled, turned and made a swift exit before anyone else clocked her.

CHAPTER FIFTY-NINE

He caught sight of his reflection in the bathroom mirror and took a step closer. Who was that staring back at him? It didn't look like him. This version of him was older, greyer, his complexion much paler. The dark circles under his eyes made him look as if he hadn't slept for weeks. Maybe he hadn't – he didn't know what was real and what was the voices inside his head. It was too hard to distinguish the difference. He'd thought he was well enough to give up his meds; that he was better and could cope without them, but now he wasn't so sure that was right. Everything that used to be so normal to him now seemed so far away that he didn't even know how normal felt anymore. The house was quiet, so he went downstairs. She wasn't in, that was good. It gave him the chance to clean up his mess before she came back. He went into the garage where he'd left his blood-soaked clothes, and the earthy, coppery smell filled his nostrils. This was so bad; what if she'd come in here? She could have gone to get the police, that meddling policewoman who had been to the church – what if she'd gone to the station to speak to her? He tugged the cord, and the garage flooded with light. He could see the pile of clothes right where he must have stepped out of them last night. He opened a black refuse sack and stuffed them inside, as something fell out of the pocket of his jeans. He bent down to pick it up; the collar was no longer white, it was now dark red. For the first time since he'd opened his eyes this morning he smiled. He would put this in with his other keepsakes. He felt the cat rub against his legs. It had taken all his restraint not to kill it. When she'd begged for a pet, he'd argued against it the best he could, knowing full well that the impulse to start killing animals could return at any moment and then she'd have been heartbroken. But she'd sulked so much for days that he'd had no choice but to give in to her. He kicked it, making it run away. Good. He wanted it to fear him. It was safer for it if it kept a safe distance, but the damn thing was too friendly and needy, always rubbing itself against him and the sofas. He was sick of the cat hairs it left everywhere. No matter how many times he ignored it or pushed it away it still came back for more.

Taking the bag outside he threw it in the fire pit, not bothering to light it. He could do that later. What he needed to do was to put the dog collar somewhere safe. He wanted to be able to look at it whenever he had the urge to relive last night. He went inside and, tugging open the drawer, he took the box out and put it inside. A loud knock at the door disturbed him, and he pushed the drawer, not fully closing it.

The letterbox opened, and a red card was pushed through. Christ what had she ordered now? She was a fucking shopaholic; he was glad he hadn't answered it. They could take whatever crap it was back to the depot. Pulling on his only pair of shoes, he grabbed his jacket and left, no idea where he was going – he just needed to walk. To try and clear his head because it felt as if there were more people living inside of his mind than there were in the block of flats opposite his house. It was getting harder to distinguish who was real and who wasn't.

He walked along the seafront, past the prom which was sealed off from the public because it was unsafe. He carried on walking until he found himself passing the police station. He didn't go near the front doors though; he wasn't ready to give himself in just yet. He didn't know if he ever would be. Standing looking at the glass-fronted monstrosity, he wondered if he ever would be ready to call it a day. A blonde woman came rushing through the sliding doors, and he turned to stare at her. It was her, that copper who was sticking her nose in where it didn't belong. Then she was inside her car and driving away, not even giving him a second glance. He turned around and began to walk back the way he'd come. He had to get away from here, what was he thinking?

CHAPTER SIXTY

Lucy made it to the hospital corridor outside the mortuary where Browning was waiting for her. He smiled.

'Remind me never to play hide-and-seek with you. I take it Simon hasn't caught up with you yet.'

She shook her head. 'No, but it's getting close. It's only a matter of time. Col has a suspect, well I think he's good for it. There's an unsolved murder from 1994, an alcoholic who had found God, used to beat his kid. The kid got took into care, four years later the dad's found bludgeoned and stamped to death with his own bible.'

'Do we have a name for the kid?'

'Darren Sharp.'

'Doesn't ring any bells. Where is he now?'

'If we knew that we wouldn't be here now. No idea.'

The loud voice behind them made Lucy freeze as she recognised Simon's deep tones. 'DI Harwin, you are a nightmare to get hold of. Can I have a word?'

She looked at Browning, who nodded once before slowly turning around.

'Have you been trying, sir? My phone's playing up, sorry.'

'Browning, can you tell the doctor I'll be a few minutes but she can start without me if she needs to?'

'Sir.'

Lucy watched as he disappeared through the double doors which led towards the changing rooms and the mortuary.

'This isn't personal, Lucy, but I can't have you working this case. I thought you would have realised that, especially after the unfortunate turn of events yesterday.'

'Which *unfortunate turn of events*? Arresting David Collins mid shag, his wife trying to kill me, or his murder after he was released from custody? There were quite a few.'

'Well if you put it like that I suppose all of them. You know what it's like, there's too much at stake. When the suspect is apprehended, and the CPS get a whiff of you doing your own thing instead of following the rules, well it will be game over; it won't even get to court. We can't afford to make mistakes like that.'

She felt her whole body sag. Damn he was right. She had been too focused on trying to make it all right, when she could be making it worse. There was no point in even arguing with him, and he knew that.

'I haven't spoken to you since you were assaulted. What are you even doing in work? Your head is a mess and it must be painful. You should be at home, sprawled out on the sofa watching crap daytime TV. Not chasing around the streets trying to find a murderer.'

'I know, but we're so close. We have a strong lead; Col is working on getting an identity for him and then we can get an arrest team together.'

He placed both his hands on her shoulders. 'I know, I've spoken to Col and Rachel. You've done everything you can; Collins's death isn't anything to do with you, but there are official procedures that have to be followed. I need you to go home and get some rest. Have a few days sick leave. Browning will keep you updated.'

Nodding, she let out a sigh. 'Please tell him to, I'll go mad stuck at home not knowing what's happening.'

He laughed. 'I know you will, but you have to anyway.'

She turned and walked away; it was pointless arguing. Her head was hurting, and she was tired; she hadn't got any sleep last night with the nurses coming in and out and the noise from the ward opposite. Doing her best to keep the scream bottled inside her chest she made her way back to the car park and her car. The best thing she could do was swallow three painkillers and go to bed, because otherwise, she would be pacing up and down the living room like she'd lost her mind.

CHAPTER SIXTY-ONE

The front door slammed jolting Lucy awake. Opening her eyes she shouted, 'Ellie.'

'Sorry, Mum, didn't know you'd be home yet.'

She exhaled, her body felt like a lead weight and her eyes didn't want to focus. Those painkillers had certainly sent her into a deep sleep. She rolled on her side and lay there waiting for her mind to catch up with the rest of her. Ellie's pounding footsteps came running up the stairs – for a skinny teenager she always managed to sound like an elephant. She knocked on her bedroom door.

'Are you ill? How come you're in bed so early?'

'What time is it?'

'Nearly seven.'

Lucy didn't turn to look at her, hoping this was just a flying visit. Ellie was having a hard time deciding which parent she should live with, so was making the most of it. If she was going straight back to George's she'd be able to avoid the awkward conversation about the state of her face.

'No, I'm tired. Been working extra-long shifts, it's been a long week.' She felt the bed go down as Ellie sat on it and realised she was going to have to turn around. As she did she watched her daughter's expression turn from smiling to horrified.

'You're face, what happened? Are you okay?'

'I'm fine, well apart from the headache from hell.'

'Who did it though, Mum, you're not fine, are you?'

She thought about telling her a different story to what had happened then realised that her daughter wasn't stupid. There was bound to be something in the news about the whole mess, and she didn't lie to her family no matter what. Pushing herself up on her elbows she smiled.

'Are you hungry?'

'Yes, Rosie made a healthy shepherd's pie for tea which tasted like shit. Then when I told her I'd rather eat tinned dog food she got mad at me and made Dad tell me off.'

Lucy laughed. 'Tact is not your thing, is it, Ellie? I suppose you take after me in that respect. Well I'm bloody starving. If you order a Chinese takeaway, I'll help you eat it, then when we've eaten I'll tell you what happened. I don't want to put you off your food.'

'I knew it was a good idea to call in here before I went to Nat's to babysit Bella.'

She felt a chill run through her body and shivered. After they'd eaten she was going to have to turn into the overpowering, bossy mother that turned her daughter into a completely different girl. What choice did she have? Natalia wasn't going to need her tonight. There was no way the Street Saviours would be running for weeks; in fact it might not run ever again. For one thing the church hall was still locked down and there was a cordon around the whole area and it could be for a couple of days. It was going to need a specialist cleaning company to get rid of all the blood from the vicarage and the hall. The nearest would be Newcastle or Manchester and it could take days for them to arrive.

'Go order the food whilst I sort myself out.'

Ellie stood up and went downstairs to phone their regular takeaway; she shouted, 'Are you picking it up or do you want it delivering?'

'Delivering, I can't be bothered going back out again.'

While her daughter was on the phone, she checked her mobile to see if Browning had been in touch and was disappointed to see that he hadn't. Then again it was highly likely he was still at the post-mortem; the number of injuries meant it would take much longer than usual as each and every one would need to be documented. With a bit of luck she'd have eaten her tea and let it digest before he rang.

They sat at the table to eat their food – there were so many different cartons.

'Ellie, did you think you were feeding a rugby team? There's enough here to last for days.'

'Told you I was starving, and you never have food in the fridge. It will last you a couple of days: I'm looking after your welfare, Mum.'

'Yeah, can't say that you're looking after my waistline very well.'

When they could no longer eat another thing, Ellie stood up and took their plates away. Then she put the lids back on the various containers and stacked them all on the kitchen worktop. Lucy stood up and went into the living room to sprawl out on the sofa; she was making the most of being told to take it easy because there was nothing else she could do.

Ellie threw herself onto the armchair. 'So, what happened then?'

Just like that, casual, as if she was talking to one of her friends. Lucy didn't know if she liked the fact that her daughter was acting so mature.

'To cut a long story short I had to arrest the vicar from St Aidan's and his wife didn't like it. She followed me home and hit me with a cricket bat.'

Ellie's mouth had fallen open as she stared at her mum. 'You arrested David, and Jan battered you?'

She nodded.

'Why did you arrest him, he's a vicar?'

'I'm well aware of that, but it doesn't mean he's above the law. It doesn't matter who you are, if you break the law then the police will arrest you.'

'I know that, but what did you arrest him for?'

Lucy didn't know how much to tell her, though it had already been in the local news about his arrest.

'He was arrested at a prostitute's address. Did you not see the news yesterday?'

Ellie's eyes opened as wide as her mouth. 'Shit, no wonder Jan was mad at you.'

'Thanks a lot for the support.'

'I didn't mean you deserved to be battered, Mum. It's just I can see why she'd be mad, what a cringe up.'

'Yeah, well it gets a whole lot worse than that.'

'How, what could possibly make it any worse?'

'Jan found David dead this morning.'

This time Ellie gasped. 'Fucking hell.'

'Ellie.'

'Sorry, how did he die? Did he kill himself?'

'I can't tell you that; what I can tell you is you won't need to go and babysit for Bella tonight because Street Saviours is cancelled for the foreseeable future.'

'Does Nat know about it all?'

'She knows David is dead, as do the rest of the volunteers. Ellie, I've been honest with you and told you stuff I wouldn't dream of having to tell a fifteen-year-old. I need you to listen to me now, I mean listen and take notice of what I'm going to tell you. You know about the murders that I've been working, yes?'

She nodded.

'We think that the killer is choosing his victims through their links to the church, so you are not to go anywhere near any of the other volunteers, and that includes Nat and Bella, until we've caught him. Once he's been apprehended and in custody then you can go see them as much as you like, but I need you to promise me, until I tell you we have him that you won't.'

'Why haven't you caught him?'

The accusation was like a burning hot arrow straight through her chest. *Yes, why haven't you caught him, Lucy?*

'I'm trying, I wish it was that easy. Sometimes people can be very clever, manipulative, secretive and very good at hiding who they really are from the people who love them. My whole team is working very hard to catch him, we're almost there.'

'So David was murdered by this maniac who doesn't like people who go to church or have anything to do with the church and because of this I can't spend time with Nat and Bella?'

'Yes, that is right. Pretty much hit the nail on the head, but this is between you and me. I'm trusting you with some very important information here, Ells, I don't want you phoning all your friends up or going back and telling Rosie.'

Ellie rolled her eyes. 'As if I'd do that, I promise I won't tell anyone.'

Lucy waited for an argument, more accusations that not only was she a pretty crap mother, but also a crap copper. They never came, Ellie nodded her head and smiled at her.

'Don't worry, I won't. I'll keep away from the church, and I wouldn't tell Rosie if her head was on fire. I hate her. Can we get a cat?'

Lucy did a double-take; she'd been expecting an argument not a request for a pet.

'Why would you want a cat? Who's going to look after it? Have you asked your dad?'

'Bella has the cutest, fluffiest cat I've ever seen. It's like a giant furball. I like the way it comes and sits on my knee purring. I've never had a pet before.'

'You had a goldfish.'

'Yeah, that was really good to cuddle when I was watching *Catfish*. I'll look after it. Dad said no because Rosie's allergic to them. It could live here; you could get a cat flap for it for when you're at work. Please?'

'I don't know, I'd have to think about it. The poor thing would be on its own more than it had company. Who would feed it?'

'Me, I'd live here all the time then, aw please, Mum.'

'I'll think about it, give me a day or two.' All Lucy could think about was Margaret's decapitated cat.

'Is that, I'll think about it you can bugger off or I'll think about it maybe?'

Lucy grinned, her daughter was one of the most perceptive people she knew. 'It's an "I'll think about it maybe", but if you keep pestering then it's a definite no.'

Ellie jumped up and hugged her. 'Thanks, Mum, I hope your head gets better soon. If I don't have to babysit can I go and see Amber tonight instead?'

'Yes, but I'll drive you there and get your dad to pick you up.' What she really wanted to do was to tell her she wasn't allowed to leave the house until they'd caught the killer, but she couldn't. Her job made her far too overprotective as it was. There was nothing to suggest he would even know who Ellie was. He had an agenda and a reason for who he was killing and why. She just prayed he stuck with the older people and didn't start working his way down the younger end of the list.

CHAPTER SIXTY-TWO

June 1995

He sat at the small desk in his room staring at the notebook, trying his best to ignore the voices in his head which were telling him how special and untouchable he was. He'd just spent the last hour drawing a detailed plan of how to murder Sharon in the back of it. He called it his murder book; on each page was a different murder weapon and method of death. He preferred it when he could watch them bleed and see the blood. That was why he liked slitting the rabbits' throats; he could watch them as their life pumped out of them. He'd like to do that to Sharon who was nothing but a complete bitch to him. He'd had to be nice to her since the other week when she'd accused him of being a freak in front of Paul. Her time was coming though; until he could kill her without getting caught the next best thing was to dream about the different ways to do it. He hadn't showered for days or changed his clothes – it seemed like too much hard work and who really cared? Why should he bother? No one talked to him at school anymore. What friends he'd had were as bad as the rest of them, all talking about him and laughing. He did his best to not go, but the school had phoned the home and Paul had gone mental about it. Angie had come back off her holidays, and he'd had to explain to her that he'd lost the rabbit. Her eyes had been so sad that it had made him feel a little bit bad; she was always so nice to him. She'd looked at him funny and hadn't really bothered with him since, only talking to him when she had to.

Paul's loud voice woke him from his trance.

'You better be ready to go because I'm not going to be late for my appointment.'

He stood up, forgetting to hide his notebook like he usually did. Leaving it on his desk for anyone to find. He hated Paul as well, maybe he should kill them all. Slit all their throats, one by one when they were sleeping and set fire to the home to get rid of the evidence. This made him smile to himself as he walked down the stairs and out to the waiting car with its engine revving. He got into the back seat.

'Don't you go skiving today either; if I get called to that school one more time about you not attending your classes I'm not going to be very happy. I haven't got the time to listen to them moaning about what a freak you're turning into. Oh, and when you get home get a shower and a change of clothes wouldn't go amiss, otherwise I'm going to stand you out back and run the hosepipe over you. Understand?'

He nodded, not speaking because he couldn't be bothered. He didn't really speak to anyone now, just the occasional grunt or nod of his head. The car stopped at the school gates, and he got out, wondering if he should go to the library instead. They pretty much left him alone in there, where he'd sit reading the books and making notes. Forcing himself to go inside, he made his way to the form room.

Today's teacher was an arse; she was a supply teacher with an attitude on her that made him want to ram his fist down her throat and choke her to death. All she did was pick on the kids like him, the freaks, the Goths, the quiet ones; Andy who was about the only person in the whole school he felt sorry for was sitting next to him, his head bent, and he knew he would be hoping that she didn't single him out. He had a stammer and when put under pressure it was painful to listen to. She left Andy alone and went for him instead, which brought a smile to his face.

'You, what homework were you given last time?'

He shrugged.

'What's the matter, don't you speak? Cat got your tongue? I'm asking you a question and I expect an answer.'

Sharon who was watching them, chewing her gum and blowing bubbles, laughed. 'Miss, he's a freak. I wouldn't wind him up, he might kill you like he kills all the pet rabbits.'

He stared at her, daring her to say anything else. She laughed at him, and he knew then that her time was almost up.

The teacher stared at him. 'That's not a very nice thing to say, Sharon. You don't kill pet bunnies, do you? Have you heard what they say about kids who kill their pets? They're weirdos who turn into serial killers. Do you like serial killers? Do you lie in bed at night dreaming about being best friends with the Yorkshire Ripper?'

The whole class, apart from Andy who looked horrified, burst into laughter. He was up and out of his chair before anyone even realised. He had his hands around the bitch of a teacher's neck and was choking the life out of her, pinning her against the whiteboard. The laughter had turned to screams as his classmates watched on as the teacher's face began to turn purple, and then it was over. He was being dragged off by the head teacher and deputy.

They dragged him out of the class and down the corridor to the empty isolation room, threw him in and locked the door. He looked at their panicked faces through the small glass window and laughed. That would teach the silly cow to mess with him. He didn't care if he'd killed her, although he doubted that he had. Strolling over to the empty teacher's chair he flopped down onto it, put his feet on the desk and gave them both the finger.

It was some time before they came back for him, this time with two coppers following behind them. He was completely unfazed by it and had managed to rip apart every book and piece of work he could find in the room. He was pacing up and down, when they opened the door and the coppers stepped in.

'You have to come with us, you're under arrest.'

He turned to stare at them. The next thing he knew he was running towards them as fast as he could yelling: 'kill you all; you can't touch me I'm the prince of darkness.'

The head teacher looked at them and shrugged. Stepping out of the line of fire, he pushed the copper nearest to him towards the angry, young man. There was a lot of shouting and the next thing he knew he was on his back. One of them sitting on his chest, the other handcuffing him. He carried on lashing out until he felt something heavy smash against the side of his head.

CHAPTER SIXTY-THREE

For the first time since the discovery of Sandy Kilburn's body Lucy woke up feeling refreshed. She'd dropped Ellie off at her friend's then gone home and gone back to bed. George had promised to pick her up, and she knew that he would. He was a lot of things but a complete pushover when it came to his daughter. Well almost; it would have been easier if he'd agreed to her having a cat. Lucy didn't really want one; she was too lazy to be responsible for a pet. Being a parent was bad enough and that had been her choice. Grabbing her phone off the bedside table she was surprised it hadn't rung or vibrated, and she felt as if she was redundant. She'd give Browning a chance to get to work and then she'd ring; if it was Mattie she'd have phoned him at home now. He'd have gone mad, but updated her, even better he'd have called in to see her on his way. She couldn't do that with Browning because they didn't have that sort of friendship. His wife might not appreciate his boss ringing him all hours of the day and night. She got up and stared at her reflection in the bathroom mirror. She looked awful. Her face didn't look much better, though the swelling had gone down a little. The bruising was darker this morning. At least she didn't need to worry about people seeing her because she had no intention of leaving the house, despite the fact that she wanted to be back at work, there in the middle of it all, hunting down the killer, only she knew she couldn't. She needed to keep her mind occupied because otherwise she'd drive herself mad.

Halfway through the second episode of *Luther* her phone finally rang. She paused it on Idris Elba's face, so she had something worthwhile to stare at. It wasn't Browning's voice.

'How's my favourite police officer this morning? I missed you yesterday afternoon.'

'I've been better, thank you, Catherine. I think you're probably the only person to ever say that. How did it go?'

'It was a long one. I think Simon was wishing he'd caught up with you after the post-mortem, if you get my drift.'

This made Lucy chuckle. 'Yeah, kind of serves him right in a way. Although I suppose he was only doing his job.'

'Well, the cause of death was the two wounds to the neck, and the slash wounds were post-mortem as I suspected. His clothes, although saturated in blood, had no cuts or tears in them. Do you want the good news?'

'If you have any, yes please.'

'I found a single cat hair, which, in my opinion, is the same as the previous two samples I've taken. That's not confirmed yet. I've just got off the phone to my friend who is testing them; he's sending me a photo of the kind of cat they're from. Apparently it's an expensive breed. Not your average kitty. He said that there will be a register of the local owners of that breed on the Active Register. So if you contact all the vets in the area they should be able to give you the addresses. How am I doing?'

'If I was standing next to you I'd bloody kiss you, that's amazing news. It's going to help narrow down the suspect list. Thank you so much. I'll get Col on with that.' Lucy stopped, remembering she wasn't in work to tell Col.

'You can phone him, or do you want me to?'

'It's okay, I'll phone him. I know you must be busy. I'll tell him it came from you if anyone asks.'

'Well it did, so don't worry about it. I've got your back, Lucy, someone needs to look after you. What's your home email address?

I'll forward the picture of the cat on as soon as it arrives. Your boss never told me I couldn't speak to you about it. So we're not doing anything wrong; anyway when was the last time he actually ran a case? He seems a bit rusty.'

'He's been an office guy for as long as I can remember. I suppose he's a bit out of his depth.'

'Yes, that's a polite way to put it. Oh, did Collins have a dog collar on at all when you arrested him? Because he had a black shirt, and in his trouser pocket was a long silver chain with a cross on it but no collar. I'd have thought he'd have one on him if he was wearing that kind of shirt.'

'When we arrested him he was stark naked and tied to a bed. He did get dressed in that black shirt, but I don't recall seeing him wearing his collar. Then again if you were getting marched out of a prostitute's house in handcuffs I don't suppose you'd want to be wearing that for the world to see. I'll find out. I'm surprised the cross was still in his pocket, because the killer took trophies from both Sandy and Margaret.'

'That's why I'm asking about the dog collar. If you killed a priest, what would be the best trophy you could take from him?'

'His collar?'

'I think so, it's more personal. Anyway, just a thought. When you find him it will be interesting to see if he has it in his collection. I know you're probably bored already, but I think it's a good idea that you're having a few days off.'

'I've got Idris Elba keeping me company, so I'm good for a couple of hours.'

'Lucky girl, I've got three corpses and a Mr Maxwell. I don't know who I prefer at the moment. Take care, Lucy, I'll be in touch.'

Catherine ended the call, and Lucy didn't know whether to jump up and down for joy or scream in frustration because she wasn't at work now that things were beginning to heat up. She stared at the screen and whispered *we're getting closer; I hope you're ready to go to prison for the rest of your life, you bastard.*

CHAPTER SIXTY-FOUR

Ellie came breezing into the house and stared at Lucy who was lying on the sofa, no make-up and her hair in a loose bun. She wasn't used to seeing her mum look so off-duty; all the years for as long as she could remember she'd either been in uniform or the smart suits that she now wore for work. Even on her days off she made an effort.

'Why aren't you at work?'

'Sick leave because of the state of my face, too scary for the public to look at.'

Ellie laughed. 'Yeah, you have a point. I can't stop staring at you.'

'Thanks, kid, makes me feel a whole lot better. Why aren't you at school?'

'I don't have to be in until eleven. I came to show you a photo of Bella's cat, so you know which one I want. I don't want you going out and buying any old moggy.'

Lucy arched an eyebrow at her. 'Erm, I haven't decided yet. The jury is still out on that one.'

'Ah, come on. It's not like it's a dog, they look after themselves. All you have to do is feed them and give them a stroke.'

'And get them vaccinated, flea treatments, neutered, litter trained.'

'Please, Mum, it can be an early birthday present.'

Lucy sighed. 'What sort of cat is it then?'

Ellie bounced onto the sofa next to her and began to scroll through the photos on her phone. She shoved the screen in front of Lucy's face. She pushed it away.

'Bloody hell I'm not short-sighted. Let me have a look.'

Taking it off Ellie she studied the photo and felt her heart begin to race: this breed of cat looked like it was the perfect match for the cat hairs taken from each victim. Trying to keep her voice calm and not give anything away to Ellie, she said, 'That is pretty cute, it's like a little fluff ball. Who's going to clean its backside when it's got shit stuck to it?'

The thought was racing around in her head: Natalia was connected to the church and both victims. Was this the break she'd been so desperately hoping for? For once she didn't want it to be, because if it was, she didn't know how she'd live with it.

'Urghh, trust you to think of that. Cats clean themselves; you won't have to follow it around with a packet of baby wipes every time it goes to the toilet.'

'I hope so. Give me a few more hours, I'm at sixty per cent. When I get to one hundred I'll let you know.'

Ellie rolled her eyes at her. 'Well don't take too long, will you, at least you'd have something to cuddle up to in bed when you're here on your own. I have to go, I'll see you later. Don't overdose on the television, you're not used to it.'

She stood up and grabbed her school bag.

Lucy shouted after her. 'By Ells, thanks for visiting.'

The front door slammed shut, and Lucy forced herself up off her comfy bed of cushions. It was time to ring Col and Browning, both of them should be in work now.

CHAPTER SIXTY-FIVE

Lucy checked her emails to see if Catherine's had come through. Relieved to see it had arrived, she opened the attachment and inhaled. Her hunch had been right. The cat was a dead ringer for the one Ellie had just shown to her. The hairs on the back of her neck stood on end. It was a coincidence, it had to be. There could be hundreds of those cats in Brooklyn Bay. *How many do you think are owned by people connected to the church?* Natalia knew all three victims – it could be her. She shook her head, surely not. She was normally a pretty good judge of character. She didn't buy it; the woman was far too nice. She was pacing up and down waiting for Col to answer his phone; he finally did. Breathless.

'Sorry, boss, was at the printer. Had to run back to my desk, is everything okay?'

'Well it would be bloody great if I was allowed in work.'

'Ah, yes. I forgot about that.'

'Catherine sent me a photo identifying the type of cat the hairs would have come from that were located at each crime scene. It's an expensive breed, a blue Persian; I've sent it to you. When you get it can you ring around the local vets and see if they'll give you a list of local owners? If they won't, go there in person and tell them you'll arrest them for obstruction. It's vital we know so we can start crossing them off the list. Cross reference it to the list of volunteers and see if any of them have connections to the church.'

'I'll do it as soon as it hits my inbox. Anything else?'

'I want you to let me know if you get any matches before you tell anyone else. Please.'

'You didn't have to ask. You're still my boss whether you're in the station or not. I answer to you, not that knob jockey they've sent through to cover. He's sat in your office trying to get up to date on everything we have. At the rate he's going it will be Christmas.'

'Who's that?'

'Some DI called Weston from the city. They've borrowed him until the killer has been caught and you can come back. He keeps rubbing his head like he's wishing he'd never walked in.'

Lucy laughed. 'Yeah, I've never heard of him. Good luck to him. I want you to make sure anything that comes in you bring to me first. You can tell him after I've evaluated the situation.'

'No problem. I'll be in touch.'

He hung up. Lucy wasn't mad about the replacement. It was pretty obvious they couldn't leave such a huge investigation without a DI, but she just hadn't expected it to be so soon. She felt a bit sorry for him – to be brought into an investigation at this late stage would be a nightmare. It would take him days to get up to speed with it. Well hopefully she would have it cracked before he got the chance and save him the bother. She jumped up, thinking she had no idea how long it was going to take for Col to get the details from the vets. If they were arsy and refused it could take days, and she couldn't stop thinking about the fact that Bella had a cat which looked as if it was a similar breed. Of course it might not be, they might be two completely different types, just look similar. There was only one way to find out and that was to pay Natalia a visit. Grabbing her car keys and phone she decided there was no time like the present.

She parked outside Natalia's house and prayed that she was home; she also prayed that it wasn't the same breed of cat because it could spell disaster for them all.

Natalia opened the door, smiling to see Lucy standing there.

'Hello again, is everything okay?'

She nodded. 'Sorry to bother you, Ellie is driving me mad. She wants a cat like Bella's for her birthday; she hasn't shut up about it. I was wondering if you could tell me what kind of cat it is. She said if I got her any old moggy, she wouldn't speak to me again.'

Natalia laughed. 'Wow, she's a girl who knows what she wants. I don't suppose there's anything wrong with that.'

Lucy shrugged. 'I suppose not.'

'Come in and you can see her, she's a lovely little thing.'

She stepped to one side, and Lucy felt her heart begin to race, praying that she wasn't stepping into the most dangerous situation she'd ever been in. Natalia led her into the lounge where she pointed at the sofa.

'Bella, is Bluebell in with you?' she shouted.

Bella appeared carrying the cutest cat Lucy had ever set eyes on.

'Oh my goodness, she's even cuter in real life than on the photo Ellie showed to me.'

Bella smiled and carried her over to Lucy, sitting her on her lap.

'She's my baby; she always wants cuddles and food, don't you, Bluebell?'

Lucy took hold of the cat and began to stroke behind it's ears, and immediately it began to purr and rub against her. 'Aw, I was hoping it would be really ugly so I wouldn't have to buy her one.'

Natalia laughed. 'Nope, she's pretty cute. Even Tony likes her and he's not a cat person.'

'I can understand why. Are they hard to get hold of?'

'You might have to search around for one and travel some distance. I don't think there are many around here. We had to go to Manchester for her.'

'Are they expensive?'

'We paid six hundred for her.'

'Really? I never knew a cat could be so expensive.'

'She was worth every penny though.'

Passing her back to Bella, Lucy looked down and saw some cat hairs attached to her trouser leg. She stood up.

'Thank you so much. I guess I better start looking, she's gorgeous. I can see why Ellie keeps pestering me now.'

She walked to the front door, her heart pounding in her chest. Natalia followed her.

'I can look up the details of the breeder we bought her from when I get a minute and text them to you, if you want. They might have some for sale, save you messing around.'

'That would be amazing, thank you so much.'

Lucy opened the door and stepped outside. Now all she had to do was make it to her car without losing the hairs. She reached the gate, turning to wave at Natalia and Bella. Then she was inside her car. They went back inside, closing the front door behind them.

She let out a huge sigh; she still had some hairs on her trousers. If she could get them to Catherine, she could take a look and see if she thought they were from the same cat. Leaning over to the plastic evidence bag on the passenger seat and a pair of tweezers, she didn't realise how much her hands were shaking until she tried to pick them up.

A loud knock on the car window made her jump, almost dropping the tweezers. She saw a man standing there; he was smiling at her. She wasn't sure who he was. Putting her window down a couple of inches she said, 'Can I help you?'

'Are you Ellie's mum?'

Lucy's throat was so dry she found it hard to answer him. 'I am, yes. I'm sorry, I don't know you.'

'No, you don't. Sorry, how rude of me to presume. I'm Tony, Bella's dad. I just wanted to say hi, I've heard a lot about you.'

Lucy grimaced. 'Oh God, not from Ellie I hope. Don't believe everything she tells you, I'm not that bad in real life, I promise.'

He laughed. 'Nope, it's all good. I didn't want you to drive away without introducing myself.'

'Phew, it's nice to meet you. I'm so sorry have to go now, I'm late for work.'

He stepped away as she turned the key in the ignition. 'Don't want you being late. See you again. Say hi to Ellie for me. She's such a nice kid.'

She nodded, placing the tweezers on her thigh, then she waved and began to drive away, hoping the tweezers weren't about to fall off and lose her evidence. Once she was out of the street she pulled over and, after several attempts, managed to get a couple of hairs into the bag and sealed it up. Next stop the mortuary, where hopefully, Catherine wasn't tied up and could spare the time to take a look.

CHAPTER SIXTY-SIX

June 1995

He didn't know where he was. He looked around expecting to be in a cell. He wasn't, there were no metal bars, no steel door, no bed even. He was in a room, a padded room; he tried to stand, but his legs felt as if they weren't strong enough to hold him up. Holding onto the wall he dragged himself up. Stumbling towards the door he launched himself at it. Hitting it with a huge thud, he bounced back. Looking down he realised he wasn't even wearing his clothes: he had on a hospital gown and a white wristband. Opening his mouth he began to scream over and over, until someone came to the door. It was unlocked from the outside and standing there was the biggest man he'd ever seen. He was wearing a nurse's uniform, and in his hand was a tray with a needle in it.

'Either shut up screaming or I'm going to jab you and send you back to sleep. Your choice.'

He looked at the needle; he hated them. He felt sick, how long had he been here?

'Where am I?'

'The General, psychiatric unit. Do you not remember coming here?'

He shook his head, trying to clear the fog. The last thing he remembered was fighting with the two coppers at the school.

'You had a bit of a breakdown. It was bring you here or the cop shop, so they decided here was the safest place.'

He sat down, trying to process what he'd been told.

'Look if you stay calm, I'll get you some food and a drink. If you kick off, I'll jab you and send you back to cloud cuckoo land until the doctor can come and speak to you.'

He nodded. He needed to think, act normal. He didn't want to be locked up in the crazy unit for ever. He had stuff to do; he was still going to kill that fucking Sharon. She'd started it all off, making him a laughing stock. The door shut and the big guy locked it again. He began to rock back and forth; there was nothing else to do.

Half an hour later the door opened and the nurse came in with a sandwich. He passed it to him along with a plastic glass filled with water. He gulped the water down; his throat was so dry he felt as if he was choking. Emptying the glass he handed it back and ripped open the sandwich. Stuffing it into his mouth and swallowing it down.

A woman came in wearing a white coat and smiled at him.

'I'm glad to see you're awake, I'm Doctor Pearson. I'd like to talk to you if you're in the mood.'

He nodded.

'Good, we'll go into the recreational room. It's not very comfortable in here.'

He found himself being lifted to his feet by the nurse and marched along behind the doctor. He realised that he needed to be a model patient if they were going to let him go. Despite the panic building inside his chest, he knew he could pretend. Maybe he was nuts, but he wouldn't let them know that. He'd do what they said, take his meds and keep calm. Then when he got out of here he was going to go back and kill the fucking lot of them. The whore who his dad had used to replace his mum, the priest, the teacher and anyone else who got in the way.

CHAPTER SIXTY-SEVEN

Lucy drove to the hospital way faster than she normally would, unable to stop the butterflies in her stomach. She desperately needed Catherine to compare the cat hairs and say they weren't a match because the outcome was unthinkable if they were. Who could it be: Natalia or Tony? They seemed like such a perfect, happy couple. Everything going for them, successful business, gorgeous daughter, nice house, pretty much the happy family. But if either of them was the killer, they needed to get Bella out of there and fast; there was no knowing what would happen. She ran through the hospital foyer, clutching the clear plastic evidence bag as if her own life depended on it. Catherine's office door was shut, and she hammered on it, hoping she was inside. It opened, and she passed her the bag.

'I think I found the cat and the killer, only I'm not sure which one is the killer. Can you compare these hairs and see if you think they're the same?'

She took the bag from her. 'What do you mean you're not sure which one is the killer?'

'They're a married couple, both are really nice, successful, playing at happy families. It's the perfect cover; I mean they could be working as a team. The wife is a volunteer at the church, she knew all three victims, and they have the cutest kid. I need something, so I can get an arrest team together and get the kid out before they know what's going on. I can't afford to fuck this up, there's far too much at stake.'

'I can tell you if they look similar, Lucy, but I'm not the expert on this stuff. It wouldn't hold up in court.'

'It doesn't matter; you tell me if you think they're similar or not. Fuck, I hope they're not. I need a good enough reason to bring them both in. Once we get them into custody a full search team can go in and rip the house apart. We can get official samples to send off to your university friend and hopefully find the missing trophies. There's bound to be evidence somewhere in the house or garage.'

Catherine pulled on a pair of gloves; carefully removing the hairs from the bag, she put them on a slide, then pushing it under the microscope, bent her head to study them. Lucy didn't know whether or not she was going to throw up, her stomach was churning so much.

Catherine lifted her head. 'They look similar. I've kept a sample. It's in the mortuary; come on, I'll have to compare it in there. You need to gown up because I have a body being prepared on the table.'

Lucy would have dressed up in an astronaut costume if it meant getting the answer she needed. She followed her into the ladies changing room. Neither of them spoke as they scrubbed their hands, pulled on plastic aprons and gloves.

Thankfully whoever was lying on the gurney hadn't been removed from their body bag yet. Lucy was used to dead bodies, but she didn't need any distractions. She had her fingers crossed as she stood and waited for Catherine to retrieve the sample she'd kept. There were two microscopes side by side. She put the slide under one with the sample that Lucy had brought in. Then taking the slide she had in storage from the drawer, she put that in the other one. Bending her head, she went from one to the other, scrutinising them for any differences. Finally, she lifted her head. 'You look, see what you think.'

Lucy did the same, going from one to the other. Stepping back, she nodded. 'They're the same or pretty much look the same.'

'Yes, they are. But we won't know for definite until the DNA has been extracted and compared.'

'It doesn't matter, they look identical. It's enough for me to get an arrest warrant for now. We can work on the scientific stuff when we have them both locked up. Thank you so much, have I told you how much I bloody love you?'

She grabbed the doctor. Pulling her close, she kissed her cheek. 'When we go out, cocktails are on me.'

Catherine laughed. 'Well, there's an offer I can't refuse. Lucy, I know that you know this, but please be very careful. You're dealing with someone who might be having a psychotic episode. There's no telling what they'll do. How were they? Did you speak to both of them?'

'Nice as anything, both seemed pretty normal. They didn't look crazy or sound crazy to me.'

'That's what I'm afraid of.'

Lucy walked out of the mortuary, ripping off the apron and gloves. She dialled Browning's number.

'I have two suspects. I've managed to get a sample of cat hairs to compare, and Catherine has just confirmed they look identical. I need you to get a warrant and an arrest team together; meanwhile, I'll go to the address and keep watch until you get there.'

'Whoa, hold on there, boss. What? How have you even come up with not one, but two viable suspects when you're on gardening leave? Supposed to be taking it easy.'

She began to explain the last hour of her morning to him.

'And you went there on your own, with no backup, are you fucking mental, Lucy? You're lucky we're not out looking for your body.'

The magnitude of the danger she'd put herself in crashed over her and she felt her stomach lurch once more. 'Look, I know it was stupid. How else would we know? I'm very doubtful it was Natalia. She's so lovely, I'm more inclined to say it's her husband, Tony. But it's Natalia who has the links to the church and was in contact with all three victims. I honestly don't know at this point who to think it is. What I do know is we need to get that gorgeous kid out of there and fast.'

'Leave it with me, I'll get everything we need together. I'll go see the Super now. Lucy, please don't go back to the house. It's far too dangerous.'

'I'm not going to knock on the door or anything, I'll just park at the top of the street and keep watch.'

'Yeah, well keep your engine running and if either of them gets as much as fifty feet near to the car get out of there.'

'I will, thank you.'

She ended the call, then began to run back to her car.

CHAPTER SIXTY-EIGHT

Natalia hoped Lucy could find a cat for Ellie's birthday, she was such a great kid and Lucy seemed lovely too. She hadn't slept well last night; too upset to tell him, she'd feigned sleep so she could think about poor Margaret. He would have no sympathy for her because he had such a strong dislike of the church and its parishioners. Tony had stayed at the restaurant until late. Then he'd tossed and turned all night long. She still couldn't get over the shock of David's death, if she was honest. The newspapers had run a front-page story with huge headlines saying there was a serial killer on the loose in Brooklyn Bay. It was unheard of and terrifying; she wasn't going anywhere near to the church or letting Bella out of her sight. At least not until whoever it was had been caught. She wanted to pass her condolences on to Jan, but it was too dangerous. She supposed she could send a card and some flowers, but would she still be living at the vicarage? It was highly doubtful; as far as she knew it was still all cordoned off with officers still guarding the scene. She shuddered, maybe she should tell Tony to start spending a bit more time with his family instead of every spare minute he had at the restaurant. She was scared. What if whoever it was decided to come for her next?

Taking the polish and a duster out of the cupboard under the sink, she decided to knuckle down and do some cleaning to take her mind off everything. She ran upstairs to check on Bella, who was curled up on her bed with Bluebell, watching her favourite film, *Beauty and the Beast*, for the hundredth time.

'You okay, Bella?'

She nodded.

'I'm going to clean up, then I'll make us some dinner.' Walking into the room, she bent down and kissed her daughter on the top of the head. 'I love you.'

'What about Bluebell?'

'I love her too.'

'Give her a kiss, she'll feel left out.'

Natalia smiled, kissed her fingers and stroked the cat's head.

'Mamma, would you marry the beast if you were Belle?'

'Yes, it's not what people look like on the outside. It's what's on the inside that counts, and he's a big softie deep down.'

'He's always angry though.'

'Well that's because he was a handsome prince who got turned into a monster. I think you'd be angry too.'

'Daddy is always angry. Do you think someone turned him into monster?'

Natalia laughed. 'Sweetie, your daddy is tired. He's been working too hard; grown-ups get grouchy when they're tired and overworked. He needs a few days off and then he'll be a handsome prince again.'

Bella stared at her. 'I hope so, I don't like him when he's mad all the time.' She turned her attention back to the television, and Natalia felt her heart sink. He had been angry and moody the last few weeks, and it made her furious that Bella had picked up on it. When he came home she was going to have it out with him and tell him he either hired a manager to run the restaurant or he stopped working so hard. Her daughter was her world, and if she was troubled by his behaviour then it was time to do something about it. As much as she hated confrontation there was no way she would have Bella living in a house where the atmosphere was always fraught with tension.

Pushing her earphones into her ears she went into the dining room, selected her playlist and began to dance her way around, dusting. When she reached the dresser, she noticed the drawer was open. Pushing it shut, her fingers touched something sticky. She pulled them back and looked at them; they had some dark liquid on them which she thought was probably jam off Bella's little fingers. Lifting them to her nose she recognised the coppery smell: it was blood. She knew she hadn't cut herself, and Bella certainly hadn't. Tony must have. Pushing the drawer back into place, it wouldn't close. She shoved harder – it still wouldn't move. There was something sticking up inside it. So she tugged it open, and found more drops of dried brown blood on the papers and envelopes inside. She saw the gift box that she'd thrown away ages ago was the reason it wouldn't shut. How did that get back inside? She'd put it out in the red recycling bin. Pulling it out she noticed it was covered in reddish-brown splotches. Tony must have taken it out and cut himself on a can while retrieving it, but what did he want to keep it for?

Lifting off the lid, she stared at the contents inside, trying to make sense of what she was looking at. She recognised the big, white, plastic button earrings, and there was a delicate gold chain with a crucifix which she had seen many times before. The thing which made her heart race and her stomach drop like a lead weight was the once-white priest's dog collar. Now covered in dried brown blood. Her own blood rushed to her ears as she realised what she was staring at, and the panic which filled her chest made her heart race so fast she thought she was going to pass out. The music still playing in her ears, she hadn't realised that she'd gasped so loud. She needed to get Bella and get out of the house, now. She also hadn't realised that her husband had come in and was standing behind her, his arms crossed, watching her every move.

CHAPTER SIXTY-NINE

Lucy positioned her car at the top of the Costellas' street. She had no police radio, cuffs or CS gas. All she had was her phone. She kept replaying her earlier visit over and over again in her mind. There was nothing to suggest that Natalia was having a psychotic episode at all. She was calm, friendly, funny and not acting strange. Her husband, although she'd only spoken to him briefly, seemed okay as well; she'd never met him before, so it was harder to judge. All she wanted was to get that little girl out of there safely. She was in the middle of what could turn into an explosive situation. A car parked behind her, and she watched Browning get out of it. He came around to the passenger side of her car and got in.

'Christ, these cars aren't made for well-built blokes, are they?'

Lucy didn't know, she didn't have a problem getting in or out of it. 'You got here quick.'

'I've left Col and the new boy sorting it out. I couldn't risk you being here alone with nothing to protect yourself. I never realised how much of a pain in the arse you were until the last few days. I can't wait for the golden boy Jackson to get back off his holidays. There's a plain car parked at the top end of the back alley that runs behind the house watching that.'

'Thank you, I'm good though. A lot tougher than I look.'

'Who's in the house?'

'I don't know if anyone's in or not. When I left he'd just turned up. For all I know they've all gone out shopping.'

'What car do they drive?'

She shrugged. Browning began writing down the registration numbers of the cars parked nearest to the house. Pulling out his radio he began to pass the numbers over to the control room operator to check the PNC database. Lucy felt helpless, but at least she was here. He hadn't been told to send her home which was a good sign. The white Audi A5 came back as insured to both Costellas.

'I think they're all home. Do you think whoever it is knows that we're onto them?'

'What did you say you were doing there?'

'Asked her about her cat, told her Ellie wants one for her birthday. Which is actually true, she keeps pestering me for one. Do you know how much they paid for that cat?'

'Tenner.'

'Six hundred quid.'

'You're kidding me, right? Who in their right mind is going to pay that? For a cat.'

'Nope, honestly that's how much it was, and not me, although it is pretty cute.'

'Play your cards right, you might be able to buy that one cheap if we lock them both up for murder.'

Lucy looked at him, pushing him in the arm. 'That's terrible.'

'But true, you've got to look at the positives in situations like this.'

She turned away from him to hide her smile; cop humour was bad but sometimes humour was the only thing they could use in these situations. 'I wish we could do something.'

'Like what?'

'I don't know, go knock on the door and ask to speak to her. I just want to get Bella out of there. I feel as if my heart is racing so fast I'm going to have a heart attack sitting here doing nothing.'

'I know, but that wouldn't work, would it? If you had to take a guess, which one do you think it is, providing there isn't some weird partnership going on? Like Fred and Rose West.'

'It has to be him. I don't know how she would get Collins hoisted up on that cross. Even if she was flipping out, I just can't see it being her.'

'Right, so when the door entry team gets here we need to go after him first. Get him secured, then get her and the kid out to safety. Simple, it will be okay, Lucy. Stop panicking, like you said they won't know that we're onto them.'

Lucy stared at the house, hoping to God he was right.

CHAPTER SEVENTY

Natalia pushed the box back into the drawer. Turning around to go and get her daughter, she screamed to see him standing there watching. Pulling her earphones out she smiled at him.

'I didn't hear you come in, honey, you gave me a fright. I was busy dusting.' Her heart was hammering inside her chest.

'What were you looking at?'

She stared into his eyes, which were darting from side to side, not sure whether to lie or be truthful. There was a film of perspiration on his forehead as if he'd been out for a run, but she knew that he hadn't because he wasn't wearing any trainers or shorts like he usually would.

'The drawer wouldn't shut. I was just trying to close it.'

He walked across so he was standing next to her. 'Why wouldn't it shut? All you had to do was shove it.' He pushed the drawer so hard that the whole dresser shook and a couple of plates tippled off, falling to the floor and smashing to pieces.

'There, problem solved. Any other DIY jobs around the house you need me to take a look at while I'm here?'

He was smiling, and she felt cold fingers of fear rising up her spine, because that wasn't a smile she'd ever seen before. It was more of a smirk; he was laughing at her.

'No, everything is good, thank you.' She looked at the door. It would take her a few seconds to reach it. Then she had to run up the stairs and get to Bella. She could lock them both in the bathroom and phone the police. 'Would you like some lunch, I was about to make some?'

She was trying to distract him, normally he lived for food.

He shook his head. 'Not hungry today.'

'Oh, okay. I'll go and fix something then.' Food was the last thing on her mind; she'd throw up if she ate. She deliberately didn't mention their daughter's name, hoping he wouldn't be thinking about her.

'I'll come with you.'

That smile again; she tucked her hands in her pockets so he wouldn't see how much they were trembling. He let her leave the dining room and followed her to the kitchen, where she kept her back to him and went through the motions of preparing a sandwich to buy some time. He was leaning against the fridge.

'What did that fucking copper want, coming around here? Being nosy, why did you let her in?'

'It's the babysitter's mum. She wanted to know where we bought the cat.'

'Why?'

'So, she could buy her daughter one.'

He marched over to her, grabbing her by her ponytail. 'Are you lying to me? I'll know if you're lying.'

Her hand reached out, grabbing hold of the nearest thing to her, which was a heavy-based milk pan. She swung it as far as she could and hit him on the head with it. He let go of her, and she made a run for it. She knew she had to get to their daughter before he did. Letting out a loud grunt he stumbled forwards.

Natalia had never run so fast in her life. She didn't turn around to see if he was following her, there was no time.

She ran into Bella's bedroom, grabbed hold of her and dragged her into the ensuite. Locking the door behind her, she sat on the floor her back against it.

Bella looked at her, shocked, and whispered, 'What's up, Mamma?'

Natalia tugged her phone out of her pocket. She dialled 999 but the phone kept on ringing. Ending that call, she found Lucy's number and pressed it.

CHAPTER SEVENTY-ONE

Lucy's phone began to ring. She answered it and heard a frantic voice whisper: 'Please help us, he's gone mad.' A loud scream filled the car.

Lucy jumped out and began running towards the house.

Browning got out after her. 'Lucy, get back here now.' He began to shout orders into his radio. 'Backup now, armed officers to Beach Lane.' Shaking his head, he did his best to follow and catch up with her.

Inside the house, Tony was kicking and throwing himself at the bathroom door to get to his wife. It was shaking and buckling under his weight. Bella huddled in the corner crying, and Natalia was bracing herself trying to stop the door from being kicked open. There was loud hammering on the front door, and he stopped. Running over to the window, he looked down to see that fucking, meddling woman hammering on the door.

'Police, open up now or we'll break the door down.'

*

Lucy was thankful to hear the sirens in the distance, because if he did open the door, she had no idea what was going to happen.

Tony opened the window and shouted, 'Get the fuck away from my house now or I'll kill them both and you.'

She stepped away, holding her hands up. 'I'm going away, but I need to talk to you, Tony. Come down and we can have a chat. Come on, you don't want to hurt them, do you? They haven't done anything wrong. Please Tony, just you and me, we can talk. Let me inside, I'm not armed I just want to help you.'

Browning, who was standing at the gate breathing heavy, was shaking his head. He hissed, 'Lucy, what the fuck are you doing? You can't go in there, he'll kill you. We need a negotiator; this is out of both our hands now.'

She shrugged, looking up at the bedroom window where Tony was watching their every move.

'Tony, I need to talk to you. Come on, just me and you. No one else. I promise you we can sort this out. Get you the right help. It doesn't have to be this way. Let me help you; this is a mess and it's only a matter of minutes before they arrive and break down the door. Come out and I'll take you in, no fuss. It will all be calm, no big drama.' Lucy's voice was trembling as she tried her best not to let it show. She didn't want him to know how terrified she was.

He slammed the window shut, and she turned to Browning. 'Fuck, now what?'

'Now you step away and wait for task force and a negotiator, there's nothing you can do.'

A police van, closely followed by another one, turned in, lights and sirens deafening in the normally peaceful street. The task force sergeant, Graham Brock, got out, running towards her.

'What's happening? Get away from there, Lucy.'

She did as she was told, backing out of the gate while watching the windows for movement as Browning relayed the past few minutes to him.

'I want you both back at the van. Do not come back towards this property. This is under my team now; I don't want you jeopardising anything.'

Browning nodded; grabbing hold of Lucy's elbow he pushed her towards the van. She turned around and asked, 'Who's the on-duty negotiator?'

'Inspector Wilson is on his way; he's silver commander today, so he'll be taking over at the scene and doing the negotiating.'

She looked at Browning and mouthed: 'He's a cock, they both are.'

She leant against the van out of sight of Tony while she tried to get herself together. Praying that he wouldn't do anything stupid to his beautiful family.

CHAPTER SEVENTY-TWO

The whole street was cordoned off with armed officers; the houses either side to the Costellas' were evacuated. There were vans, cars and an armed response vehicle surrounding the house. Lucy had started shivering, not sure if it was the cold or if she was in shock. She climbed into an empty van, turning the heating on full blast. Browning was talking to Brocky who was strutting around loving every minute of this. She thought about phoning Natalia to see if she was okay and still alive, but knew that it could make everything much worse. If she wanted to be here, she needed to swallow her pride and take a back seat. It was out of her hands now despite the overwhelming need to take control. She'd not taken her eyes off the bedroom window, wanting him to put in an appearance. It was too quiet out here; there were lots of officers and no action.

Wilson finally appeared, strolling casually towards Brocky, and she felt her fingers begin to twitch. *Yeah, take your time, mate. It's not like it's a life or death situation, is it?* She glanced at him and realised they were talking about her when Brocky kept stealing sly glances in her direction. Next thing she knew Wilson was at the window; he knocked, and she put it down.

'What did you say to him?'

'I told him to come down and we could talk about it. Not to do anything stupid, that I'd take him in.'

'Why would you tell him that? You bloody idiot, you should have kept your distance until I got here.'

Lucy glared at him. 'You just called me what? Don't you fucking come here and tell me what to do. I answered the phone to his wife screaming at me to help her save her and her child's life. I did the only thing I could think of and that was to distract him.'

He turned and walked away. She sat there trying to take deep breaths and stop her knuckles from clenching into tight fists. Christ she was so mad with the situation and everyone here that she'd go into the house and take him on single-handed, while the pack of pussies waited around for hours, drinking coffee and laughing about what was the best way to handle the situation.

Browning came over; she looked at him.

'He had the audacity to call me a bloody idiot. He's a prick. I swear to God I'll punch his lights out if he doesn't make a move soon.'

'I know he's a prick, he always has been. We should have kicked the door in and dragged him out before they got here. This is going to last for hours.'

Lucy felt her eyes fill with tears, visions of Sandy's and Margaret's bodies filled her mind, and the blood flowing around her veins had turned into iced water. She was terrified for the woman and child inside.

'I know, but will Natalia and Bella last that long? He's lost it.'

'Here we go.'

Lucy looked at Wilson, who was on his phone. A hush had fallen around the officers in the street and it was eerily quiet. She could hear the phone on the other end ringing, and she prayed for him to answer it. Just when she thought it was about to ring out, Wilson lifted his hand and began to talk. He slowly walked towards the front garden of the house, waving towards the windows. He was out of earshot now; she had no idea what he was saying.

There was a loud boom, and the shattering of glass echoed around the street as a small stool came flying out of the bedroom window. Wilson and everyone behind him ducked to avoid the flying glass, which made Lucy smile.

'Shame that didn't hit his extra-large head and knock him out.'

The broken blinds were flapping in the breeze out of the jagged shards of glass still left in the window frame. Wilson had backed off. His phone down, he huddled around the police car with Brocky and a couple of armed officers.

'Well that didn't go to plan.'

Wilson stood up and walked back towards her. 'He wants to talk to you. I'll brief you on what to say. Will you speak to him?'

Lucy nodded.

'I'm going to give him a few minutes to calm down and then try again. If it doesn't work, I'll put you on the phone. Whatever you do try not to do anything to agitate him even further.'

'What, like you just did?'

'I had to make contact and see what the situation was. I didn't know he was that unstable.'

She had to bite her tongue in case he wouldn't let her try again. She had to do her best to make him let his family out alive or she would never live with herself. If anything happened to them, Ellie would be devastated and blame her.

'Wait here until I give you the go-ahead and then you can try. Do you think he has a gun?'

'How would I know? I think if he had a gun we'd have known about it by now. He wouldn't have had to throw that stool out of the window, he'd have just shot you.'

For a fleeting moment the look of concern on his face gave her great satisfaction. He clearly hadn't thought that one through. Then her stomach lurched once more at the reality of the situation they were in. Tony could turn on his family before they could get to them.

CHAPTER SEVENTY-THREE

Tony kicked the bathroom door so hard the lock splintered, cracked, and it flew open, sending his wife sprawling across the bathroom floor, winded. He stepped inside, to see Bella crying, leaning over Natalia's stunned body. He smiled at his daughter. 'Don't cry sweetie, I didn't mean to hurt her. I just wanted to speak to you both and she was being silly. Come on let's go downstairs and get something to eat. You can watch the cartoons.' He held his hand out towards her. Terrified and sobbing, she took hold of it.

Natalia watched in horror. She forced herself to get up and follow them, just like he'd known she would. There was no way she would leave Bella with him on her own, which was what he was relying on to keep her obedient. She glanced at the broken window; the blue flashing lights of the police vans were flickering off the white walls. She could hear him talking to Bella, and she was praying to God to keep them both safe. Why was this happening to her? She was a good person; she gave to charity, she volunteered at the church, she loved her family and this was how she was being repaid for being a good citizen. Her husband had turned into some wild-eyed stranger she didn't know, and both her and her daughter's lives were at risk. She hoped that Lucy was out there figuring out how to save them both. She knew then that Lucy had probably had her doubts about her husband's innocence. Had she really wanted to know about the cat for Ellie or was it all a show to get inside the house?

She went into the kitchen, where Tony was chattering to Bella. He opened a packet of chocolate biscuits and passed them to Bella.

She was staring at him, terrified to say no. Sneaking a glance at Natalia. She smiled at her daughter, nodding to her. Encouraging her to take them so she didn't make him madder than he already was. The whole time she was looking for something to protect them with or an escape route. But he sensed her not paying attention and turned to show her the huge butcher's knife he had tucked down the back of his jeans. The handle sticking out enough for him to grab hold of. She hated that knife. He'd brought it home from the restaurant a few weeks ago, and she'd begged him to take it back. She'd only used it once and almost severed her index finger. She didn't like it in the house and now she knew why.

She limped across and pulled a chair next to her daughter who had bent her head to watch the cartoons on his iPad that he'd given to her with a pair of headphones over her ears. Sitting down, she put her arm around her shoulders and pulled her close. Natalia knew that she would die to protect Bella; as long as she didn't get hurt it didn't matter what happened to her. Her daughter was her whole life; she just hoped that wherever the Tony she knew was, the doting dad and wonderful husband remembered how much he loved his daughter as well.

The house phone began to ring, and he strolled off to answer it. She stared at the back door. The key was missing: he'd locked it and hidden it. A feeling of complete and utter despair began to take over her and she had to stifle a sob. She could take another knife, rush him and try to kill him first. But could she risk that in front of her daughter? She didn't want her to grow up an orphan with nothing but the memory of her parents stabbing each other to death in front of her. Her phone was in her pocket; she thought about dialling Lucy's number and leaving the line open so she could hear everything and know when to raid the house. But before she could take it out, he was back again, pacing up and down the kitchen demanding to speak to that interfering bitch of a copper. He ended the call and stared at her.

'If you hadn't found that box, we wouldn't be here now. This is all your fault, by the way, you should have left it well alone. At the end of today, no matter what happens, you will have to live the rest of your life knowing that you could have prevented this, Nat. You've always been too damn nosy for your own good. If you hadn't gone to that fucking church and met that vicar, I wouldn't have known any better. I'd forgot all about him, that whore and the teacher. When they let me out of the nuthouse with enough medication to drug a horse I did as I was told. I was a good boy: I took my meds, I kept out of trouble, I went to college, I changed my name. I was a different person when you met me. I was happy, content; I loved you and Bella so much. Now that's all gone: only you could decide to help out a church that was run by the local sleazeball; only you could take pity on the whore he used to fuck in the vestry, and only you would make friends with the bitch of a teacher who caused my breakdown when I was at school. Do you know how long I was in that hospital for?'

She shook her head.

'No, you wouldn't because I never told you any of this. I didn't want you to think I was fucking crazy. I had you fooled, didn't I? Four years I was in there. When they let me out I'd forgot that I was going to kill them. The drugs did that, they took away the anger and the hatred. It was as if God decided he'd had enough of those sinners and lined them all up to be in the same place at the same time for me to realise that I had to make good on the promise I made when I was fifteen. It was as if they'd been reunited for the sole purpose of dying. I tried to ignore it. I really did. I tried not to listen to the voices. I worked longer hours, I upped the tablets, I even spoke to my psychiatrist. Did you suspect I went to see one of those? No, of course you didn't, why would you? I was Mr fucking perfect to you. How did you repay me? You spent more time with them than you did me. You betrayed me, Nat, and now look what a mess we're in. They're all dead because of you.'

She tried to stifle the sobs threatening to erupt, so her daughter wouldn't hear, but they exploded from her chest, and she clung on to Bella trying to block out his hateful accusations.

CHAPTER SEVENTY-FOUR

Lucy dialled the number and listened to it ringing. She hadn't planned what she would do if he answered. She could sense a lot of movement behind her and knew something was going on, though she didn't know what.

'Yep.'

'Tony, it's Lucy. You asked to speak to me?'

There was a long pause and she thought he was going to hang up. 'Tell that prick if he tries to speak to me again they're both dead.'

Lucy turned and relayed the information to Wilson, who nodded, then turned back to whisper to Brocky and the armed officers behind her. She couldn't concentrate with the hushed voices behind her and walked into the front garden.

'Don't come any closer.'

'Sorry, I need to get away from them. I can't concentrate. What can I do to help you, Tony? What do you need?'

'I don't need anything; there's nothing you can do to help me. It's too late for that.'

'If I can't help you, let me help Bella and Natalia. You don't want to hurt them, do you? You love them and they love you very much.'

The line went silent. 'Of course I love my daughter, and I loved Nat, but she betrayed me. She chose the church over me.'

Lucy was frantically trying to process what he'd just said and make sense of it.

'She was trying to help, that's all, she didn't know about any of this. She's innocent, they both are. Please let them come outside to me. I'll take care of them, I promise. Then I can help you.'

She was holding her breath, waiting for his reply.

'If I let them out, will you come in for me?'

'Yes, I promise. I will, on my own. Just you and me.'

Lucy sensed a rush of movement behind her and turned to see the armed officers running through the gate towards her with the door entry team. She dropped the phone, running after them, screaming.

'Get back he's sending them out, get back now. He's going to let me go in.'

Her shouts fell on deaf ears as they began to hammer at the front door repeatedly with the red metal battering ram. The noise was deafening, and she turned to Wilson.

'What have you done? He said he was letting them come out?'

The door finally went through, and the armed officers ran inside shouting.

Lucy ran after them.

She knew by the silence that it was bad.

She pushed through them and stepped inside the living room. As she took in the carnage, her legs buckled and she fell to her knees. Lying on the floor were the bodies of Natalia and Bella. She crawled towards them to see if there was anything she could do, screaming: 'Get the paramedics now.'

She reached Bella, pressing her finger against the side of her neck. There was no pulse; she couldn't do a damn thing to save the beautiful girl lying in front of her. Unable to stand, she crawled the short distance to Natalia, whose eyes were glassy. She did the same, again there was no pulse.

A groan from behind the sofa caught her attention. The officers who had been staring open-mouthed turned their guns in that direction. Lucy pulled herself up, walking over to see Tony lying there, blood covering his stomach, the handle of a large knife protruding from it. His eyes closed, he groaned again.

She ran at him screaming and kicked him as hard as she could.

It was Browning that pulled her away from him. He dragged her outside, and she fought him every step of the way until she saw Wilson standing there with his hands on his hips. Shouting down the radio demanding to know what the state of play was.

She pulled herself free from Browning and ran towards him.

'You fucking bastard, you killed them.'

When she was standing in front of him she drew back her fist and hit him straight on the nose. The loud crunch as the cartilage fractured and the blood began to spray out of it made her feel a little bit better. Browning, who had caught up with her once more, dragged her away; two patrol officers came running to help separate them all.

'He was going to let them out, how could you? Why didn't you wait? They're dead and they shouldn't be. You're going to pay for this. You killed them.'

Lucy could no longer hold herself up as she felt her knees give way again; she let the officers carry her to the van, where they helped her up into the cage. She didn't fight with them, it wasn't their fight. They were only doing their job, and she had no fight left inside her. As the cage doors slammed shut and the light was blocked out, she welcomed the darkness as she slumped down burying her head in her hands and began to sob.

CHAPTER SEVENTY-FIVE

It was Col who drove Lucy home. She'd been in the station for hours and had had to give a statement. Then be interviewed by the Chief Super who had told her that, luckily for her, Wilson wasn't pressing charges, but that she was being signed off with work-related stress and would be on a managed return to work after various psychological assessments. She could hear his voice now:

Lucy, I'm trying to understand how you feel, but why did you have to punch him?

A woman and child are dead because of him. I had almost talked Tony around, he was agreeing to let them come out if I went in for him. Ask Wilson why he didn't listen to me when I told him to stop them from going in. He had no intention of letting me go in there and defuse the situation; the man is an idiot and as far as I'm concerned he might as well have been the one brandishing the knife, because he killed them both in cold blood.

Col stopped at her house, and she breathed a sigh of relief that it was all in darkness. She couldn't face Ellie. How was she going to tell her? It would break her heart – nobody should have to hear that kind of news.

'Are you going to be okay, boss? Do you want me to come in? Make you a coffee, something to eat?'

'No, thank you. I don't think I'll ever be okay again after today to be honest, Col.'

'I bet you won't. I'm sorry about that. I'm not sorry you punched Wilson though, Browning said you were like a woman possessed and he'd bet on you any day of the week to win a fight with the best of them.'

This made her smile. 'Will you keep me updated as and when you can on Costella's condition. I hope to God the surgeon slips and severs an artery so the bastard bleeds to death. He doesn't deserve to live, let alone survive his injuries.'

'If I hear anything, I'll let you know, of course I will. What are you going to do with your time off?'

'Something I've been putting off for a long time. Pack this house up and hurry up the sale of one that I can call my own. I want one with a small back garden, big enough to put some raised vegetable beds in. Not like this monstrosity: the gardens go on for ever and George would never let me dig them over. I'll keep myself busy until they decide I'm sane enough to go back to work. Thanks for all your help, Col, I really appreciate it.'

She got out of the car and waited for him to drive away, then she turned and went inside her house where she threw herself on the sofa and let the tears fall until there were no more and she fell into a deep sleep.

THREE WEEKS LATER

The winter sun was so bright and refreshingly warm, Lucy was glad she had her sunglasses with her. It was standing room only at the crematorium and she'd been relieved that she hadn't had to go inside. It had been heart-breaking watching the hearses pull up with the two white coffins inside that were adorned with beautiful floral tributes. Ellie had refused to come; she hadn't spoken to Lucy since she'd broken the news to her. She didn't blame her really, at the end of the day she'd been heavily involved in the case and still not managed to save them both. Browning had picked her up and driven her here. He had his best suit on and was doing his best not to stand out or pay too much attention to what was going on. She knew he was upset, though he didn't want to show it. Lucy cried silent tears. She hadn't stopped crying since that night when Col had taken her home. Tomorrow she had her first counselling session, and she had no idea what good it was going to do. She'd never been one to share her emotions and feelings with anyone except for George.

The music filtered out through the open doors, and she bowed her head. Life was far too short and hers would never be the same again. The coffins were put back into the hearses to be driven to the graves for burial, and the mourners filed out of the crematorium.

She turned to Browning.

'You can go now, I'll hang around for a while. Watch the burial and then walk home. I need to clear my head. Thank you for coming.'

He was tugging at the collar of his shirt. 'I don't mind waiting for you.'

'Honestly, you go. I'm okay, I have nothing else to do. I need to stay for a while.'

A look of relief crossed his face, and he nodded at her, turning to walk back to his car.

Lucy let the hearses and mourners go then she followed behind them at a slow pace. It was pretty where the graves had been dug in a quiet corner at the top of the hill. The view over the bay was beautiful and from here the sea looked as blue as the sky above. Keeping her distance, she found a bench to sit on until it was over.

When the last mourners had gone, and the grave diggers had filled in the grave in which they'd both been buried, together, she finally stood up. Walking over to the grave, she lay the spray of pink roses and white baby's breath on top of the mound of soil and whispered, 'I'm sorry, I'll never forget you both.'

Wiping a tear with her sleeve, she turned away and saw Mattie's familiar truck waiting for her at the end of the narrow footpath.

She opened the door, and her breath caught in the back of her throat at the look of concern etched across his face.

'What are you doing here?'

'Browning phoned, said you were hanging around in the cemetery. I don't know what you've done to him, but I'd swear you've almost turned him soft in his old age.'

A smile spread across her face. 'He's actually been okay.'

'Get in, Lucy, I'll take you home or wherever you want to go.'

She paused, turning around to give one last look at the fresh graves. Then she climbed inside.

'Oh, I almost forgot. There's a present for you on the back seat.'

She turned around to see a cat carrier with Bella's cat sitting inside staring at her.

'Where did you get her from?'

'Told you Browning was going soft; the neighbour has been looking after it. She rang him and said she didn't want it permanently and was going to take it to the cat shelter. He went straight round and collected it. He said you would know what to do with her.'

She laughed. Reaching back she grabbed hold of the carrier and lifted it over. 'Not so much me, but I know Ellie will love her to bits.'

'So, where to, Lucy. Pub or home?'

'I'll go to the supermarket to buy some cat food then can we take Bluebell to George's house for Ellie.'

'You can take her wherever you want.'

'Thank you.'

*

After explaining to George about the cat, he took it from her despite Rosie's protests in the background about her allergies. Lucy walked back to Mattie's car with a smile on her face. Hopefully Ellie would be thrilled, and it would help her with her grieving.

*

Mattie dropped her off at home, where she waved him off with the assurance that she'd be fine. Needing to be on her own, she looked around the house she'd thought would be her for ever home. Everything except the essentials had been packed in brown cardboard boxes. There was nothing like wallowing in self-pity, anger and grief to make you kick arse. George had collected his stuff yesterday; the stuff she didn't want she donated to the furniture warehouse for St Mary's Hospice, asking them to drop the bags of clothes and handbags off at the charity shop. This was stuff from her old life – she didn't need it now. It was time to start fresh; all she had left after ten years of marriage were five cardboard boxes, and two of those were filled with her favourite books. Her offer had been accepted on the house, with a small back garden, which was half the size of the one she lived in now. It didn't matter how big it was really, as long as it was hers she'd be happy.

Mattie had helped her with the packing. When he'd come back from his holiday and found out what had happened he'd come straight around. She'd cried in front of him for the first time ever and he'd held her, and it had felt good. What she needed. She'd wondered whether it would have made a difference if he'd been here – would it have all gone as spectacularly wrong as it had? She decided that, yes, it probably would. Despite the deep-seated feelings of guilt, she had no idea about Tony Costella or his mental illness: the blame lay with him not her. She hadn't wielded the knife that had so cruelly killed his family. There was one thing Lucy did know, however: she would never let anything like this happen again. It was time to move on, make a fresh start. She owed it to Natalia and Bella whose lives had been cut short before they'd even begun. Life was for living and as soon as she was up to it she would begin to start living again.

A LETTER FROM HELEN

This story was a tough one to write, it gave me sleepless nights and made me cry. Writing a prequel was certainly a challenge for me as a writer. I hope you enjoyed this story as much as Lucy's other adventures. If you'd like to be kept up to date with news of what I'm writing next, please sign up to my newsletter here:

www.bookouture.com/helen-phifer

I'd like to thank you, my amazing readers from the bottom of my heart for buying this book. Your support is wholeheartedly appreciated. If you did enjoy it, I would be eternally grateful if you could leave a quick review. They make such a difference and are a fabulous way to let other readers know about my books.

I'd also love to hear from you and you can get in touch with me through my Website, Facebook, Twitter or Instagram.

Love Helen xx

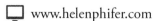 www.helenphifer.com

Helenphifer1

helenphifer1

helenphifer

ACKNOWLEDGEMENTS

A huge thank you to my amazing, gorgeous, editor Keshini Naidoo for all her expert editorial input. I'm forever in your debt, you take a rough draft and turn it into a work of art. I'm so lucky to have worked with you on my last three books and I wish you all the luck in the world with your new venture. I'll miss you, thank you. Xx

Thank you to the lovely Jessie Botterill for taking over where Kesh left off. I'll apologise now for the rough drafts that will be coming your way.

Thanks to Jan Curry for the copy edits.

Another huge thanks to Mamma Bear, Kim Nash and the amazing Noelle Holten for all their hard work and looking after the Bookouture authors so well. It's amazing to know that you're there any time, night and day to offer advice, hugs and support.

What can I say about the rest of the amazing team at Bookouture? I owe them a huge debt of gratitude for everything. It's an honour to work with such true professionals and I thank you all.

I'd also like to thank my fellow Bookouture authors. I'm truly amazed to be amongst such a super talented, bunch of writers. I'd especially like to thank Angela Marsons for always being there. You're such a huge inspiration to me Angie.

Bloggers and reviewers are the lifeblood of a writer and I'd like to thank each and every one of you from the bottom of my heart for all your support, it means the world to me.

A special thank you to my coffee girls, Sam Thomas and Tina Sykes for the love and laughter. Xx

A heartfelt thank you to the wonderful, patient, life saving Paul O'Neill for casting his expert eye over my work and writing such excellent surveyor's reports. Xx

It goes without saying that I'd like to thank my family for always being there, for making my crazy life fun filled with love and lots of laughter. Sometimes there are tears, but mainly laughter. I'm truly blessed to have you all in my life and I appreciate and love every single one of you, most of the time.

Printed in Great Britain
by Amazon

85713767R00167